With best wishes,

J. J. Dixon

FACE VALUE

Jack James Dixon

With love to my Mum, Delia,
without whom, this story would not have been possible.

And very special thanks to all my friends at
the Liskerrett Writers' Group.

"Man is least himself when he talks in his own person. Give him a mask, and he will tell you the truth."

OSCAR WILDE

CHAPTER 1

All mortal flesh is yet to keep silence…

Metallic sighs from the church organ charm the pews into a jitter as motes of dust and fibres swirl in reds, blues, and yellows under the glares of saints.

Waiting for a funeral service he did not arrange, waiting for lunch he did not arrange, Neville Pike turns his dark head to scan around the populous of fellow black suits and black dresses. He sees from the frontmost row, some younger attendees are dressed in mournful jeans-and-t-shirts, tapping on their phones.

How fucking rude.

A long-held chord from the organ is followed by stillness. Everybody – living, of course – stands. Smartphone keys continue to chirp behind Neville, under reverent organ strains.

There's too much privilege. The least people can do is pay attention so we can all 'die' equally.

Dark-suited pallbearers waddle sombrely in, each with one hand on a trolley underneath the coffin.

Come on! He was no bloody saint, but where's the dignity in that?

Squeaking wheels insult Neville's ears, and injure his heart further still.

What's the point of it all, when you're gonna be discarded in the end anyway, while every other bugger carries on without a care?

A storm brews in Neville's chest with each furious breath, as the morose penguins slow their roll before the vicar, an apparition of white with one hand formally clutching the other. He watches through round glasses, under thick greying hair.

It should've been me assisting as well, shouldn't it? Why aren't I? Who are those goons?

Steering Grandad's *lumbersome* cocoon into full view, the pallbearers fill the front row of the *not*-family side of the church.

I've never seen any of those men in my life!

The congregation sits; a brief shower of rumps on pews, like hailstones crashing against windows.

The old man of the cloth speaks, with a voice of a thousand years, "Today, we celebrate the life of Maxwell Pike, who went to be with his beloved wife Ellen, in the arms of our Lord, on the ninth of September this year."

There's hope for us all if he managed to make it up there.

"Maxwell had spent much of his life travelling with the army..."

First I've heard of it!

"...when home on leave he met Ellen Tremaine, and then he left the service to be with her."

More specifically, to have Mum...

"They soon married in this very church, and in the following year bore their first child, their daughter Annabelle."

Neville's arms fold – the closest semblance of a loving embrace with his mum he is yet to recall.

"They lived in Saltash, where Maxwell would soon set up a business with…"

A hard cough from the – *not*-family – front row stops play.

The vicar glances just beyond the pallbearers for the source of the controlled explosion, before drawing his next breath to resume.

"…*within* a local warehouse, soon to become *Pike's Museum of General History and Antiquities*, where he worked diligently to provide for his family ever since. Then, once their daughter Annabelle was at school, Ellen started work at the museum as well…"

But you were going to say something else, weren't you, reverend? What was it?

Neville studies the well-dressed ghouls who manhandled his grandfather in his wooden overcoat. It had to be one of them who 'coughed.'

Any other speeches to come? No? Just the rest of the show, then. I'd love to know what they wanted to keep quiet…

***

The tang of old varnish congeals the air… at odds with delicate floral fragrances staged around the stark wooden hall.

Old women with cauliflower hair, and stuttering old men busting out of tweed suits and waistcoats, garble over pastries on paper plates.

Most of the younger crowd have not stuck around, while the hurricane building behind Neville's ribs changed course, having followed everyone else back to the wake.

Anyone would think they were all paid *to be at the service… Good turn-out, but why such a huge attendance? Where've all these people come from?*

Neville bypasses the stack of paper plates and reaches to claim a pasty. He crab-walks left of the be-plated savouries spread over the lace tablecloth, to the tray of mugs, and picks up a ready-made tea.

Every mug *in its place…*

He takes a bite out of the pasty for a bit of Cornish courage. Armed with food and drink in each hand, Neville approaches the group of suited gentlemen he is certain was in the other front row during the service. Yet, conversation stops before Neville. He nods, attempting to reignite the talk, "Glad to see so many people make it, chaps. Thank you all for coming."

Each gentleman, wearing a different shade of grey, smiles blankly. The lightest shade's frothy brown hair shakes as he finally responds, "Nice service, wasn't it?"

Who the hell are *you people?*

"It was, it was…" Neville stalls. "So, how did you know Grandad?"

The man looks at the darker greys to meet their glares before looking back at Neville. "Our firms- uh… *traded* with Mr Pike's Museum."

"Really?" Neville *eyebrows*, "What sort of stuff?"

The greys watch with stone-chilled stillness, like gargoyles ready to come to life if their cohort drops so much as a crumb Neville's way.

"Oh, just materials for display… Stationary… gift shop merchandise… that sort of thing."

"Ah, of course." *And what else, my chatty chum?* "Will business still go on?" Neville rewards himself with a bite of hot steak and potato.

"Well, I expect so, as long as someone at the museum keeps the books open. And the funds rolling."

A growling cleared throat draws attention. The darkest grey shares a brisk, slight smile and a nod with Neville, before turning away with the rest of the group.

"Sorry, the... *team* and I have appointments this afternoon. Nice chatting, Mr Pike." He turns away and follows the rest of the pack out.

The silence seems to leave with them, as noise and chatter saturate the little hall once more.

Edgy, aren't we?

Neville's appetite must have double-booked as well... He puts his mug down, bundles up his pasty, and flees.

It's just a museum.

***

Neville hooks his fingers under *the noose*.

Hoping it will snap, he grips and pulls at his tie as it stretches against his skin. Neville gets out of the car, sporting a low-hanging knot. His gale of rage had petered out on the drive back.

Home shitty home...

He swings the car door shut as the town clock strikes 3. Locking his grey Volkswagen, he flees, desperate to get out... of these clothes... of this skin...

He heaves himself over the threshold into the building, into the pungent odour of nicotine. Taking big steps, he inhales as little as possible. Most evenings, Neville can avoid the sight of scuffed white walls and the abrasive beige carpet; but today, the glare of overcast sky through the window lights up the realm in all its glory: a different atmosphere. A different world.

How far hath I fallen...

Treading hollowly up the stairs, Neville goes *round the bend* and faces the door to his flat. His own personal purgatory on Earth. He unlocks the door which whispers open over the cold wooden floor. Residents, *revenants,* in their own adjacent hidey holes would hear that *nobody* has walked in. The door shuts and locks behind him, heralding the rest of his indefinite sentence.

In cleaner airspace at last, Neville barrel-rolls out of his black jacket, throwing it over the couch in front of the kitchen. In defiant oblivion, he passes by the answer phone and its winking red eye.

Bollocks to that.

He shuffles off his shoes and socks, while undoing the top buttons of his shirt. Neville's feet stroke along the carpet in the *unliving* space until he lands on the couch, hauling his feet up to rest on one arm. Drooping his head over the other arm, he lies like a patient desperate to talk to his therapist.

Who would've thought that Grandad would finally up and cop it just like that? Gran said he'd live forever and then take shooting…

Neville glums over his abode: the white front door before the kitchen arena, the milky walls, the open door to his beige bedroom and his empty bed, the dirt brown armchair in the corner – *for guests to keep their fucking distance* – an airing cupboard, a black, forbidding widescreen TV with nothing on, and a *bloody great* window to the street, beholding every other mug with a place the exact same layout as his.

A 'Will' indeed… there's still his bleddy museum to think about.

His head sinks into the arm of the couch. He stares up at the deceptively vast empty canvas overhead. Clear ceilings today, not a cloud in sight…

I can't to go back to my sodding day job. I don't want to be a miserable bastard the rest of my life, I don't want to be wheeled into my funeral 'cos no-one can be arsed to carry me. After all, I'm so worth my weight in love and affection…

Neville swings his feet back onto the floor and stands with the momentum. He approaches the phone on the small table beside the bedroom, pulls out the desk drawer underneath, and scrabbles around inside until he snatches up a scrap of paper. Neville opens out the receipt and turns it over. "Yesssss."

He picks up the phone and dials the number for the museum on the grubby receipt. It rings and rings and rings and then… a woman's voice, "Hello, this is Pike's Museum of General History and Antiquities. Opening hours are from nine till five, Monday to Friday, and from nine till four-thirty on Sat…"

Neville plonks the phone down.

Stupid bugger, it's gone half 5! What now? Guess I'll call tomorrow…

He stares down at the machine, and then looks over his shoulder.

That's another thing I hate about this place. The quiet. *It's just me… and the voice in my head!*

***

A new day dredged from the depths of the one before.

'Didn't you want to leave it 'til next week, Mr Pike? I imagine this would be a bit soon for you, just days after the funeral.' She sounded nicer on the answer phone than when I called her earlier. I seem to have this effect on people…

The VW drifts down the road with Neville's hand resting on top of the steering wheel. A breeze through the open window rests on his hand and tickles his face. Suspense tickles his mind into an irritable haze.

"The sooner the better," Neville rehearses, "I feel I need to take responsibility for the museum now that Grandad's no longer with us."

Yes, the sooner I take my rightful place on the throne, the better.

The car dashes forward… drifting over of the white lines.

Careful! Don't dream and drive…

Neville *has reached his destination*. He parks the car just before the surprisingly tall heap of reddish bricks that makes up some kind of warehouse. He steps out in a navy suit and tie, locking up, *looking* up at the hipster building looming over him and ventures up the steps.

7

Neville walks through the wooden double-doors of the museum, into an empty reception. The concrete floor ushers the echoes of Neville's steps through the two halls each side of a mahogany desk, fixed a few feet before a wall of tan wooden panels.

A slim woman in her thirties wearing a black, pin-striped skirt and blazer, with smart, mousy brown hair, approaches, not exactly keen to shake Neville's hand… "Mr Pike?"

"That's me," says Neville.

"I'm Tracy."

"Yes, of course you are."

"…Let's talk in the office." Tracy turns about face and walks back the way she came, expecting Neville to follow as her shoes clip along the corridor.

Those sharp heels are well under the table…

Sickly yellow walls… with a pale green hue cast by jealous shadows.

Well, this is 'nice'…

…for a quiet walk to the office.

Not even a 'How are you after the demise of your dear Grandad?'

Neville and Tracy step defiantly out of sync with each other.

I can't wait for this bit.

She holds the door for Neville as he walks in, and then leaves it open…

She thinks this'll be a quick meeting, does she?

No pleasantries, as she sits in the throne behind the desk.

'Please have a seat…' 'Don't mind if I do!'

"Did you go to the funeral?" He pulls out the chair in front

8

and sits. "I don't think I saw you there."

"I didn't," says Tracy, "there was a family emergency, so I had to drive down west to see to that."

"Oh. Sorry. I hope everyone's okay."

"Yes, *amazingly,* we all survived…"

"You know, if you were actually having a get together with your friends, or you wanted the day off or something, you can say. Grandad *was* a bit of a sod."

Tracy blushes. "How was the service?"

"He had a surprisingly good turn-out. I'm sure he smirked inside the coffin when they *wheeled* him in."

Try to be nice to the one person sitting between you and this place.

"Well…" she says, "anyway, we're here to talk about what happens to the museum now. *And…* I have a few ideas."

As do I.

"While you're, *no doubt,*" she continues, "busy with your current job, I can continue to run the museum for the time being, while its future is being decided."

"That sounds very good," says Neville, "but…"

Christ. Watch her face go! Can't break eye-contact now…

"I've already left my job, so I can step into the breech and manage the museum myself."

A sharp intake of breath from Tracy, like stormy waves crashing against a stone harbour wall, the sound of a slap in the face. *Hush…*

"Okay," she says. "Have you had any experience of this kind of thing?"

Neville sighs, a submissive wave dispersing upon impact.

"Well, Grandad might've told you, I've been working at an accounting firm. For several years."

"Actually 'crunching numbers'?"

"Yeah, amongst other things. But listen, I know how this looks. *Neville* Pike, out of nowhere, waltzes in and expects to take over, but it's the *family business* after all. I just want to come back and do my bit."

"But you left your job for it? I could've covered the workload here, and you could've kept your position at that accountancy firm."

"Spending any more time working in accounting just didn't *add up* like you'd think it would… My wife and I are separated at the moment… This would be a great opportunity for me to take some extra time to try and patch things up…"

And make as much money as I can with my newfound freedom. How could she refuse me with my sob story, especially when it's true?

"I'm sorry to hear that," Tracy – resigned – brings her hands together. "Well, maybe, we can come to an arrangement…"

How desperate to run the place is she?!

"How about you try managing the museum for a just week or two? Even a trial month?"

Oh. Good. Glad I'm not misreading the situation!

"Just for you to see what it's like," she goes on, "and if you find that it doesn't work for you, why don't you look for somewhere else in the meantime? And *I'll* take care of the museum."

You're determined, aren't you? Probably thought 'ooh, this could be a nice little nest egg, couldn't it?' This one's a schemer, isn't she?

"Great. I'll give it a go," he smarms. "And I *do* want to stay."

"…That's fine," sighs Tracy, taking it squarely on the chin. "If you come back on Monday, this office will be set up for you. I've got to go now. I'm off to another meeting, with a buyer in town."

"Great. Thank you."

She did not like that, did she? Not one little bit.

Neville gets up from his chair – *my chair* – and holds his hand out to Tracy, in an effort to squeeze just one handshake out of his potential enemy. "I'll see you on Monday."

"First thing," she grips his hand. She gives it one firm shake and releases it.

Neville got his one handshake alright.

I'll take every victory I can get.

CHAPTER 2

Buffeted by shoulders, all manner of coated crowd crashes against Neville's cheap grey blazer.

With everything else against me, why shouldn't *I continue to swim upstream, through a school of dead-behind-the-eyes pedestrians this fine morning?*

The circumference of one obstructive man in front encompasses two.

It's supposed to be a short walk to work from the station. This is exactly why I've taken the car this last month, and not get stuck amongst the cattle…

With the stiff texture of the man's coat under his palms, shoving *this great bowling ball* into the wandering skittles ahead would greatly satisfy Neville.

But instead, he continues to brave the populated strip of pavement, in his dark grey suit and tie, with his combed hair, like a *good* citizen.

Of course the bloody battery died. Of course it needed replacing. It's always one thing after another, isn't it?

Further down the hill he ducks left to break away, but an aimless young man in ripped jeans and a dark red hoodie bumps into him, without even a glance.

FACE VALUE

Having paused for the oik to drift past, Neville raises his foot to step out of the crowd, but more bodies cross his path. He watches for an opening, in-between the stubbly slaves to sunrise tailgating one another.

Neville rushes forward through the slightest gap, knocking against an older woman dragging a trolley, who huffs in disgust.

I'm late as hell anyway.

Neville brushes himself down. He strolls onward, up the white-splattered steps and pushes open the museum double doors. They clatter against the walls as he enters majestically, the man of the hour… for two whole seconds.

Far away at the reception desk, Tracy types at the keyboard, unfazed by his dramatic appearance.

The doors fold back, one knocking into Neville's shoulder, making him jump. It closes. The other door slows to a halt, slightly ajar. He whips around vengefully to shut it.

Tracy stares at her computer screen.

Neville takes a musty deep breath and straightens himself up. With a bold posture, he moves towards her as she types. Her mousey fair hair is sculpted into a bun. Her flimsy lavender blouse flatters her petite frame.

That's a nice look for you. I wonder, with my baggage, if I'd have a chance?

He approaches, like a cheetah closing in on a gazelle. "Morning, Tracy."

"Morning, Neville." She barely notices him. No enthusiasm: 'Neville'.

Well… tried that.

Smoothly, Neville picks up his pace left to pass the desk.

What does it matter? I've already won back control of the museum. She knows her place now.

13

A clatter of doors echoes behind Neville. He looks back over his shoulder.

"Oh, hi Mark!" says Tracy.

'Oh, hi Mark'!? She's genuinely pleased to see him. The deliveryman!

"Hi, Trace." Mark greets her on his approach. A tall, Y-shaped Adonis – *twat* – in shorts and a hi-vis orange vest.

'Hi, Trace.' A relaxed, high-pitched 'hi,' like slipping into a warm bath! I bet he's slipping into her. She'll bid a sullen 'Good morning' to me, but any other Tom, Dick and Harry that walks through those doors she'll greet happily!

"Hi, Mark!" Neville chirps.

"Morning, Neville."

In that second, Neville's right arm turns to stone, restraining the fury that would find Mark's face. He walks on around the corner, following the hard floor to his office.

'Morning, Neville.' That was at least two whole tones lower than me! I made the effort, the bastard. 'Morning, Neville.' Like a discreet burp you try to cover up, that somehow escapes anyway.

Neville stands before his office. His incandescent right claw reaches for the door handle and strangles it, until the door opens and swings away in submission. His steadier left hand slides up the smooth, chilly magnolia wall until his fingers stumble over the switch and snap on the light. The cold, morgue-esque lighting reveals the cluttered desk, stranded in a sea of bare, beige carpet.

He sighs and steps inside, to withdraw into his colourless shell, but turns back out at the corridor.

Why do they get to be so happy?

He gazes over the desk at the other end of the room, with sheets of paper and derelict pens scattered all over the top.

Neville closes the door… with no intention of re-surfacing to the cruel outside world.

***

Having broken his silent promise to remain in the stark office, ravenous Neville lurches along the grubby pavement, returning with his cold, plastic-packed meal-deal lunch.

He climbs the tatty museum steps, spotting three men in dull coats lingering near the door, muttering to each other. Two of them, facing the door, hold smouldering cigarettes while the third faces away, hunched over the thin wavy plumes. The men fall silent on Neville's approach.

He glances at their dark-circled eyes, and then turns his attention to the double doors, when the sandwich packet falls out from under his arm and hits the ground.

"Shit." Neville bends down to pick it up. The bottle slips from his fingers. He growls and claws up the goods. He looks behind and catches the three men staring at him. Neville stands, cradling his lunch in both arms and then shoulders open the left door, dismissing the strange crowd.

Inside, Tracy sits at the computer, part of a tableau perfectly preserved from earlier this morning.

Neville trundles along with his lunch, trying more cheerfully to get her attention, and to disguise the miserable creature of the dark he is. "Alright, Trace!"

Tracy shivers.

What did I do wrong? Do I disgust her?

"Alright… Neville…" She – *is actually bleddy tense* – recoils before settling.

He ruminates his way to his *damned* prison-cell office…

What the hell is wrong with her? I'm making the effort. I'm her boss now and she won't even pretend to be interested!

Neville turns the corner and walks the doomed 'green mile' to his office once more. Inside, he drops the crisp packet onto the table, placing the drink and sandwich beside it. He faces the door, charges at it, and shuts it hard.

How long am I gonna be trapped in this *fucking dungeon before I die?*

He circles around the worn, brown leather desk chair and lands in it heavily. It squeals under the sudden pressure. He digs his fingers into the sandwich box and snaps it apart.

Fifteen years chained to a desk, and I have nothing to show for it.

He pinches the crisp packet with both hands and pulls it open with a breaking pop and crackle.

Here's to fifteen more years of the same misery in this dump.

Neville picks up the bottle of drink, and with a silent toast, he brings it to his lips for a swig.

What's the point of my life?

The hand holding his still untouched sandwich falls to the table, as one little madam skips into his mind: his precious Gem.

Little Gemma. Six years. That's how long it took me to lose sight of everything I had. I still had dreams. I do now! But I'll not be living inside my head forever…

***

Pitch-blackness has swallowed the world outside the window…

Plastic percusses as a biro hits the wall in the office. Neville's patience dries up like the pen which, in its last act of defiance, lands on the floor just short of the bin.

The museum has long-since closed. With everyone else gone home, messy-haired Neville sits hunched over the desk. His tie hangs in a strained knot over his chest while he shepherds forms, bills, and cheques into the appropriate trays, because there is *no-one to fucking go home to!*

He rubs his eyes in the pale light.

Where will I sleep tonight?

16

Neville spins his chair to the right and yanks the drawer open. He rams his hand inside and rustles up an open packet of humbugs. Pinching one, and then another, he drops the bag back into the drawer. He smuggles one into his trouser pocket then pops another into his mouth, rolling the bittersweet creamy mint around his tongue.

Home is here now. At the museum. Dull. Full of shit… Left by the wayside…

He reaches in to pluck up another lidless biro and slides the drawer shut again. Hunching over the desk in his sweaty grey suit, he puts the pen to paper, but it moves no further.

Will *I sleep tonight?*

In just ten hours or so it will be time to open again. He will not need to shower because *customers don't come in on a Friday, do they?*

He drops the pen onto the desk and surrenders his head to his hands.

Why am I here?

The chair creaks as he sits back and pinches the moist shirt away from his skin. *'Bad' always seems to cling to me.*

A distant crash in the building sits him up. Neville stands and creeps over to the window behind him, ducking beneath it.

Through the open door to the hall, shadows dance onto the floor. Neville sits beneath the window and spits out his humbug, which clacks off the desk and onto the carpet.

"Oh fuck… *Why* am I here?" He shuffles across and peeks around the door frame. The 'shadows' have moved elsewhere. Hard to hear, but Neville can *feel* them… shifting through the building, collaborating.

Time to get out… I've got my mobile. I'll call the police when I get outside.

He stands. The way should be clear if they move further on. Just the matter of getting to the foyer and sneaking out through the front entrance, giving no impression he was ever here at all.

They are burglars, aren't they? Surely, I can check, get a look at them…

Neville stalks the wall to the foyer and pokes his head around the corner.

Please steal something, so I can claim a bugger-load on the insurance.

Three men in black, wearing balaclavas, wander around the room. Not one glass case has been broken into. All the vases, old maps and pieces of 'armour' remain in place.

Small wonder the museum is in the red… it's all just shit!

The three men meet up at the entrance to the next exhibit.

Do the British Museum use lasers that detect intruders and shut them in? Pike's Museum of General History and Antiqui-titties can barely afford a bolt across the door!

The burglars march forward, leaving the first exhibit hall untouched.

Do they want something in particular?

Neville, the cowardly curator-turned-helpful-merchant, scurries after them as quietly as his flat feet can muster. At the next corner he glances around at the Arts History exhibit, where the three men separate to prowl up each aisle.

The exit to the car park is behind me… but this is too exciting to miss!

There is only half an inch of glass between the thieves and their prizes, but they show no interest in stealing demi-famous paintings, moth-eaten Victorian costumes, or broken props from Charlie Chaplin films.

Creeping as close as he can, Neville finds himself exposed in an open space of floor. The nearest place he can hide is to his right, behind the display of masks, with chins seated on top of fixed silver rods…

Neville scuttles behind it, but one flat foot clips the side.

One of the men looks back. Seeing no-one, not even Neville crouching behind the display base, the man continues browsing past a row of strung-up, snarling puppets.

Neville stands behind the masks, with no glass case over them, and looks through a horned mask of the Devil on one of the rods. He stares, dumbstruck: 'balaclavas' and 'hiding behind masks'…

'Jinkies,' I've stumbled into a bloody cartoon!

Through the eyes of The Deceiver, he watches the three men rendezvous at the other end of the room, proceeding into the Prehistoric exhibit.

That was too close… Better go and call the police.

Neville gives the burglars a head start. The room gets warmer… The milky-painted interior of the mask seems to get tighter around his face.

I want to get home. And peel off these sticky bleddy clothes!

He tries to stand up straight… but he cannot.

Neville claws at the mask… but it does not come away. Neville stands, and as he struggles, it unhooks from the rod.

He tries to pry The Devil from his skin… but the Devil's face is a perfect fit.

What is this? I can't…

It refuses to let go. His lungs are squeezed from within…

No- I can't…!

CHAPTER 3

A greedy gasp of air fills Neville's chest.

Opening his eyes, he lifts his head with a grunt, and then drags up the rest of his weary body from the hard floor.

The Devil's red face stares up at him with hollow eyes; it bears a sharp set of teeth fixed somewhere between a smile and a snarl. Two bone-coloured horns protrude from its head.

Neville looks away and then back down at the mask. He crouches to scoop it up, as if it could explode at any second, and replaces it delicately onto the silver rod that held it before. He turns and rushes for the back of the museum…

Shoving the door open, Neville stumbles into the merciless glare of daylight. He jolts against the acrid smell of car exhaust clinging to the air, as commuting cars growl past the alleyway behind the museum.

"What? It's morning?!"

He fumbles through his jacket pocket to pull out his cheapo mobile phone, but it slips through his fingers and dances over the tarmac before falling flat. Neville's hands swing down by his hips. His jaw follows as low as it can go.

How long was I out?

He bends down and snatches up the phone; it is 8.33. He dials 999 and brings it to his head… but it is upside down – an easy mistake to make…

"Stay calm…"

Neville clears the three sixes from the screen and dials the correct number. He hears it ring at the other end of the line.

So far so good!

He requests the police and gets through.

Finally!

"Yes- Hello! My museum has been broken into just now- last night, I mean. I don't know if they – the intruders – are still inside."

"Alright, sir," says the stern policeman, "which museum is this?"

Maybe I can claim on the insurance…

"It's Pike's Museum of… General History and Antiquities."

A pause, and then at the other end of the call, a sharp exhale…

Did this prick just scoff at me?

"And your name please, sir."

"It's 'Pike'. Mr Neville Pike."

Another scoff from the man pulls Neville's face into a frown.

"Oh *yes*, Mr *Pike,* we have your address. A couple of officers will be with you as soon as possible."

Neville hangs up.

I bet that copper's belly-laugh could shake the Earth… Bastard…

Fixated on the blue sky, he drops the phone back into his pocket.

"It was nearly eleven pm just now… wasn't it?"

Maybe it was exhaustion… It had to be, for me to have passed out and lost the entire night…

Neville faces the door again.

Are they gone? What else can I do but check?

Sunlight presses hard against the museum as *His Lordship*, now *returneth to the castle*, marches over the threshold into the smothering warmth.

Neville's shirt now clings tightly to his skin in the humidity. Thankfully, with no stairs ahead, all exhibits are accessible to wheelchair users, the hot and bothered… and *burglars*…

Yeah, suckers of all creeds, colours, and shapes, welcome!

He pauses before Arts History, where he had stopped shadowing the burglars the night before. Entranced, Neville retraces their steps into the Prehistoric exhibit – most popular among the few children who ever stop by. Neville had convinced himself it is worth keeping the dinosaur bone 'replicas,' for *educational purposes*, but the parents know better. As he speeds past the seven-foot-tall wooden models, he sees the raptors themselves have not been molested, although after millions of years of extinction, chance would be a fine thing. Neville treads into the hall which leads to…

Blood?

On the floor, a dark red smear… like a predator has marked its territory. *Red* trails ahead, to the left.

Under the battleship grey storage cupboard door, the blood has… pooled.

Although the toilets are directly opposite, Neville feels a pressing urge to 'mark his territory' right here… He holds on, and then extends his cautious paw towards the handle…

But his arms betray him.

Hesitant, Neville steps forward.

Just open it!

He grabs the handle, twists... and the door swings open, pushed by red sticky hands, boots, and blue-bruised heads, poking out in all directions...

Piled one on top the other, broken bodies in black clothes spill out.

Neville stumbles back and falls onto his arse.

He sits up to look, into the tangled chaos again. The sight, the *stench,* snatches his breath away.

Three bodies, *or more*, stuffed into the cupboard... mangled cadavers contort into a tormented chimera... with limbs outstretched at all angles. One of the heads, at the centre, hangs upside-down facing Neville, staring at him with its desperate eyes and its mouth wide open, just like Neville's... but here there are no signs of life. The creature should not stir, to crawl out from the cramped space with a desire to pounce, but Neville flails onto his feet and runs back the way he came, just in case...

***

Orange, creamy, bitty grains of pasta spill over the black tarmac, leaping from Neville's stomach.

Outside the rear of the museum again, he stands upright, breathing heavily, as if a phantom hand has just released its tight grip over his innards. He could not have gone into the toilets opposite the storage cupboard, and then come back out with *those... dead eyes... staring at me...* supposing the jumbled mess of bodies could still crawl out, find him, and with his back turned-

Neville retches, but nothing else comes up to paint the ground, in the colours of his evening meal.

Can I turn around?

Breathing as steadily as he can, Neville faces the building.

He smirks... and walks back inside, pulling the door shut.

Now *the police will take Neville Pike seriously!*

Neville chuckles, assuming it *is* alright to laugh?

Fuck people, of course it is! I've just found a bundle of bodies in the storage cupboard, who cares how I react?

Each step excites him. The door behind him springs ajar, letting in light.

So, this must be where they broke in.

Neville heads towards the foyer, and around the corner towards his office. The first door he sees is on his right: the surveillance room…

He enters, scanning the claustrophobic duck-egg *cell* on his way in; one swively computer chair on the left and one hard, blue, plastic chair on the right, behind a desk. Multiple screens display CCTV recorded on tapes, instead of a hard drive.

Dear old Grandad was stingy. During the day, stingy, and paranoid of the public being around his prized junk. They'd be safeguarding a heap of crap anyway, why waste the money?

Empty chairs…

The security guys are only on the clock morning till teatime! He's got a lot to answer for, lumbering me with this hopeless place.

The remote control lies on the desk; Neville snatches it up and squeezes the stubborn rewind button. While waiting, he glances to his right at a poster against the wall of Halle Berry, also against a wall, in air-tight clothes.

The recorders grunt. Neville presses the eject buttons to check each of the tapes, but-

Gone… Why? Where the hell are they? And where the hell are the police? Didn't I call…

He pulls out his phone and wakes it up…

"It's almost nine! About half an hour ago I rang… They'll be here any minute! What the hell do I tell 'em?!"

Neville looks down at the remote control and picks it up. He takes out his pocket square wipes off the remote, and then the buttons on the recorders.

He wipes is brow, caresses his head, but his clammy paws feel dirty, even though they look as clean as can be.

I need to wash my hands.

***

People in working clothes, aprons, and uniforms, walk into the pastel-coloured shops and cafes across the street to open up.

Neville waits outside the drab front of the museum, while a young, uniformed constable glances up and down at him.

He must think I'm full of it.

"I came in early to set up as usual," says Neville, "and the front door was damaged, so I slipped inside."

"Oh yes..." the constable condescends, as he scrawls onto his notepad.

Just wait till your colleague gets back, you smug little prick.

"Nothing was disturbed, except, on the floor leaving the Prehistoric exhibit, there were these trails of... what looked like *blood.*" Neville is not over the stomach upset. He perseveres. "I followed the trail to the storage cupboard... I felt I *had* to open it."

The museum front doors shudder open. An older police officer rushes outside, with the back of his hand over his lips. He uncovers his face to gasp for air but recovers... his mouth...

You'll take me seriously now, won't you?

Pale-faced, he stands surprisingly tall before his colleague and Neville.

"Three..." he breathes putridly into his radio, "deceased males... all *crammed* right into the..."

Today is a good day to be sick.

"The storage cupboard?" says the *boy*. Officer *Lofty* looks down at him, at Neville and then winces.

I wish I could've showered.

"The forensics team is on its way in."

Today is a good day to keep my mouth shut.

The younger officer, suddenly on the ball, turns to Neville. "CCTV?"

"I don't know. Possibly," he replies.

"Do you have any?"

"We'll have to check…" Neville turns to walk back in, but a hand grabs his modest bicep.

Lofty's hand. He shakes his head before letting go. They stand in awkward silence as the autumnal-plumed early bird crowd flocks all over town.

A siren wails as a police van emerges from around the corner, followed by another, and then one car, close behind. Things keep coming in threes, turning Neville's stomach like a fried egg spoiled by one too many flips.

The vans park up. Doors slide open. Men and women in white overalls step out with metal cases in hand and approach. Officer Lofty breaks away to lead them into the museum. He pushes the doors open, leading the spectres inside.

Neville faces the vans again, but in the way now are two suit jackets on another older, greying man, and a piercing blonde woman in a navy power suit flipping open her police ID.

"Mr Pike," she announces, "I'm Detective Inspector Lake. This is my colleague, Detective Sergeant Tout. We'd like a statement from you, but first, would you show us to your surveillance room?"

No, don't go to the surveillance room.

Neville looks at the old chap to the right, DS Tout, and the bags sinking deep under his eyes.

I bet necromancy is all that's keeping you awake! I'd better keep quiet...

Neville nods, "Right this way."

Christ's sake, I can't even keep my trap shut for that long!

He leads them inside. Police units are dotted all around the room, wandering further into the museum...

There's nowhere to run.

Neville pushes the doors open, with his blood-lusty bodyguards behind, and heads toward the hall on the left.

Wait, I don't need to run! Stay calm...

The seedy surveillance room door is suddenly much heavier this time around as he struggles to push it open. Neville lets the detectives through first.

DI Lake pulls out the comfortable computer chair, leaving DS Tout with the hard plastic chair.

Neville tries not to smirk.

Tout looks around the room, giving Halle Berry the once-over before facing the screens again.

DI Lake presses PLAY on the remote, but the player squawks in denial as the screens remain black. She looks over her shoulder at Neville, stopping him cold. "Where are the tapes, Mr Pike?"

"I don't know. They..."

"What kind of place do you run here, Mr Pike? I see that you don't even keep this door locked. Someone obviously waltzed in here and stole the tapes. I'm surprised they even had to *break in*."

If the museum had those laser tripwires, I could've shut the burglars in and got out. We just don't have the budget.

"We just don't have the budget, Miss Lake."

"*DI Lake,*" she threatens.

"…*DI* Lake… even to keep staff here overnight."

"And you don't have the budget for a lock and key, either?"

"…It's only a small business. And I've only just taken it on."

"I think we've seen enough here." *DI* Lake stands, followed by DS Tout.

Neville steps back out, to *make way for the queen.*

Exit Lake-*Trout*, but as Neville shuts the door her icy gaze chills him.

"Now," she says, "tell me everything you found. Starting from when you first got here. When *did* you get here, exactly?"

Do not dare roll your eyes… Will Lake-Trout take the bait?

"Half-eight…" Neville goes on to recount everything he had *supposedly* found from when he *supposedly* came in early to set up. Of course, he tactfully leaves out his being at the museum last night and passing out after putting on an evil mask.

That would just be fucking strange…

DI Lake jots the story down in her little notebook of doom. Everything is running smoothly.

"I have a business to run. Is there any chance the police could hurry up this investigation? Even… tidy up? Then I could re-open as soon as possible, right?"

The inspectors stand silent. Digesting. DS Tout, The Grim Reaper, shifts his sombre gaze over Neville.

Has he come to take my rotten soul?

"Where were you last night then, *Neville?*" Of course the Grim Reaper has a London accent.

"I was home. Just like everybody else. Well, like *they*

should've been…"

"Is there someone who can vouch for that? Say, your wife?"

Neville clears his throat and swallows his fear. "No. I'm afraid we're separated at the moment…"

Tout's gaze chills him further to the ninth circle of bone.

'Of course you are.' I know he's thinking it!

"I think we're done here," Lake states.

"So… What next… detectives?"

"You can go home now, have some brunch, and we'll continue to look around, Mr Pike."

"Right…" Neville steps carefully around them.

Brunch? Who the fuck could eat, after being around… that…? As soon as I get round this corner, I can leg it!

DS Tout's grave voice booms down the hall. "Don't stray too far, Mr Pike."

Feebly, Neville escapes around the corner, hiding this unshakable, unmistakable stench of death… from the being itself, who has *his* scent.

My time will come…

CHAPTER 4

Plunging hands into the depths, she hauls up another willow pattern plate from a baptism of bubbles.

Kat scrubs it clean. Smooth and fresh-faced, she places it onto the rack, as if it had never been abused before.

Her hands crinkle as she scrubs the next plate, squirming, like cat's teeth piercing meat, while it drowns underwater.

The kitchen is just like any in every show home suited to family living. Natural wood colours above unnatural disputes… Warm white walls that are not easy to scrub free of hot blood… And enough burners to burn food for the family during an altercation.

Now, Kat washes Gemma's little dish. Plastic, pink, no hard sound as she wipes it. The smiling, coloured ponies do not squirm under the scrubber. There was a time when they would gnaw at Kat's heartstrings. But now, nothing.

Kat sets the dish on the rack, then shakes her hands and dries them off with the towel. She turns to observe the kitchen, swinging her chestnut ponytail. It is an irritation, an affectation, doing herself up like a samurai warrior so she can launch an assault on the housework. She refrains from untying it. Everything hurts a little less with the warrior mindset. If there is an obstacle, she can remove it. If there is an attack, she can fight.

She turns around to fill up the kettle… "If only with the blood of my enemies..." She smiles.

Scalding hot tea might burn her mouth and throat, but at least she might feel something... Alive...

One cup follows another, and another, and another, to drown the day away. How many more before she has to pick Gemma up from school?

The kettle bobbles and boils... again...

Kat opens the cupboard and shifts Gemma's little dino-mug out of the way. "'Mummy,'" Kat utters.

Only 'Mummy,' now. No longer 'babe' or 'dear' or 'darling.'

She pulls out a willow pattern mug and closes the cupboard door on the matching set of willow pattern plates, willow pattern bowls and willow pattern saucers. A matching set for a family, that is not.

Her thumb caresses the rim of the cup, but it nibbles at her skin. She checks it, to find a small chip by the handle. All these sets have blemishes.

"Don't we all..."

A pinprick streak of red dribbles from the rim of the cup, under the shadow of Kat's thumb.

CHAPTER 5

Tall, gaunt lampposts lean over. *More* crooked figures peering into Neville's life.

He clutches the steering wheel which goes round, like the police investigation in his head. With the battery replaced at last, his car rolls through town at a *risky* thirty-three miles an hour, so late after the morning rush. Red-white signs drift past on Neville's way home. Not the shithole flat on the other side of town, but *home,* to see his little Gem.

But it's not my *home anymore.*

Neville turns off the road and into suburbia.

It's better that Gemma lives with her mother. I can only bear 'The Flat' for so long. And there's no living under the same roof as Kat, not since…

He pulls the car into *my* old driveway. *My* white gravel, crackles under the car as it pulls up to *my* house…

I need to see Gem.

Neville opens the door and steps out of the driver's seat: *crunch.* He plants his feet onto the stones. He reaches in and grabs the little book of dinosaurs from the passenger seat – *she likes dinosaurs.*

The car door slams shut. His key twists in the lock. The point of no return…

A surprise visit should cheer us both up.

Neville walks towards the front door, *crunching* with every step, as if creeping over thin ice.

Finally, on a slab of solid land, he wipes his feet and rings the doorbell. Neville kneels. He can dream, that *she* might open the door.

I just want to see my family.

The door opens to a pair of sturdy legs in blue jeans. Neville looks up at the merciless face staring down at him.

"Oh. Hi Kat. I know it's a bit sudden, but… could I see Gemma?"

"Nev… it's *Friday.*"

Neville stands up to find even ground, *equal* ground. "I know… but work's not on today because something- Well… I just really need to see her."

"Nev, you can't see her… It's a school day."

"Oh. Christ, of course it is! I'm sorry, it's just… how are you, Kat? Am I alright to come in?"

"You came to see Gemma, *not me*… Bye, Neville." She shuts the door.

Neville steps back, to avoid the impact against his nose.

Stupid! Of course my six year old is at school…

He steps back off the porch… *crunch.*

She didn't have to be so nasty about it. I couldn't just tell her about the break-in… The deaths…

He sulks back towards the car, his heart breaking with every *crunch…*

I'm trying to be a good father, why is she making it even harder?

Crunch.

It was a mistake, fuck you if I care.

Bitch.

I should get to see my child whenever I want!

Bitch…

"Where are the fucking keys?" Neville seizes them, stabs for the keyhole and misses, leaving a dent. He has scratched a darker silver under the dull grey.

More gently, the key slides into the door. He gets in and drops the dinosaur book on the passenger seat, but it bounces off into the footwell.

Neville turns the key in the ignition. A furious growl starts the car. He wrestles with the gear lever until it grunts into reverse, backs the car out onto the road, and roars out of suburbia.

Damn it, I look a bloody fool!

He stares ahead, up at the grey skies over the conveyer belting road.

It's been a fine day for it so far…

Now cooler now, sweatiness pervades Neville.

I'm still in yesterday's clothes! I stink. No wonder Kat wouldn't let me in!

He sweats more.

I hope she didn't notice…

Neville turns right for the way 'home'. His stomach in knots, but with some space in between.

Nearly time for lunch.

He slows, halfway through the town... littered with pedestrians.

Wasters, under-achievers... I fit right in...

Above the population of jeans, hoodies and tracksuits, a grubby yellow sign shines like a beacon for the greasy and the hopeless. The stench of curry, burgers, and bubbling fat inflates the car, and Neville's belly. The craving can only be sated by clamping grilled red meat between his teeth. Neville perks up. And parks up.

Nasty food. But reliable, day and night.

He gets out of the car. The musty clothes constrict him. Neville's warm wallet dislodges from his outer thigh, falling to the bottom of his trouser pocket as he shuts the door. He walks around the car, onto the dirty pavement, and steps into the glow beneath the yellow sign, half-expecting to find St Peter.

Neville approaches the stainless-steel counter as a spherical older man wearing glasses and a flat cap leans against it, waiting for his order.

His mind's tongue samples the pictures on the overhead display.

A bronzed Middle-Eastern man with a black moustache turns away from the chip fryer, steps up to the counter, and nods to him. The beige grease stain on his dull white shirt is the only label he needs. "Yes please?"

"Hi, a cheeseburger and... large chips, please."

The man's fingers blur over the touchscreen till.

I don't even like 'hi'.

The bright cyan five pounds seventy-five flashes on the display. Neville reaches into the bottom of his pocket and pulls out his wallet.

The man declares the price and then turns around to retrieve the other customer's burger. He places it into a copper-tinted polystyrene container and sits it on the counter.

The old chap takes off the top bun, showcasing it in all its glory. He squirts a zigzag of red sauce over the disc of cooked flesh and sliced onion, lettuce, and tomato, piled on top of each other, like-

Mangled multi-coloured organs.

Neville's stomach tenses, cold fingers wrapping around it. He opens his wallet but finds no notes.

The old man replaces the bun, pushing it down. The burger *bleeds* ketchup and bits of garnish protrude from under the bap, like-

Red, sticky hands and feet.

The phantom hand squeezes Neville's stomach even harder.

The old man puts the lid down on the box-

...the lid down on the coffin...

Neville holds his wallet to his chest and missteps back, for the door... "Sorry," he stumbles, "I... have to..."

He runs outside before the front of his car and hunches over, staring at the grubby, grain-speckled pavement while struggling for air.

Neville stands, breathing sour carbon, and tries not to faint on his way round to the driver's side. He gets in and lands on the seat, tucking his legs in. He shuts the door. He rests his head against the steering wheel with a thud. His eyes fall shut.

One car rolls past, tailed by another. His eyes open. He looks up ahead... The road is clear... and no-one has followed him out from the takeaway.

Good. Keys, keys... slide into the ignition.

Neville pulls onto the road and drives to the only place he can go...

***

Neville's shirt falls to the floor as he shuffles off these mortal clothes.

He carries his bare little self into the white, en suite bathroom with tasteless fudge walls – an even more neutral plane than the rest of the flat.

He glances at the mirror... a grave error. A tired man of thirty-nine, looking forty-nine on a bad day, stares back, with pale skin and dark hair *just* starting to grey. He wears dishevelment with his clothes. Yet in this flat, this space, in Neville's life-in-between...

...I am a man...

Not just the separated husband, frantic father, or failing museum curator. He had disrobed himself of all that as soon as he walked in.

Neville gets to be *just* a man here.

His feet stick to the chilly tiles. Perhaps this place is *not* his prison.

Maybe it's in my clothes.

While constricted by his desire to be a good parent and to run a successful business, as long he stays naked, Neville does not have to worry about things like fixing his life...

I'm just a man after all.

Neville Pike, a mere man... standing in the bathroom, naked... staring at himself in the mirror... starting to shiver... starting to shrivel up...

Better get into the shower.

He pulls the cord and the shower sucks in air and water, to spit on him. Neville stands in the cubicle and washes off his bad day in the artificial rainfall. Warm water runs down his back. He is preserved in a white wet space where time outside no longer matters.

On the search for inner peace, *a legendary Kung Fu master* meditates under a cold, back-breakingly heavy waterfall...

Neville turns the shower off and steps back into the present. His toes rest upon the cold floor, followed by the arch of his foot and the rest of his person. Baptised from all stress, this new man reaches for the towel and dries himself off. Unbound by the constraints of this material world, Neville walks into the bedroom. His feet stroke against the rough carpet, ready to find new purpose. He breathes in the musty rising damp.

"I am a free man."

But a free man needs clothes. Naked Neville strolls over to the wardrobe and opens it, in search of what wonders he had left behind from his past life. He pulls out a small selection of trousers and throws them over his shoulder onto the bed, like a toddler rummaging through *Mummy's and Daddy's* things.

Neville opens a drawer, pulls out a pair of blue boxers and slips them on. He stands up and looks behind at a pair of black trousers, faded blue jeans, and pin-striped suit trousers. Separated husband… Frantic father… And failing museum curator…

No.

"I can do *anything*…"

Even commit a triple homicide and get away with it.

"What?"

Who are you trying to fool? There's no running away…

Neville looks around…

No-one else here.

"That couldn't have been me. I was out like a light when all that happened!"

He faces the dresser and pulls out more clothes.

"There *must* be more trousers in here…"

He stands as it dawns on him…

"Of course, they're in the wash. Isn't there anything else?"

He digs further, panicking.

"There's *nothing* else! No, I'm *not* just a loser!"

Were you really out of it, at the museum?

The voice slithers into Neville's ear, like liquid silk swirling around the plughole, before tumbling down the drain.

"I didn't do anything."

There's a devil in all of us, or so they say.

"I'm just stressed. Therapy, that's what I need! Better still, I'll go abroad…"

Neville picks up a pair of black trousers with tiny white fibres magnetised to them, slips his leg inside and then the other.

Separated husband… Now, there's someone with a fresh start ahead of him.

He turns away from his old clothes and stomps briskly out the room. Bare-chested, Neville can do whatever he wants. He approaches the fridge by the front door to his left and opens it… but there is too little inside to alchemise into a substantial meal.

There's no escaping who you are…

Neville shuts the fridge… but this new, tenacious voice in his head jams its foot in the door… grounds him… digs its claws into his head….

How can you get a fresh start with your history? Do you even deserve a fresh start?

Neville stands, staring at the pseudo-wood floor and his naked feet. As soon as he puts on his shoes he will be tied down again to a number of very real, very adult responsibilities.

Wherever you go you simply wander around in your cage.

"This damned town…"

The space in Neville's stomach, a whirling black hole, grows, tearing him apart from the inside. He looks to the fridge again for comfort… but behind the storage cupboard at the museum, *those bodies*, push against the door, wanting *out… Those eyes…* upside-down, stare at Neville…

He is sick with hunger.

"A holiday would be a great getaway. It doesn't matter how much it costs."

You'd be surprised how broad your cage is… Your responsibilities, your whole pathetic life, will still be here, waiting for you.

He turns away from the fridge and walks into the bedroom, past his wide, lonely bed and the clothes draped across it.

Besides, it would be suspicious to leave now… you, being a suspect.

He pulls open another drawer for a t-shirt, *anything will do*. Neville then inserts his feet into a 'fresh' pair of shoes.

He buttons up a clean shirt on his way out with tired, feeble fingers, grabs a mould-green jacket and opens the door.

Wait.

Reality check. He backtracks into his bedroom and fishes his wallet and keys out of his sweaty suit-trousers. Re-pocketing his effects he rushes across the threshold, blanking on the mess of his flat and his life.

Dreams of a fresh start, forgotten…

But the phone rings. A rare occurrence.

Who knows? It might be good news.

Neville picks up. "Hello?"

"Neville… This is Tracy."

"Hi Tracy. I s'pose you know what's happened!"

"Yes. I do. Look, I can understand that you must be in shock, Neville – disturbed, sure – but I needed more than to find police tape and a note on the door to tell me that we're closed for the next god-knows-how-long! I had to find this out from some bobby who stopped me from going inside. What the hell?"

"I dunno, Tracy, I was stuck. The protocol for dealing with a triple homicide wasn't in the museum management handbook."

"You don't need to be smart with me, Neville. I should've been one of the first people you called."

"Well, next time this happens I'll be sure to call you. I'm sorry…"

Tracy sighs. "Do you want to… talk about it? Have you had any lunch yet? It's gone *one*…"

***

The dark wooden table is sticky under Neville's hand. Pub chatter bubbles away…

The remains of a dissected jacket potato lie on the plate before him, with his knife and fork placed together neatly on the skin.

Tracy places her cutlery together too, over the red memory of a lasagne. "It's like pulling teeth getting an answer out of you."

"Sorry. I didn't want to spoil anyone's appetite. That *is* the jist of it though. But…" He looks around at empty tables and chairs.

Safe enough here, I guess.

He faces Tracy again. "…that's only what I could tell the police."

She shifts in her seat with bated breath, uneasy.

"I was actually there," he sighs, "I was already at the museum…"

She watches Neville, scanning his face.

41

"I heard the break-in, from inside my office…"

"Oh my god…" She gets up to leave.

"No, wait!" He grabs her wrist, careful not to crush it. "What do you think you're going to hear? It's not that bad! Please, Trace, sit down just a bit longer."

He lets go of her.

She sits back down, with her handbag on the table, prepared to make a quick exit. "I don't know, Neville, it sounds pretty bad already… And please don't call me 'Trace'. I can only just stick 'Tracy.'"

As if 'Neville' wasn't a stab in the gut every single time I hear it!

"How do you think *I* feel? It's like people stop the conversation just to rub my nose in it, being called '*Me*-who-shall-not-be-named.'"

"What, *Voldemort?*" Tracy smirks.

Hell, there's a snigger! See? I can be funny.

"But anyway," he continues, "I followed the noise and saw the burglars in the act. They were looking around for something. Something specific, I thought. I didn't think we had anything valuable enough to steal… do we?"

"Well… that depends on what you would call 'valuable'. This is this first time this has happened. Since *I* started working there, anyway."

"Oh… Well, that's when I decided to sneak away to call the police, but I…"

"You… *what*, Neville? What did you-?"

"I passed out! That's all… Maybe it was a blow to the head or something because I woke up on the floor. You didn't think I could do something like… *that,* did you?"

"We've not really known each other for that long, Nev… aha!

See? I did stop myself!"

"Well done… But I'm not telling *the fuzz* I was already there. It looks bad."

"It *is* bad! You should've said you were there in the first place."

"The tapes are missing. And I'm not taking any chances. I only told them that I came in early because that's… what I *remember*."

Stop. Please. You're lying to yourself now. See, you do know where…

That voice is definitely not Neville's. He looks again at Tracy, more aware of the pub silence as he stops talking.

You're just aching to open up. Let it all out, like cider tumbling into a nice tall glass… Too much will rot your gut.

"…Neville? I'd better be going. Your secret's safe with me. No-one needs to hear about this."

"Thanks…" He sinks, more burdened than relieved. "Hang on, how long is the museum closed, for? We're just barely keeping our heads above water these days, aren't we?"

"For as long as necessary, I suppose." She stands. "We're just going to have to brave these uncharted waters…"

Neville gets up and walks out with her.

Pedestrians drift by. Cars, vans, and trucks groan up and down the road.

Could this have been a date?

Neville looks to Tracy for… *a hug? A kiss? God forbid… a handshake?*

Go on, be bold! Give her a nice wet kiss…

He freezes. Afraid to show any signs of activity behind his eyes.

"Bye, Neville. See you whenever." She turns, walking briskly in the opposite direction, before he even gets the chance to lean in… The *bastard* voice laughs.

So, she went for the abrupt walk away. How very interesting…

"Shut up!"

A couple of passers-by turn to look at Neville.

Careful. You don't want anyone to think you're losing it.

Neville's thoughts are no longer his own. He cannot hear himself think. 'It' has the mike now. He mutters to the voice, "I don't know what you are or where you came from, but I don't want this, and I don't *need* it. Just. Fuck. Off."

Oh, but you do… I helped, even though you don't know it…

"You're not even real."

You've already seen what 'real' can do. Or does that not hit you close enough… to home? You should secure those tapes. Watch the show…

"Why? I'd have to find them first. *I'm* not looking for that footage, dammit."

Even if that footage might concern you?

"Why should it concern me? Who the hell *did* take them?"

He corrects his posture, having collapsed slightly with the embarrassment of talking to a voice that no-one else can hear, and not thin air.

Where would I even look?

CHAPTER 6

Teeth sink into a sour green apple.

Detective Inspector Christina Lake, chews, with a view of Pike's Museum of General History and Antiquities from the passenger seat. And she *will* get to the core.

This hour is just the same as any on surveillance beside Detective Sergeant Mickey Tout in their blue Astra. Watching and waiting. Waiting and watching… but never in all her career, all her life, has she known such an ungodly stench, as the atmosphere of a vehicle after Mickey has had his cheese and onion pasty. One might think her partner's most basic skills in deduction would tell him, after years of dairy-related treats and the various flavours of gas they generated… said treats do not agree with him…

It is coming up for five o'clock. Christina must 'be professional.' She might make DCI. Maybe soon… Never in all her career, has she ever been more certain that she is *this* close to finding a killer.

Mickey scrunches up the paper packet that held his flaky pastry, at long last. He just *has* to talk with his mouth full of that last bite.

"So, you still like this 'fish' for sardining those burglars then, Chrissy?"

If only his skills in deduction rivalled his knack for sarcasm.

After all his years in the service, there has to be some kind of worldly wisdom to show for it.

"Yeah," she says.

"I do enjoy our trips out." He buzzes the window down and throws his balled-up paper out; it lands straight into the bin's mouth. "Yes! Ha!"

Christina grunts in frustration. Eyes on the museum building.

"We used to play 'I Spy,'" he says. "The most intellectually charged games I ever had were with you."

She could invest in a pair of binoculars, but that would be going a bit too far. Her eagle eyes would come to rely on them, and she would look conspicuous in the middle of town.

"I spy…" says Mickey, "time-to-get-back-to-the-bleddy-station."

"No," Christina dismisses, still fixated on the museum. She takes another bite of her apple. "Not yet."

"'The culprit always returns to the scene of the crime?' Is that really what you're going for? That's not, in fact, always the case."

"In this instance, Mickey," she nods, "it will happen to be true."

"Because he *works* there."

"If he's innocent, he'll have no reason to come back here today, but if he comes back, well, at least we can follow him and see for ourselves."

"Still no chance at 'I Spy', then?"

With her eyes still on the building, she smiles. "Sorry, Mickey. Not this time."

The two detectives settle, watching the building.

A mobile phone rings. Christina does not shift her gaze from the museum even as she wriggles the phone out of her trouser pocket. She glances at the screen: Hawkins.

"Bollocks," she says.

"Hawkins?"

"Yeah."

"Can't ignore the DCI..." Mickey starts the car. "Don't answer. Let him think we're on our way back."

Christina answers.

Mickey throws his hands up in the air, fussing quietly. 'What did I just say?!'

"Yes, Guv," she says into the phone, while holding up a finger to *wait*.

Mickey collapses back against the head rest.

"Back to the station? No... Okay, that's fine. We'll see you in five."

She hangs up and turns to Mickey. "We've-"

"Got to get back to the station, yeah, yeah, I know..." He pulls out into steady traffic. "I don't know why I bother... and I don't know why you want to nab that dopey sod Pike for this."

Christina does not answer. There is no hard evidence in a hunch. Just something in Pike's eye. He seemed so innocent at the centre of it all. Too innocent, indeed.

He seemed to love the attention.

CHAPTER 7

Traffic rushes by from both directions, never slowing, ever flowing like a river. A part of nature.

It's after five now. The police should already have left the crime scene.

Neville stands at the foot of the museum steps, before the yellow tape stretching across the entrance.

"There are probably cameras nearby with a view of the front, but the burglars went in through the back..."

No surveillance there, so Neville walks down the street, to head around to the back of the building.

Yes, you won't look as suspicious this way...

If *only* the voice would leave him be…

Yellow tape spans the back entrance as well, like a fresh web left by an absent spider. He tugs it away and opens the door, looking into the dark…

"I don't think I'm supposed to be inside here."

You want answers, don't you?

Neville creeps inside… Within, he finds the building as quiet as it was left, yet the distinct sense of a dozen strangers poking around lingers, as if they are *still* loitering inside...

"There are so many places to look. Where would I find them?"

No answer.

"Oh, now you shut-up? Marvellous!"

Neville begins at the Arts History exhibit, but *it* catches his eye.

The Devil's face is suspended on the metal rod as if nothing ever happened. Its mouth gapes open, ready to bite down on Neville's hand should he touch it again... Hungry for more... He approaches the mask and snatches it from the rod.

This is it. This is the one I looked through, before I passed out.

According to the blurb, '...Devil masks were often used in Japanese theatre. *This* mask was said to drive its wearer mad.'

Of course it was. Of all *of them, I just had to stick my face into* this *one!*

The soft, fleshy mask seems innocent enough resting in his hands. Every line defines the crimson face and teeth of a demon. Yet *calm* seeps into Neville, holding the smooth cool cheeks as if cradling the face of a lover. He shakes free of his trance and replaces the mask onto the rod.

I'll be looking you *up later...*

Retracing his steps through the Prehistoric exhibit, he finds the dinos hiding *nothing* about their persons... But, beyond the Jurassic era, Neville slows before the storage cupboard. The blood smears are still caked to the floor, a duller colour than earlier. Cool, calm burgundy.

He passes wide of the stain, and *the door*, to browse *Little* Ancient Egypt. Canopic jar replicas fill out the collection around the real article.

Maybe I'll add to the caption, 'Guess which one is the real one!'

Neville even heaves a peek inside the hollow, fake sarcophagus.

Empty.

Next, the Victorian section. A collection at Pike's Museum that spans an extra hundred years before, and after, the era. It consists largely of moth-eaten dresses, suits, and antique jewellery.

The hunt goes on…

He picks pockets, opens chests, and wrestles with whether to look under the skirts of mannequins…

But no tapes.

The accumulating indignities spur Neville's search for truth about last night, as he blurs into the twentieth century, pre-war, war and *post*-war, various collections of biscuit tins; saturated reds and blues, fifties women blushing before men holding bouquets of flowers. He bursts open one after another, until… he finds they are all empty as well.

There's only so many other places I can search! Dare I look…

But Neville glances each side of him for spying eyes. Having come full circle to end of the tour he, like most of the museum's visitors, is put out by the waste of time. The building is empty… for now. No-one else can be inside if he is going to warm his hands over this burning curiosity.

He braves to step once more through Arts History. Marching past the mask, avoiding eye-contact with the Devil's eager, hungry stare. Those hollow eyes burn into his spine, urging him forward… but Neville welcomes the momentum as he passes the static raptors and *tiny*-ranosaurus rex.

The smears on the floor grow the more he sees them, the more he gravitates towards them.

Surely, when you come into contact with blood, it touches you. It stains your soul. It leaves you unclean… Don't look down…

Neville treads around the murderous marks and presses forward. Each step becomes harder and harder as if one magnet repels another, pushing against him more and more until he makes himself stand, at last... once again... in front of the grey storage cupboard door.

I've done this before, haven't I? Why stop now?

He snatches the handle and pulls the door open, and the reek of dead meat rushes out to greet Neville, as if the broken spirits of the damned have come to hug an old friend. He winces, in grief more than disgust, at the rancid air.

"Empty... They've been taken away..." Neville steps inside, looks under and around mops, buckets, and other cleaning supplies.

How did three bodies fit in here, in that *state?*

Lying one on top the other, crushed, beaten...

Neville sighs, finding nothing. He breathes again, calmer... until he realises *what* air he is breathing, in the middle of the cramped space that barely contained three fresh *corpses*...

Neville rushes out of the door before it closes... He looks back around...

Of course it wasn't going to shut!

With a keen hand, he swings the door the rest of the way... but it stops, ajar. It drifts open again...

Neville raises his leg and shoves the sole of his shoe against the door, slamming it shut. He lowers his foot, wary of the door, and the invisible force that might still be inside.

At last, Neville turns and rushes behind, into the visitors' toilets opposite to look under the sinks and inside the cisterns. Or to throw up again...

No luck, either way.

Is it this other 'will'? Who is this, what *is this thing, riding shotgun? I'm a nervous driver at the best of times...*

He exits the toilets and stops before the storage cupboard… "Still shut."

Thank God, right?

"Stop wasting my time. Where. Are. The tapes? Tell me!"

But you're already getting warmer.

As the light dyes orange beyond the windows, Neville notices the museum's back door. "

Clever boy…

He runs as quick as he can for the exit. If the *voice* knows what happened to the footage, and it does concern Neville… then black, sticky, video tape could have him bound at the hands, feet, and mouth.

***

Soft plastic wrapping, and unknown specimens of cold slime, caress Neville's hand as he reaches down to the bottom of the bin.

Nicks and scratches from scrunched-up cans and pointed corners breach his skin, as if he is molesting a nest of angry scorpions.

Neville pulls out his hand to once again bathe in the peach-tinted sunset.

The police will've looked through the bins right outside the museum, but those fucking tapes had better be in these, opposite, or…

He slips his hand into the other slot, bracing against the bitter, sickly smell that permeates the rubbish. Pushing down, weaving his knuckles through more wrappers, papers, and bottles…

Almost to his shoulder in waste, Neville's hand dives further, stretching out fingers until they clip against something hard. He seizes it and hauls up a greasy, black video tape.

Fucking yes! The other two have got to be here as well. It

52

just wouldn't be bleddy practical!

Neville rams his hand down through the slot again, his fingers wrap around another hard object.

He drags out… the second tape… and stacks it on top of the first one.

Neville places them onto the pavement, beside him. He reaches into the putrid bin once more.

This thing would *be almost full…*

A lot of rubbish to sift through. A lot of slime. Not a lot of luck…

Neville pulls out his hand, somehow holding the last sticky, red-stained surveillance tape.

He grabs up the other two black boxes and stands, clutching them, while quickly scanning his surroundings like a squirrel holding a nut.

No nearby witnesses, aside from one very confused, very old lady who slows before Neville staring through large thick glasses. She clutches her bag to her chest.

Neville forces a smile and then turns away to charge inconspicuously across the road, rushing back to the rear of the *prestigious* Pike's Museum…

***

Finally!

Sitting in front of the screens in the surveillance room, Neville wipes off the videos with a tissue before he inserts them into the recorders, and then pushes the buttons on the sets to rewind them quickly. He balls up the tissue and chucks it into the bin, through the hoop of a mini-basketball set.

Neville faces the screens again… And the three blurry burglars wandering rapidly backwards around the exhibits.

Where the fuck's the remote?! There! PLAY:

A blurry Neville onscreen is frozen, hiding behind the mask display as the burglars leave. He struggles to pull his visage away from the face of The Devil. Neville stands, with the mask as his face, trying to pry it off again… He panics, clutching at his throat, and then collapses onto his back.

Seconds pass… when suddenly, he springs to his feet, and marches off into the Prehistoric exhibit.

Fascinated. Awestruck. Neville leans in, closer to the screen.

Which one's the next screen? REWIND, dammit! PLAY:

The masked figure struts past the static raptors.

Neville points the remote at the next screen, displaying the hall beyond.

PLAY… I pressed it, you bastard! PLAY:

The three burglars approach the Ancient Egyptian exhibit. One of the men stops to look around.

The masked figure walks up to the trespasser, grabs his collar, and punches him in the face one, two, three times… *More…*

The other two burglars rush back. Each throws a punch at the figure, but he avoids them.

The figure lands one in return, knocking back one trespasser. He strikes the other man and continues to beat him to a pulp. The figure approaches the first – and now last – man standing, knocks him back to the floor and kicks him in the ribs… until he stops twitching.

The figure returns to the other two on the floor and, with absurd strength, kicks them nonchalantly towards their third man, like rubbish. He grabs each of them, like dolls, and flips one on top of the other. He circles behind them, holds up his hands against the bodies and pushes, sliding them forward. His feet slip around the floor as he achieves momentum, pushing them to the left, leaving blood smears all over the floor from leaking faces.

The figure steps around the mess to open the storage

cupboard. He steps back behind the bodies, kicks, and punches the deceased trespassers until their remains finally fit inside. He swings the door shut, but it does not close against the stray limbs. He forces the reluctant appendages inside and then pushes his back against the door until it closes.

The figure leans against it to get his breath back… and then jumps to his feet again. He sways from side to side, clicking his fingers and kicking his feet out. He jives to and fro, dancing victoriously back the way he came…

"Who *is* that psycho?!" Neville erupts. "That can't have been *me.*"

Neville stares, agape, with the urge to retch… but manages to resist the aspiring geyser of stomach acid. He turns back to the screens when, in perfect sync with the previous scene, the Devil-masked figure glides into the shot…

…dancing through the Prehistoric exhibit, stomping, twirling his way into the middle and then all around the room… moving gracefully into…

"A *waltz?*" Neville leans forward. "But *I* don't know how to waltz!"

Full of dread, he watches the next screen…

The figure sidesteps gracefully into the Arts History exhibit, with wiggling jazz-hands. He jives back and forth and spins around flinging his limbs out repeatedly… slowing to a halt, when he falls back onto the floor, panting.

The figure lies still…

"He's fallen asleep! Where's the fast-forward on this thing? Here…"

Ten fifty-seven; twelve-midnight; one am; two; *three o'bloody clock!*

Five-six-seven-eight, who-do-we-app-re-ci-ate?

The mask slides away from Neville's face. He wakes. And stands up at…

"Eight thirty-one! I… was this really because of that mask?".

It couldn't have been. You were just delirious.

"Yeah, I *was* delirious."

That's what you want to think, isn't it? That you are not really mad, or indeed murderous?

"What?"

Someone threatened your business. Your life! You had to do something about it. It was all in self-defence…

"Wait…"

And you loved it.

"Stop it! No, I didn't!"

Liar…

Neville sinks into his swivel chair which squeaks – or did it snigger? He clutches at the rough fabric, a desperate grip on reality as he digs his nails dig into its dark, tightly woven threads.

"Even if that *was* me… I've been under stress. A *lot* of stress… I can't go to prison. Gemma needs a father. What could I do if I go to *trial*? Plead insanity?!"

Remove the incriminating evidence.

Frantic, he presses the relevant eject button… The three recorders stick out their black plastic tongues. Neville pulls out the tapes and holds them together. He stands, boxed in the middle of the room, looking around as if carrying a bomb.

"Fuck! Where do I put them?"

A woman's giggle reverberates from the foyer. He opens the door, to peek-

Wait. There's a camera in the hallway.

Unsure if this *is* really his voice of reason, Neville takes the mini-basketball hoop off the bin, drops the tapes into the innocuous, half-full, white plastic bag, and ties the knot.

Tying the knot... Another commitment! Well, my dear Kat won't be finding out about this!

Neville places one tentative foot out of the room and shuts the door as he ambles towards his office, trailing the bag behind. Having escaped the imposing, objective eyes of the CCTV, he places the bag on the beige office carpet, unties it, and pulls out the three tapes, one by one, cradling them on his left arm.

The giggling gets louder. She is getting closer.

Neville pulls open a desk drawer.

No, can't put them in there.

Though more at ease with his own 'head' voice, the tapes weigh down on Neville's arm, eager to pull him down to Hell for what he has done.

Where will I end up, in the end? – 'The' end... I haven't been good all my life. I try to be nice. I really do! But it's just another mask. I'm a bitter, jealous creature. Among blissfully ignorant cattle.

Despite managing to blend in up to this point, as Neville finds red sauce smeared across the labels like the drag marks on the floor, he fears a similar fate.

Looking down at the carpet, he sees a stray humbug. Neville crouches and picks it up, not that he got the chance to finish it last night... but in front of him, a dark space under the drawers of the desk waits... still... hungry... looking just wide enough for the video tapes to squeeze underneath.

Neville chucks away the humbug, and then sits two of the tapes on the floor beside him. He places one on the gristly carpet with one narrow end facing the desk. The carpet purrs as he slides the tape underneath. A perfect fit. Neville positions the second tape the same way, next to where he pushed the first one in. Another contented purr from the carpet assures him as he pushes it in. Neville picks up the third tape, sets it down in the same space as before and pushes it beneath the desk.

Purr… Click.

Stopped. One end of the tape is still exposed. He slides it to the left, then pushes. *Click.*

Oh god, it's caught on the fucking beading! *I need it to fit!*

Neville turns the wider side of the tape to face him, and eases it in. *Purr…* Click, gently, as if the hunger has been appeased.

It fits!

"Hello?" Tracy opens the door.

Neville stands quickly. Unstable.

"…Neville?" she struggles with putting on a resistant earring.

"Yes! Hello again, Tracy."

"What are you doing here?"

"I needed to come back and see if I left my mobile… charger… but I thought I'd clear out the bins while I was here."

She doesn't look too convinced.

"What about you?" He asks, "What brings *you* back here?"

"Ha… well, I thought I saw you come in. Just wanted to make sure everything was all right."

"Thanks… I was just passing by, and I was getting pretty desperate to get my mobile – charger – and to see what they've done with the crime scene. Have you seen it since you came in?"

"I thought about it, but I usually faint at the sight of blood."

You could've fooled me.

Tracy and Neville exchange a stilted 'How was the rest of your day?' as Tracy puts a foot back over the threshold.

It's always the bloody same thing people say to each other. 'I'm terribly sorry, Tracy, you've just caught me in the middle of trying to get away with murder! Cue the intermission! Neville Pike will still be just as guilty when we return again...'

'...Well, that was Tracy with How her day has been' and now, over to Neville, with the weather...'

With small talk out the way at last, Tracy puts the other foot out the door.

Ready to escape, no doubt.

"Well, I'd better leave you to it then," she turns rapidly around.

"I've got what I came for. We shouldn't really be here, anyway. Let me walk you out." Neville follows her.

"That's okay, Nev, I'm actually in a hurry." Tracy marches out of the office.

Neville follows sheepishly. "They say the killer always returns to the scene of the crime. *I* wouldn't want to be alone around here."

Don't say that, you creepy bastard...

Tracy looks over her shoulder at Neville as she nears the end of the hall.

"That's okay, I didn't come here alone..." she bumps into a tall fellow as he comes round the corner.

"Hey, *you*..." he puts his hands tight on her hips.

"As I was *trying* to say," Tracy clips Ben in the chest, and slips from his grasp, "I'm *not* alone. This is Ben. He... really wanted to see the crime scene, so... seeing as no-one else was here..."

And by 'no-one' else that includes me, Miss 'I-thought-I-saw-you-come-in'?

"Oh," says Neville, "fair enough. If you don't get caught... What did you think of it then, Ben? I'm *Nev*, by the way."

"Yeah, it's pretty interesting actually. Not every day you get to see a crime scene like that."

Funny, how trivial it is to anyone who isn't at the centre of it. Even dear Tracy isn't that connected to the bloody 'venue.'

"Great." Neville catches up to Ben and Tracy and overtakes them. "You know, while you're here, why don't you take the tour? It's on the house!"

"Thanks, Nev!" says Ben. "See you around!"

Gullible tit.

"I'll leave you to lock up, Trace." 'Nev' races for the exit, not looking back.

"Bye, Neville," Tracy blushes.

The full 'Neville' again, is it, 'Trace?' Oh well, you stick around and hook up *again. You deserve it…*

CHAPTER 8

This could be the end of me… if anyone finds out.

Full of panic as much as food, a nervous smile pulls at Neville.

But no-one will *find out. No-one can…*

Unsettled in the pub, he picks up his lager for a cool, refreshing sip, a drip feed of Dutch courage…

…a 'sip feed' rather…

…having seen his murder spree on the CCTV.

Neville looks around once more at the barely populated bar. Sitting at the end, a zombic, pre-thirties oik in a green hoodie plucks out crisps to crunch upon, one at a time. The walls are peachier than Neville's temperament. He sits surrounded by empty round tables placed before plush bench seats, flanked by dark wooden chairs.

Out of the corner of his eye, Neville sees a folded newspaper on the table behind him and turns to reach for it… He has to stretch… *got it…* He pushes his plate out of the way and opens the pages.

What a treat. Teatime, sitting before an empty plate… Nursing a drink and reading the paper… Peace and quiet… I should kill more often.

Neville shivers.

Ordering a meal in a pub twice in one day… I'm not on holiday!

He glances over the black and white shapes that fail to register as words.

Will those bodies make the front page? Tomorrow's headlines will be advertising 'my work…' Is this how killers think? Is this what they do? Perhaps I'll order a steak. It could be my last meal anyway. No wonder these people feel the need to... treat themselves… to a good murder…

A door whispers open over the carpet as a dainty blonde woman in a blue coat slinks in on matching shoes. She locks eyes with Neville for one long second, and then turns to the bar to order a drink.

Neville hides his face behind the paper. But, too unsettled to read, he peeks over the top and watches the blonde take her something-with-lemonade to a small round table in the centre of the room.

Of all the empty tables she had to pick that *one? She wants to be the centre of attention?*

Neville watches from the side lines… a nobody, peering in.

Only for science, mind...

Hush… the door opens again, as a well-dressed fellow, with a sculpted face and chin, and well-kept hair, struts in… well-smug before the lady… who greets him with a polite smile.

A totally different breed, the snobs among us… I should've been one *of them! I* would've *been, were it not for such terrible luck…*

The man breaks away to go to the bar, with affected, pointed, white shoes gliding across the floor.

The woman watches him – and his arse – saunter gracefully

away.

People are so transparent they may as well be made of glass.

…and Neville wants to throw stones.

Gorgeous, privileged… Why do they get to be so happy?

The blonde glances over at Neville.

He drops his eyes down to the newspaper. As she notices him, he feels suddenly that he actually *exists*. He *slowers* the paper away from his face.

The fancy man saunters back to sit in the chair opposite the blonde.

Is that what constitutes appeal to women now? Metrosexual poodle-headed ponces who and carry themselves around like they're wearing leotards?

Snapping the paper shut, Neville drops it onto the table and gets up. He marches for the door, followed by the couple's eyes.

I hate people who put on a front, and the others who inevitably fall for it. Well, I hate people, full stop. Why can't they just be honest about the wicked selfish bastards they are?

Neville steps outside under the dulling pink sky and turns right, down the empty, crazy-paved street for the longer way back.

A walk around the block will buy some time before getting back to the flat.

He walks against the wind, whose cold fingers stroke through his hair.

"Excuse me, mate, have you got any change?" Sitting cross-legged over a mat on the pavement, a man in lived-in clothes looks up at Neville.

Automatically, Neville digs into his pocket for a couple of coins, and glances down at his palm as he hands them to the guy.

"Oh, thanks! Much obliged…"

Neville nods near-smiling before carrying on.

A whole two pound fifty! It was the decent thing to do, I suppose. I can do it!

His hands sink into his pockets as he savours every step on his way back towards the dingy flat.

I'm still a doomed failure of humanity.

As he stands by the traffic lights, a shiny red convertible glides past. The couple from the bar, in sunglasses, drive nonchalantly around the next left turn, out of sight.

Every other bugger goes on, so fortunate, so privileged, not a care in the world. Everything and everyone I have always breaks or abandons me. It shouldn't be like this. It can't just be bad luck.

Like succumbing to 'possession' and killing three people…

Neville stops. "But why put me towards the tapes? I would've been better off leaving them."

You had *to know the truth.*

"My life is over. After everything, anytime now I'm going to be found out for something I didn't choose to do. I'll get arrested… or worse…"

He looks ahead, the only way is forward. Neville steps around a corner as various cars continue to drift past him. "Fuck you. All of you."

No-one hears under his breath.

It's safer to hold onto this loathing inside. Safer for everyone else than wearing it on your sleeve.

"Well…" he muses, "what can I expect when I hate everyone?"

The flat is just ahead. "At least I hate everyone equally,"

Neville answers to himself as pushes on.

No, everyone besides Gemma. I could never hate her. If it wasn't for Gem, I wouldn't hold on. And the jury is out on Kat for now...

Neville finds himself at his flat at last. His one safe place.

***

The cold white sink shifts slightly under Neville's hands, too late at night.

He looks up into the bathroom mirror, at his face, baring the toll of a frozen income, exclusion from his family. A loss of purpose.

"I'm sorry."

Who are you sorry for?

"I never meant for my life to end up this way..."

Which part? Dead-end jobs, broken family, murder?

Neville's reflection listens as *he* does, and speaks as he does, "Who are you? *What* are you?!"

You know, this could all be traced back to separating from your formerly beloved Kat. So needy... and then she goes and discards you as soon as she gets what she wants!

"Answer my damned question!"

Not too loud, or the neighbours will hear...

"Where did you come from?"

Where do you think I came from?

"That mask..."

No... I've been around, since long before... Long before you first started to think.

"I don't understand."

You could say... I know you as well as you know yourself.

"Tripe!" Neville storms out of the bathroom.

You dwell and feel sorry for yourself now, but you know where it started to go downhill. Besides being born, that is. Everyone's still trying to recover from that one...

"I just want to go to sleep."

You can sleep long enough when you're dead. Speaking of... you must really miss your mother right now.

Neville glares into the bathroom, clenching fists.

...Always there for you, someone to talk to when you lost your toy...

Neville storms towards the mirror.

How inconsiderate of her to just up and die, so ahead of her time.

He slams the bathroom door shut.

No more from the voice…

Maybe it is *all just me. It's understandable. I'm bound to talk everything over with myself, considering the trauma I've endured. But, given the body count at the museum, this can't just be my 'common sense' talking back to me…*

Neville hauls up the duvet and slips into his safe, cotton cocoon, as if he has a chance to sleep.

The very teasy cater-pillock might wake up a mellow man by morning...

CHAPTER 9

Blood on the floor. Blood under the door. The storage cupboard full of bodies. Death…

…wherever Neville Pike goes.

What makes crime scene photos so haunting is that they depict the wake of a ghastly event. It is not staged. It is not art. There is no humanity in such brutality. Or, perhaps, there is an abundance of it…

"Like an animal defending his territory?" Christina can only ponder aloud as she stands and stares at the board, all alone in CID. She is immune to the stupor of stark lighting, dark windows, and quiet.

"Or…" barks a male behind her…

She whips her head round to find Mickey…

"…like a man who's snapped." He dawdles closer with his coat over his arm. "You haven't snapped, have you Chris? You know what they say about talking to yourself…"

"No," she chuckles, "just little old me. It's the only way to have a sensible conversation around here."

"Speak for yourself. I was only wondering if you wanted to stop for a swift half on the way home, but then I thought you had company." He steps closer. "Are you making your way home anytime soon? I don't want you falling asleep at the wheel tomorrow. Or tonight, for that matter."

"Sure…"

Mickey faces the door, leading the way out.

Christina turns. "But how could one man overpower three, just like that?"

He stops, weary. "What? I don't know, Chris. Maybe it wasn't just one man."

"There's no evidence to suggest anyone else was there."

"Exactly, there *is* no evidence! The tapes are missing, and it's suspicious. Pike is a creep, but he's a desperate creep. That's all he is. He's not our man." Mickey marches over to the door and flicks a switch on his way out.

The lights blink off around Christina.

Footsteps… The lights flick back on again.

Mickey turns to find she has caught up to him, to argue, "What about where the bodies were found? How were they all squeezed into such a tight space?"

Mickey faces her again, taking his time for dramatic effect. "I don't know, Chris. How would one man-who-isn't-necessarily-Neville-Pike manage to squeeze three men into such a tight space?"

Christina's eyes shift from side to side, scanning her mind for any hint of a rational explanation.

Mickey reaches for the light switch once more when Christina interrupts, "Freak adrenalin."

"Eh?"

"Like… that phenomenon of how a mother can lift a car to save her baby."

"How often has that ever happened?"

"It's not impossible, Mickey. We're just not sure on the means, but Pike would still have the motive. He was defending himself, or rather, his territory."

"His territory? Yeah, alright… Why not? We'll go with that." He turns to walk out of the door, to leave for a home-cooked meal with the wife at last.

"You really don't believe me, do you, Mickey?"

"I think… scratch going for that drink. You sound like you've had a few already. I'm driving you home."

"I am not drunk. And I'll drive myself home, thank you very much."

"Will you? Right now?"

She looks back over her shoulder at the *bloody* board of bloody crime scene photos.

"The victims will all still be dead tomorrow," he says, "Look, you're not a *robot.* Just imagine how much clearer your head will be after a good night's sleep."

Christina faces Mickey again with a sigh. She flicks off the light switch like a stroppy teenager and steps around him, leading the way out.

CHAPTER 10

It's been okayed at last.

The shiny, grey VW rolls along red brick *Stepford* houses.

I suppose it's too much to hope that all of yesterday was just a very long, very tedious, very traumatic dream.

Neville pulls up to his – his wife's – house and gets out of the car, with the dinosaur book in one hand, and in the other a plastic, green, goofy-eyed T-Rex from that film-

What's it called?

The front door opens and…

"Daddy!" Before Neville even gets to the door, a cheer from a golden-haired munchkin brings him to his knees. He sees the crystal blue sparkle of her eyes as she runs on little legs, into him for a tight hug.

The stony ground sinks its teeth into Neville's kneecaps.

Ow…

Gemma releases him and stares with a milk-toothy grin.

Neville feels all the lighter. "Hi, Gem."

With his radiant, blue-moon smile, and sore knees, he

stands while Gemma chuckles adorably at his mild agony.

That's my girl.

"Come on, walk me inside!"

As Neville clamps her gifts under one arm, Gemma grabs his free hand and pulls him towards the door with all her might.

Strong child, for her size…

He utters a pained groan as she tows him over the gravel.

Kat – the gatekeeper – leans against the doorframe, watching this magic reunion. Perhaps his presence is all the sweeter for not always being there.

"Only for a couple hours, mind," says Kat. "You're going off to spend the rest of the day with Nanny and Grandpa, aren't you?"

Gemma's only grandparents. Another stabbing reminder of what Neville has never been able to provide. He stops before Kat.

Gemma releases him and wanders inside, oblivious to her mother's words.

"What, *why*? You don't have to spoil it, Kat."

"Did you think I wouldn't find out about what happened… at the museum?" Kat's voice is a harsh, scornful whisper.

Neville returns the tone. "I would've told you… but I was in shock. And you sent me away, remember?"

"You came over here with the dates mixed up. In *that* state, no less! I thought… while Gemma's over at Mum and Dad's… we could talk."

That sounds sinister.

"You *could've* told me, Nev."

You didn't give me that impression yesterday, darling.

"Come in," she turns away to lead him inside, not giddily up the stairs, as in times gone by…

71

Does she still care? At all?

You *shouldn't*.

Neville follows Kat right into the living room and stops before Gemma sitting on the floor. He kneels down on the softer-than-gravel carpet…

Oh carpet, thank you! I've missed you!

"I've brought someone along who wants to meet you…" He holds out the green, scaly, smiley T-Rex.

Gemma spreads out her arms for a big hug. "Rexsy!" she cheers, wrapping her little arms around the rigid reptile.

"*And* I brought you this!" With the thick little dinosaur book in his hands, Neville attempts to dazzle as she takes it.

Every child-appropriate present you get for your offspring is a gamble.

Gemma studies the book with an eerily grown-up scrutiny.

She hates it.

She lifts her face with a cheeky grin and holds the book over her head. "Read it to me, Daddy!"

Oh, thank goodness for that!

Neville cosies up beside her and reads aloud. Sneaky compensation for hearing less of her father's voice these days.

The book takes about an hour to read. *Twice.* The rest of the following hour is spent playing. Kat peeps in from the kitchen every now and then…

Perhaps Gemma doesn't get to have so much fun without her dad around…

What about your *fun*? You didn't seem to be having much before!

Neville lies on the floor beside Gemma, watching her draw

a pair of black outstretched wings, a horn, and another horn…

Neville catches his breath… when there is an affected knock on the door.

No! We've still got quarter of an hour!

Kat strides through the living room and disappears into the hall. Monstrous, aged footsteps creep inside.

What fresh hell hobbles in through the door, besides her parents? They're fifteen minutes early, the bastards!

Gemma does not shift despite hearing them stumble in and croon over Kat.

That's my girl.

Kat's parents waddle in, each wearing the face of *loving grandparent*.

"Hello, my darling!" says Moira with open arms.

Gemma looks up at her.

"Go on, say hello to nanny," begrudges Neville.

Gemma climbs to her feet and wanders over to Moira, less than animated.

It's just as much an ordeal for her as it is for me, bless her. That, or she knows what's really going on.

Hugh loiters in after Moira. Little white wiggly fibres springing from Hugh's cardigan catch Neville's eye.

"Hello, Pickle!" Hugh hugs Gemma captive, as Moira releases her.

Already, she has to be all things to all people…

"Hello, Neville." Moira suspends all emotion. Apparently, Neville is not even worth expressing her animosity.

"Alright, Moira?"

No response, just the way he likes it.

"*Neville*," Hugh acknowledges, not looking him in the eye.

As he carries Gemma out, she leans over Grandpa's dark fleecy shoulder. "Bye-bye, Daddy..."

"Bye-bye, Gem..." Neville tears up. He puts up an arm to wave. Indeed, to snatch her back in his mind's eye.

But Hugh disappears into the hallway.

Is that it? 'Bye-bye?' Aren't you even going to put up a fight?

"Bye, Love!" Hugh says to Kat.

"See you later!" She stops before the hallway. "Bye, Gem, be good!"

I *won't be seeing you later, you sanctimonious old codger.*

Moira turns to Kat and hugs her warmly. "Lovely to see you, Darling."

"You too, see you later."

Moira faces Neville and looks him up and down, keeping perfect composure as if in the face of a fresh turd on the doorstep.

"See you, Moira."

"Bye, Neville." She scuttles off.

Neville smiles as he pictures Moira walking out of the room and right into an industrial woodchipper...

Kat follows her out and shuts the door.

Never mind, there's always a chance the winter will claim the old fools... Then you can have Kat and Gemma all to yourself, without Hugh and Moira's petty whispers spoiling everything further.

Neville stands in wait, looking down at the dinosaur, the book, and the fiendish doodles Gemma had to abandon...

Kat lets out a massive sigh as she returns to the living room.

It's such a weight off her mind? This is what being a single parent does to someone. I really should be here.

"Well," says Neville "they behaved rather well, didn't they?"

"It's not them I'm worried about... Please, let's sit down."

Is she that tired?

Kat and Neville sit on the couch. The canyon of space between them is marked by the join between the two seat cushions.

"How are you holding up, Nev?"

"Fantastically, considering."

"No, you're not. You're really not."

"Don't be silly, I'm not at rock bottom yet..."

The only way now is up, after all!

"It wasn't that long ago that your grandad died. I know you weren't close with him, but it must've really shaken you up. And then you up and left your job..."

"I thought the museum would bring opportunities... money, and flexibility. That way I could be there more for you and Gemma."

"That's great, Nev, but what about this *break-in*? You found the bodies afterwards. Don't you feel the need to take time out?"

An intervention. One woman attacking on all fronts! Do I stay on the defensive? ...Do I retaliate?

"I don't have much choice at the moment," he says, but Neville's rage still has a say in the matter.

Permission... to engage?

He sits, a statue of flesh, desperate to keep the scene in his head from playing out... Beating Kat into submission... dominating her... *worse*...

75

"The museum's closed for the investigation, so I have all the time in the world… For about a week or two. I hope."

"I mean, to take a break, not just from thinking about work, but thinking about Gemma and me. I know you mean well, but-"

"I do. Mean well. That's why I moved out for the time being. Kat, you know what that job was doing to me. And I thought that would be fair for both of us."

"I don't want to go there today, Neville… I just wanted to talk about *you*."

"We *are*, Kat. If you're gonna talk about me, we *have* to talk about *us*."

She jolts up before Neville, baring her teeth. "Do we really? Or are you going to hit me again?"

Blood chills Neville's veins. No one in the whole world has any desire to console him, comfort him… or even hug him.

"That happened only *once*." Neville rises softly, "and never again. I am not my grandad. And I'm certainly not going to just up and disappear like my bastard father. But I suppose that doesn't matter, does it? You don't trust me at all…"

Neville shivers. Unwanted. Every particle of his being is willing to die right here and now.

"I know you love your daughter, Nev, and she loves you too. My god, she adores you! But I'm worried you're holding onto each other too much."

"What are you talking about? She's the only thing that's keeping me going."

Oh, cue the trash *talk-show intro*!

"That's my point! You're a grown man and you need to do more for *you*."

"Like I *deserve* that."

"Nev, it's not about deserving it. You *need* to take care of

76

yourself."

Words no longer pull their lips together to soothe them in moments of despair. They no longer connect even just for the hell of it. Their fingertips no longer kiss and stroke the other's hands.

"I'm trying, Kat. That should matter. It matters to *me* that I got it wrong. Doesn't *that* mean anything to you, too?"

"We took our time apart so we could heal. *Both* of us... But *I* haven't healed. *You* haven't either... I don't think we can ever be what we were."

Neville's fingers coil timidly, tightly, into his fists.

Kat's hands sit in her pockets, hiding her nails as they scrape against her thighs as she braces against another awkward, painful encounter with her once-loved man.

Having not so much as touched each other this day, how can they not help but wonder if the person standing before the other is really there?

Neville struggles to even see Kat right now, through his blurry, watery eyes.

"I think..."

"Don't say it, Kat. Please."

"...it's time we get a divorce."

Her shape melts through the lens of tears.

CHAPTER 11

Crunch, crunch, crunch, *bitch, bitch, BITCH!*

Gravel buckles under Neville's march to the car.

Kat runs out of the house in tears, "Nev, wait!"

He rips open the car door.

"Neville, please, don't do anything stupid!"

"Oh, don't worry. I've had *my* fill of stupid mistakes." He gets in and slams the door shut. Neville starts the engine and launches out in reverse… into the horn of an oncoming car.

He stops short of it. Neville collects himself, reverses out, and drives…

Kat shrinks in the rear-view mirror.

What about Gemma? What do we tell her? What will she think? Why didn't I stop to say all this before I-

Neville swerves to avoid a lorry and its bellowing horn… He drops to the speed limit… on the correct side of the road.

It would just suit her if I copped it, wouldn't it?!

***

In the black mirror of the telly, Neville watches the pathetic sap sitting on the couch, surrounded by the four drab walls of his flat.

The grey afternoon falls over him like a heavy blanket. His blurry reflection loses any definition of him as he ruminates upon the meaning of his life.

Well, enough's enough…

***

A gold-filled glass that chills his fingers makes Neville a day drinker. But patrons will bring the night with them later anyway. Meanwhile, black clouds still loom over Neville, to drench him with woe sooner or later.

You've always been miserable.

"It's not my fault," he whispers.

Permanently absent father… Mother died when you were seven…

"And held back by controlling grandparents…"

Even now, you are still held back. Waltzing in to run Grandad's museum, ballsing it up… If anything, you've made things so much worse.

Neville stares into the amber reflective nectar of false wisdom ever shrinking from his glass. He would be kicked out if seen talking to his drink in the middle of this establishment.

The museum has ensnared him.

"That place is drinking me dry. And now I'm cut off from my own child."

No chance of redeeming yourself through her now, eh? Poor Neville, so much of him gone to waste…

"I was supposed to be a success by now. Rich. Famous! I haven't endured all I have to come only this far. Any futile ambitions to be free and create were put out of reach by my *bastard* grandparents, pushing me into an office job and sitting me behind a desk."

Watching better opportunities pass you by?

"Damn you, Kat... I was enough for her once. I even took my job more seriously. Sure, it was a strain, but we were together, we were happy... We had a home, a baby on the way... I worked *hard*."

But it wasn't enough. It wasn't enough to fulfil expectations...

"When Gemma was being born, Kat screamed every decibel for the both of us, for the *three* of us. I was so proud of her... That naked squawking child was proof that we survived thus far. We still had our heads above water by then. But the stress, and the pain we endured to make it all work... We were going to make it work. We had to."

But willpower isn't enough.

"The strain, the pressure... It was too much. I lashed out. Now it's *all* gone."

And now you're a curator, to 'a diverse, fascinating historical centre, full of character.'

"Is she even going to stay in our house? Or will she take Gemma away with her, to some godforsaken hole miles and miles away?"

You might as well expect the worst.

Neville takes a hefty swig of his cider. More hefty swigs tally up as he puts away more pints that can be counted on one hand...

Students trickle into a flood on the Saturday night floor.

Time to leave... Time for beddy-byes...

"Drink reshponshibly, kids..." He wanders out the door, past one or two smug, chuckling, turning heads... yet another nail for his coffin.

Neville stands in the middle of the drifting nightlife to take a breath. Neon signs and glowing shopfronts mark the path each side of the pub. Colourful blurs drive past under streetlight. He paces unsteadily forward to the edge of the kerb.

I could end it all here…

He steps…

Left… and walks the wobbly walk home… but a figure stands among the pubbing and clubbing stragglers, absolutely static before Neville in the shifting tides of night.

The well-kept man in a dark suit, stands with his hands in his pockets. The light does not touch him, but for his pointed white shoes… He stares fiercely at Neville. "Excuse me, Mr Pike… could you please tell me exactly what your opening hours are these days?"

"You what?" Neville is dizzy.

"When does your *museum* open? I'm *very* interested in seeing what you have in there."

"Um, the muzeum's closed till furva notish… pending a murder inveshtigation, you shee." He stumbles past and totters for home.

Neville glances over his shoulder at the man facing him with a sigh.

Tired, Neville looks ahead. A pisshead Moses before a stream of people parting like the red sea.

He half-sleeps the rest of the walk home with muscle memory, his only guide, puppeteering his body through the opening and closing of doors…

Somehow Neville's key finds the lock and with a twist, he drifts into the black hole of his flat. The door falls shut.

"Ohhh…" He collapses onto the couch like a felled tree. "…fffuck it…"

***

Yellow streetlight leaks into the box of shadows and onto Neville's bed.

He stirs under the covers, having migrated from the couch, when his bedroom door opens… and something shuffles across the carpet.

Fingers coil over the edge of the bed, followed by the rest of a hand. And another hand…

And *another* hand…

Neville stirs, under the alien mass over the duvet around his toes. He looks down at his feet…

A head – stubbly chin first – rises, *grey*, with a gaping mouth that sucks in desperate air. The nostrils, like black eyes, stare closer and closer into Neville…

He watches, petrified as the hands press down onto the bed. Neville's feet and legs tilt down towards the pale, grey creature as it looks up. Its dull, dead, blue human eyes bear a frozen expression of fear, reflecting Neville's current state during his *last moments on Earth*…

The creature pulls itself onto the bed, so clumsily at first it nearly falls off, but it snatches at Neville's leg and holds on. With a third, reversed, hand the creature pushes down on the bed so it can bring up its right foot. *Both* right feet.

The will to scream fills Neville's lungs more than air. Instead, he shivers. His body's *silent* scream.

The slow, black-clothed, and bloody arachnid beast crawls over him. Its upside-down head at the front, hangs from the top body, whining and whistling as it inhales. The left and right hand of the lowest body claw at the sheets, bringing the creature forward. A broken neck carries another drooping, drooling head. It walks on two reversed arms belonging to the top body, while the black slacks and shoes of the sandwiched middle body hang over the front like mandibles. The lowest body's legs push the beast from the back. Neville might only assume the middle body's head watches out for an attack from the rear… but that is the *least* of his problems as the bloody chimera grabs at Neville and scuttles until it sits over his chest.

I can't breathe!

Neville's ribs buckle under the weight of three dead men, as the lower body's half-dead head dribbles all over the duvet. The upside-down head at the top leans into Neville. Its open mouth lets out a raspy, corpsey breath in his face.

The creature's mouth expands like a huge python and engulfs him from the face down, covering his body in pitch black darkness.

Cold floods him within…

CHAPTER 12

Pathetic!

Neville's eyelids pry themselves apart. He lies paralysed under a shroud of duvet, heavy with the morning sun. His eyes are the only mobile part of him.

No sign of any monster. No trace it was ever in his bedroom.

A relieved sigh escapes him, as he savours waking from disembodiment, before starting a new day as 'Neville Pike.'

He shuts his eyes again, enjoying each breath before he has to move… with the alcohol-induced vice around his head.

Look at you… discovering the inevitable, and then 'boohoo, I'm off to get pissed again.'

Neville lies still, eyes shut, but the voice does not stop at 'cut to black.'

There are far more productive ways to spend your time.

He breathes louder.

I can't help but wonder… if those tapes are really safe…

Neville's eyes snap open. "What?"

Given the… 'other' strange man that tried to catch you

84

last night, and his interest in the museum, you should reconsider how secure the footage really is… or rather, 'isn't.'

"No-one's gonna find them. I'll do it tomorrow…"

Tomorrow – Monday – the police might be back for a more thorough poke around. And if they find the footage, well… Think of your family! 'Ahem,' or Gemma, at least…

Neville grumbles. Swinging one foot off the bed and onto the floor, he stands under the crushing weight of his throbbing, cider-soaked brain. "Maybe the divorce thing was just a nightmare, too?"

When have you ever been so lucky?

Neville gets himself ready… for a *different* kind of work…

***

No police cars outside the museum.

No police inside, then.

Neville makes his way in through the back door.

Sneaking into my own museum had better not become a habit!

The probing feel of police inside has faded, but the journey to his office, his only other sanctuary, stretches out more than usual. Neville quickens his pace to avoid the very walls of the museum that appear to close in on him.

"What will I do with the tapes if I do find them?"

You destroy them, of course! And… you mean 'when.'

Neville treks onwards with last night's alcohol circling his system… weighing down each step.

Why are you dragging your heels, now? Hurry up!

"You seem agitated. That's not like you."

You need to secure those tapes. Otherwise, divorce will be the least of your troubles.

Neville reaches the office *at last*. "Tracy didn't see what I was doing the other day. *Of course* the tapes are still here…"

He crouches to look under the desk, and finds the space underneath…

Nothing but carpet and shadow. And no tapes.

"No… No! Who took them?!"

Could be the police… Could be Tracy wondering what on earth you were doing down on the floor. Could even have been Kat, coming to check up on you and the museum. All she'd have to do is watch the footage and, just like that, she can finally tell you to your face the perfect reason why she wants the divorce.

Neville kicks the *bastard* desk so hard his toes curl, sore…

Blackmail looks good on her…

"What do I do now? Hope and pray the tapes aren't found? Deny everything? Plead insanity?!"

That won't get you anywhere. The attempt to cover up your involvement was too obvious.

"But *the Devil made me do it!* So, who's fault's that, then?"

Silence…

"Well?!"

Alone again.

Of course… I guess you're not in control of everything after all… Which begs the question…

"Who the fuck has me by the balls?!"

Neville hammers his fists onto the desk… and then once more. His socks absorb sweat. Underarms leak. He falls to his knees, wilting over the tacky desk. The chill of chipboard kisses his forehead as he sobs.

The arms of a good woman are not there to comfort him. There is no voice to tell him everything will be alright.

But finally dry of tears... cold, melting alone in his quiet office, his desperate breaths are not joined by company.

Neville clamps his mouth shut. Breathing through his nose, he stands, finding some semblance of clarity.

Stomping out of his office, Neville wades through the murky silence. He might stumble onto anything... that could surface and devour him.

"If my last days of freedom are going to mean anything, I may as well see what I can find out about that night..."

He makes his way to the Arts History exhibit.

I should really 'Katch up' *and cherish the time I have left with Gemma.*

But there he stands, suddenly before the Devil's crimson face.

Neville crouches and peers into the duller inside of the hellish mask.

Even the interior is carved in immaculate detail, marking the shapes and lines of a face... a *living* face.

A huge pressure suddenly falls upon Neville, like heavy rain soaking him.

This side of the mask entices Neville, a perfect fit pleading to be worn.

His hands float up to each side of it, gripping each demonic ear.

The air around him changes...

The cool painted face warms up in his palms, bringing heat to his chest, his stomach, his very core. The mask sucks his face inside and softens... as a second skin. Neville's true face...

He breathes the freshest air he has ever breathed. Old paint and varnish… dust and must…

…never smelt so good.

The fear of…

…the ignorant pigs…

…that broke in…

…never felt so good.

It is now *that* night once more. Tingles run up and down his arms and legs. His hands curl into fists. He feels the impact of his knuckles against one of the burglars… *never pelt so good…* Two more come at him and he avoids their punches. He beats them down and feels them implode as each kick collides with their broken bodies…

Neville felt so good…

Neville rips off the mask.

He stands, in the present, at the museum with no-one around… and shudders. "What the fuck?!"

Why, you were having the time of your life, that's what.

"But I never wanted to kill anyone…"

He puts the mask back on the fixture, mindful that it might actually bite.

But you thought about it. A lot… People are nuisances, aren't they? And you have so much to get off your chest! 'Want' has nothing to do with this. It just feels right.

"This doesn't tell me where the tapes are!" Neville storms for the back door. "What's the point of all this? I have a daughter who needs me. I can't go to prison for this!"

He steps outside, at the rear of the museum.

"The tapes won't be anywhere inside now, anyway," he

muses aloud.

"What tapes? I'm intrigued!" Opposite the door, a man in a suit looms, with his hands in his pockets. He sounds not unlike the voice in Neville's head…

Neville's stomach turns. Such a slick, cold entity *standing* before him, in white shoes and a grey suit, no less – this is *not* merely some disembodied 'will.'

"The museum's closed this fine Sunday," says Neville. "Can I help you?"

The suave man steps boldly forward like the museum is his.

I wonder who looks shadier right now.

"Isn't that police tape stuck on the door? You don't look like a detective."

"It's *my* establishment."

"So you *say*… But I knew Mr Pike senior. He… very inconveniently *died* before he could give me the something I was after. I was hoping you might know where to find it."

"I don't know what you're talking about. Grandad and I weren't exactly close. I don't know you and I can't help you right now. Sorry."

I'm not dealing with you, you creep.

"My name's Nick… Nick White. And I'd *really* like to take the tour."

"Like I said, the museum's closed until the police are done with it."

You *were outside the pub when I left for home!*

Neville presses the police tape back in place. It comes away, but he pushes down harder. It sticks… just. He steps away and *have a nice day's* past Nick.

"*Today* would've been as good a day as any…" Nick turns

towards Neville… who has already gone.

Around the corner, Neville hurries streetward. "What the fuck was Grandad up to before he died?!"

But his new alter ego has not followed him out of the museum this time. At least Neville has the *mike* back again.

And did he really snuff it *from natural causes?*

CHAPTER 13

His second-in-command picks up...

"Morning, Tracy." Neville wanders the flat with the phone to his ear.

"Hi, Nev, I just stopped by the museum. The police have been in touch. We can open it up again!"

"Oh. Great! That was quick... When exactly?"

"Tomorrow. Didn't you get the email?"

"No... I mean I did, of course. I just wanted to hear your dulcet tones! In fact, I was wondering... if there was more to Grandad's death, given the incident with the burglars... Was there something else that brought it on?"

"I couldn't say. I... I was the one who found him, but..."

He freezes. "Sorry. I didn't know."

"He was in the chair. In the office..."

"Oh..." *The chair I've been using for weeks!* "Right. Was he under any stress at the time?"

"Funny, you say that..." she answers. "Why do you ask?"

"I was thinking, it seemed very odd the break-in happened

not that long after he died. And then there's the way those men were... dispatched."

"It could just be coincidence, Neville. We've never had a break-in – in all the years *I've* been working at the museum – let alone murder."

"That's *so* reassuring..."

"I can't think why they'd want to steal anything from the museum. The value is 'purely intellectual', as Mr Pike Senior would say."

Senior, indeed!

"What about that Devil mask?" Neville paces.

"What?"

"That *ugly* thing. The one in Arts History?"

"Oh. It's from Japan. Like it says on the plaque. Why? You're not thinking of taking it home?"

"No, *god*, no! It just... caught my eye, that's all."

"We're supposed to have some new stuff come in tomorrow – well, *old* stuff, obviously – so our consultant, Mr Mosley, should be coming in to validate it. You can ask him about the mask when he gets in. Thank you for phoning, Nev. I'll see you tomorrow."

"Sure. Bye..."

Tracy is quick to hang up...

...Of course. She couldn't stick you for too long.

"So, the police are backing off for now..." he puts the phone down. "I should have more time to find the tapes!"

Silence...

"At least I have Monday all to myself."

Thump-thump. Thump-thump. Thump-thump.

92

The walls spring to life with their own pulse. Loud, repetitive bass from the sound system upstairs.

"That thug bastard's off again…"

Then, do something about it.

"I've already told the landlady."

What's she gonna do? Spank him?

"Well, what do *you* suggest?!"

You could kill him.

***

Tracy looks up from her monitor, at Neville passing by.

"Morning, Neville. It's good to be back… Those new exhibition pieces should be arriving dreckly."

"Thanks, Tracy."

She's always typing… Is there that much admin to do here?

On his way towards the office, Neville stops before the surveillance room. He taps on the door and looks in on the security staff… "Morning, Mike."

Mike turns, sitting upon the comfier of the two chairs. The lower buttons on his powder blue shirt fight for the high ground over his belly. The waistband of his black trousers clings firmly beneath his gut.

"Do we have the replacement tapes in the machines yet?"

"Yeah, all ready to go," says Mike.

I can't see him going anywhere, anytime soon!

"Good stuff… I'll see you around. Have a good one." Neville shuts the door on nodding Mike as he raises his steaming mug.

Stepping into the office, Neville shuts the door, drops to his knees, and looks under the desk…

"Someone has the footage of me beating those men to death…"

Well, you'll just have to be on your guard, won't you? You're not in handcuffs yet…

"That does *not* fill me with confidence!"

A knock on the door turns Neville's head like a rabbit caught in headlights.

Tracy opens it and leans in. "Am I interrupting something?"

"No… just… dropped my pen… Come in."

"I just came to tell you that… Mrs Pike is here."

This should be fun.

"Thank you, Tracy… I'll be right there."

He follows her out to reception.

Tracy sidles elegantly back behind the desk and observes Neville approaching Kat, who wears an unflattering dark blue uniform skirt and blouse. She stands with her arms folded, eyes primed and ready.

Neville stops just short of the potential blast radius. "You didn't take time out of the post office just to see little old me?"

"I had a dental appointment," says Kat. "Thought I'd take a diversion…"

"Did they find anything wrong?"

"No."

"Well, I wouldn't expect the *dentist* to find anything wrong."

"Oh, Nev, really? Here?" She maintains perfect adult cool.

"No… No, let's… talk in my office."

Tracy watches as Neville leads Kat towards his *evil lair*…

He lets Kat through and then closes the door as she eyes up the room…

…Making estimations, judgements, whether she's dodging a bullet with me, no doubt.

Please! Bit late for her to have done any dodging, don't you think? She's just here to check the exit wound.

"Are you really *happier* here?" she asks.

"Imagine *my* disappointment. But now I'm stuck with it."

"Pretty little thing you've got there working at the front." Kat wanders around to behind the desk.

It's not like I have anything to hide, is it?

"She was here before me. Cunning bugger, mind. She was ready to take over the place after Grandad died. Had every intention of doing so, too!"

"Why didn't you *let* her?" She sits in the chair and leans back. "And stay at your old job, bring in two lots of inadequate income?"

Neville smiles in spite of her multi-pronged dig.

Grandad died in that chair.

Maybe someone else should, too.

Her dainty pale hands curl over the arm rests. Ruby fingernails probe the leather at the sides.

How long has the ring been missing from her finger?

"I walked out of it. I hated that shitty job."

"This impulsiveness has got to stop, Neville. It's already done enough damage. You can't go wrecking any more of your life."

Watch me…

"Says the grown woman spinning around in my office chair?"

Kat smiles…

"Divorce, Kat? Are you sure?"

Her smile melts away. "It's been long enough since you moved out, Nev. It's only rational."

"But you don't see me more than once a week. Wouldn't it be fairer to give us one more chance? What about Gemma? She needs her dad."

She whirls away from him and then sighs. "I'm starting to wish I did this over the phone."

"It's a good job you didn't. I hate the phone."

"I know you do, Nev, but we all have to do things we hate sometimes."

"I wouldn't know. I'm busy doing stuff I hate all the time. This isn't how it's supposed to be."

"*All* the time?" She stands. "You have a daughter, for god's sake! Christ, here we go again… You're not the only person in the world who has ever suffered! It happens to be a symptom of living!"

"Well, I *am* suffering… I'm living without the only people I care about."

"Well, *I* hate to do this, too…" She steps around the desk.

She could have stayed behind for cover.

"It's been one blow after another, Kat.What is it now?"

"I just dropped in to see how you are. After you nearly got yourself into a traffic accident, storming off like that."

He's fine and dandy, my dear!

"Oh, for fuck's sake!"

If only the voice would stay out of this…

"Look," Kat urges, "it's not ideal, I *know*, but you've been out of the house long enough, and I don't even know what we're supposed to be waiting for. More of the same when you get back? Inevitably losing your temper, again? I can't be doing with it. Not for the rest of Gemma's childhood. Not the rest of *my* life. Besides, you'll still get to see her!"

"Speaking of Gem," he says, "what does she make of all this? Does she even know about the way things are going?"

"I couldn't lie to her. I *wanted* to, but she's too clever! In fact, *she* suggested that if this isn't working out between us, it could be for the best to end it."

Even your own child doesn't want you in the house. What are you kicking and screaming for?

"She's a chip off the old block, our Gem..." Neville marvels. "But I think I know what's brought this on. I *thought* you'd already met someone else."

Of course!

"No, that's just it," Kat admits, "I had one nice conversation with someone, one nice, non-judgemental, guy. And I realised we can each start again with a blank slate. We deserve to. I can't wait forever..." She steps closer to Neville. "Besides, it's not like it's that easy for me either, you know. 'Single mother seeks decent man – comes with pain-in-the-arse ex-husband!'"

'Non-judgemental!' 'Ex!' See what she did there? Hysterical!

A sigh tickles on its way out of Neville, Pulling up a laugh and indeed a cry.

But the voice is already laughing...

You have to laugh. It really is so dire...

"'Ex...' I don't know how or why I've kept... *losing it*. I thought things would be alright at last now that I'm working here, keeping up the family business... with an emphasis on *family*."

"You've always been bitter, Nev. But this museum isn't the answer. If it was, you'd have come home already."

Nothing to say there, 'Nev?' Are you 'unfulfilled?'

"I've got to get back to work. My shift starts at noon." Kat steps out of the office first followed by Neville, dragging his feet.

Silence, as they rack their craniums for anything else to say.

Have you both said all you wanted to? No more last desperate declarations of love?

They approach the entrance, and Tracy's pricked-up ears…

Oh, the all-seeing Tracy, tracing *our steps… And our* silence… *Knowing her, she can hear our bloody* thoughts!

Neville holds a door open for Kat.

You just have *to get the last word in, now, don't you?*

"It was an ulcer they found, wasn't it?"

Kat, without looking back, gives him the finger playfully over her shoulder.

He smiles, letting the door fall shut. Not a soul in the world wants to hug Neville Pike right now. Not that he needs it.

He gazes only at the floor as he ambles back to the office.

Staying out of his way, she faces into her monitor again.

Neville strolls into the corridor, into an echo of his own making. Of chuckling… or indeed sobbing…

CHAPTER 14

Murder is great for business.

The first day of opening since the break-in-triple-homicide, nearly twenty visitors this morning have already graced Pike's Museum of General History and Antiquities. Old-timers, mostly. Even midweek, the half-dead and dying get curious about a murder scene.

Neville approaches the front desk, as two more customers walk off with tickets from Tracy. Service with a smile...

I really should kill more often.

Neville burns with a question for Tracy, "When was the last time this place got so much attention?"

"I don't think I've *ever* seen so many visitors in one go! But have you seen the looks on their faces on the way out? This won't last."

"Do you know when Mr Mosley's turning up? At this rate, we'll have to put up the 'new-*old* stuff' and hope for the best till he comes to proof them."

"Oh, I had a call from him earlier," she says. "He said he's sorry, but a client contacted him at the last minute – a wealthy, foreign client."

"Oh *yes*..."

"Yeah, it's a small window of opportunity for him apparently. In France. So, he can't get here till next week... if we're lucky."

"'Lucky?' Well, we've already lost him then." Neville drifts away.

Tracy scoffs. She looks to him again, but Neville is venturing into the exhibits. "Where are you off to?"

"To get the full tour experience for myself." Neville saunters towards drab-painted colours and unwelcoming aromas of must and dust in Arts History.

Studying the reactions of visitors who stop to browse and read, he can hardly rub his hands with glee – this spike in business *is* only temporary.

Just like any paying visitor, he approaches the mask display to observe the plaques. A painted wooden African mask stares vacantly at Neville on the far right of the stand, next to a miserable *Comedia Del Arte* Old Man face.

"Expanding the collections would be a good start," he mutters, "Ugly bastards aren't they...?"

Says the man with many faces...

Left of the Old Man is a white, lightly decorated Geisha mask, but Neville slows before the Devil's face, wary of the secrets it knows. Although, if it were not for its diabolical intervention, business would not be booming like it is.

"*All* of them are ugly..." he mutters.

Beside him, a hapless man wearing a flat cap and glasses approaches the mask display.

Neville watches from the corner of his eye, the man raising his hand...

What is he doing?

He reaches to touch...

Get away!

...the Devil's painted lines...

"Don't touch that," snaps Neville.

The man drops his hand. He stares blankly, guiltless, like a cat caught stealing food.

"I... really should put up a sign for these." Neville continues the rest of the tour, observing reactions from the beer guts and silver-tops, as they regard the plaques and exhibition pieces.

Truly, like cattle... Drifting from place to place, nothing better to do...

He finds the prehistoric exhibit scarce of anyone, even though this leads right up to where *it* happened. Beyond the false skeletons and the glass tanks filled with artificial greenery and scaled-down lizards... There lies beyond, a place, where real bodies were laid to unrest...

Maybe I should take out this one and expand the rest. It's not like we'd ever have any artefacts from the Jurassic era. What were you thinking, Grandad?

As he passes through, he spots a small crowd of four or five elderly ghouls trying the door to the storage cupboard.

People are animals! Is there anything else, other than death, to keep these people interested?

This is very much the scene in Romero's *Dawn of the Dead*, where the zombies break into the shopping mall...

You know how to get five hundred cows into a barn?

"Put up a bingo sign..." Neville smirks as he wanders past them.

"Pardon...?"

In response to the raspy voice, he turns to face one of the old men. "Enjoying the tour, sir?"

"Oh *yes…*" says the old man.

"You know," Neville pulls out a key on a string in his pocket, "I'm sure you could all squeeze inside there if you stand up straight."

I might even lock you all in for the authentic experience, if only this were the actual key. Although, I'm not quite sure if the smell has gone yet…

"Would that appeal to you?"

"Uuuhhh…"

"Then perhaps you and your friends should kindly refrain from hovering around… *there.*" Neville turns and walks on.

If only people knew the mask *was behind the murders! Then, there'd be a lot more interest. 'The Devil made me do it,' indeed…*

"Here, why not try it on…" he chuckles quietly to himself… until a sobering idea surfaces…

Is it actually just me*? Hearing voices? Killing? Is this really some sort of nervous breakdown?*

As if he would know…

None of this would've happened if I hadn't walked out on my job… Stayed here till late… Found that bloody mask! There's nothing here in the Ancient Egyptian exhibit to steer clear of as well, is there?

From handsome head to shiny toes, the omni-coloured plaster sarcophagus in the middle of the room gets the full benefit of Neville's gaze.

Grandad, what was the point of all this? You faker… Am I losing? Would anyone be able to tell the difference?!

Neville stares in the vacant painted face of *'King Tit'*.

Is there someone inside? Anything at all…?

Laughter. Obnoxious laughter, reverberates…

You are your own worst enemy.

…inside Neville's own head.

Maybe, you should kill more often…

***

Rosy sunset lights up the town. Windows up and down the street glimmer and glow around Neville as he stands on the doorstep of one particular house.

How long has it been, months… a whole year?

His knuckles rap on the door.

Oh, the suspense!

"He's not exactly the quickest mover at the best of times," mutters Neville.

At last, the door opens. The chap behind it looks surprised. "Who are *you*?"

"Cheeky bugger…" says Neville. "Alright?"

"*I'm* alright. It's the others… Are you coming in or what?"

Neither is the hugging type.

What a relief… surely it hasn't been that long since we last spoke!

Si heads into the kitchen on uneven, crooked legs. His steps beat a distinct, but soothing rhythm for Neville. Familiar.

Cerebral palsy's a bitch, eh?

He shuts the door and follows Si into the spacious kitchen.

There's enough room to fling a few bodies around in here!

"Long time, no see," says Si.

"I know, right? Doesn't time fly when you're not having fun."

"I saw in the paper about you taking on the museum. That was almost as weird as the story on the front page!"

"It was me who found the bodies…"

Just dying *to talk about it, aren't you?*

"That's mad, man! Are you *okay*?"

"Still trying to recover from it, really. How've you been, mate? Everything alright with Caroline?"

Si's face drops.

What a note to start on!

But then he chuckles. "*No,* no, we broke it off a few months back. I'm… seeing another bird now, *Millie.* Taking it slow, mind."

"Oh… Well, keep it up. So to speak!"

Si smiles, leaning against the work top, but his skinny legs do not straighten. "How've you been since Kat, mate?"

Neville melts a little, "She wants the divorce."

Also, a devil mask made me kill some people, and the police are after me…

"Oh! Well… at least you have your health."

Silence.

A snigger escapes Neville.

The flood gates have opened. Laughter spills out from the two of them, threatening to wash away the whole town…

Would that be such a bad thing?

A cuppa or two later, Si walks him out with his offbeat limp.

"Thanks, mate," says Neville.

"You've surpassed yourself this time," says Si, "coming over here, with your *troubles!* Seriously, if you ever need to get away from it all, just come over. It's been way too long. And the guys haven't heard from you, either."

Ah yes, I wonder what they'd think of my predicament…

"Yeah, I'll take you up on that!"

"Good," says Si. "Listen, however things turn out with you, Kat, and little Gem… I hope you can *settle* soon. Families change shape all the time these days. So, hang in there… you miserable sod!"

"We'll see…"

"You'll figure it out. See you around."

"Bye, mate." Neville steps out.

With a coy smirk Si shuts the door as Neville, lighter and brighter than the surrounding dusk, goes over to the car, gets in, and drives for home…

How long do you think your renewed little friendship's going to last?

"As long as I can bloody well make it, mate!"

You know, hell is other people…

"That's rich, coming from you!" The accelerator sinks under Neville's tensing foot. His fingers strangle the steering wheel.

What makes you think I'm 'other people…?'

"What do you mean?"

The car swerves rapidly round the bend… A little girl looks around.

Neville gasps. The car shrieks. The girl has no time to…

"Fuck!" shouts Neville.

The car grinds to a halt. The bonnet merely brushes against her dress.

"What are you doing?! Get off the bloody road!"

She runs onto the pavement and towards a front door. She turns and waves with a cheeky smile and rushes inside.

Neville sighs with his head and hands on the wheel. He sits up and puts his foot down, but the car has stalled. He turns the key and restarts it. A shrieking vehicle catches up behind him as he moves off, just missing him.

"Oh, fuck off!"

It voices its horn as he accelerates, leaving the halted car in his rear-view mirror. It lurches forward – another car has gone into the back of it.

"Oh shit…"

It's always one near miss after another with you, isn't it?

"You call that a near miss? What if I get caught?"

Don't worry. I'm sure you haven't lucked out just yet…

"Whatever. Just… don't distract the driver."

That girl… she looked so much like Gem…

CHAPTER 15

Waking light trickles into the sleeping museum to stir every shadow.

Still walls and monuments eavesdrop on Neville and his echo.

When you organise the new exhibition pieces, that'll be the time to make the switch...

"I don't want to bring this thing home!" Neville stares at the face of the Devil as if speaking with it. He looks around to find no-one else in earshot.

But if those tapes surface, you might want some way to lead the investigation away from you. And... you'll feel better having it around...

"I don't need that thing."

It belongs with you.

Turning away from the Opposer, Neville double-takes at the reception desk.

She's already typing away. It's 8am! When'd you get in? And what the hell are you working on?

"Trace..." he *winces* over... "Tracy, when do you think we could start working the new – *old* – pieces into the exhibits?"

"There isn't really a slot until Sunday." She looks up at him at long last. "*Maybe* Saturday…"

"Couldn't I get Mike to help with the lifting?"

"Not likely. Your grandad usually saw to the layout, out of hours. He said there was an *art* to it."

"Oh. Well, it's not like my evenings are that busy these days. I'll see to it then, I guess."

Tracy faces him hesitantly. "Would you… Like me to help with that later?"

"No, that's okay, you don't have to give up your evening. I'll see to it." He approaches the front doors and pushes through for some fresh air. A bemused Tracy watches him, as if hoping a drunk will make it home safely on his own.

As he watches the peaking nine o'clock traffic, distant, bass muttering catches Neville's attention.

Three thugs meander up the road with cigarette fumes permeating their huddle. They turn their hooded heads one by one towards the museum.

Those… three were loitering before the break-in. Surely, they're *not…?*

"What do you want?" he growls.

The *weird brothers* turn into their huddle again. The thin streaks of cigarette smoke peter out as they drop their fags and stamp them into the pavement. They stalk past with pursed lips. Fierce glowing eyes strafe Neville as they get closer.

Neville watches aloofly. He steps back inside to safety… for now…

Whose safety? Just don't come in… don't come in, don't come in, don't come in, don't come in…!

He looks back, puzzled, at Tracy, a *machine* at that computer.

Just what the hell is she working on?

He faces the door again, waiting for a fateful, *fatal*, knock, as the hoodies crash their way in…

But the doors remain still. Quiet.

Neville pulls one open slightly and peeks beyond. He leans further out to see the street more clearly. The hooded pack of thugs skulk away.

"I'm sure they'll come today," says Tracy.

Neville jumps. As he turns, the door shuts heavily, making him jump again.

I hope they *don't.*

"Yes! There's nothing more enticing than a strange man hovering around the entrance, is there?" He strolls back, inconspicuously, towards his office.

***

Anoraks, strays, and small families trickle through the doors of the museum, coming and going… underwhelmed…

Neville pops back in for a break from people, and out again to check on… *it.*

It *can wait 'til the end of the day. Can't it?*

The mask's resonance grips Neville all the way to his desk. An invisible force, pressing against his chest, fingers dig through, and pull at his ribs…

It's surely… too dangerous to leave alone with the public…

At five o'clock, Neville slithers into the foyer as Tracy slips her handbag over her shoulder.

"See you tomorrow, Tracy!"

Hurry up and go…

She faces Neville, but her energetic spark from the morning

has fizzled out as the day has gone by…

…or maybe she's just teasy.

"Are you sure you want to start bringing out the new stock this evening," she asks, "all by your lonesome?"

What makes you think I'm lonely…?

"Yeah, I've got it. Thanks, Tracy, goodnight!" Neville struts immediately into the Arts History exhibit. His ears ring with the call of the mask.

After all this time, she must still want to take over the museum. Ambition like that doesn't just go away. She's biding her time, waiting for me to snap. But I won't… I won't snap. I can take the pressure… especially if people want to throw their money at the museum. At me…

He stands once more before the smug scarlet leer propped on its metal rod.

Neville scans his surroundings, shying from the shadows that have returned in place of gormless faces.

Yes… the coast is clear…

He brings his hands up to the mask. Tentatively, he lifts it off. The pointed teeth under parted lips invite a kiss… a bite… Its enraged hollow eyes invite a look into the abyss… but his stroking thumbs savour the smooth surface of the devilish red visage. Neville turns the mask over in his soft dainty hands. His fingertips explore the carved lines of every inverted feature, tracing over every ridge and curve and dip from its eyebrows down to its chin. He expects his fingers to release the mask, but they are welded to it…

Should I really be doing this?

There is no-one around. He could put the mask back and go home.

But I've come this far. I may as well…

Neville aligns his nose with the Devil's and pushes his face into the mask, as if into a bowl of cooling water.

The mask sucks Neville in, hugging him tight.

Not again! I can't breathe!

He claws at the mask to pry it off from the sides… *Deville* savours the air filling his chest.

His lungs like bellows stoke the fire. He lowers his hands, letting his fingers follow the contours of his face, his burnished face, acquainting with his lips, his fangs, and his horns.

Deville's hands hang at his sides. His fingers flex, finding soft delicate palms as knuckles whiten. Lightning courses up and down within his arms and legs. Flames roar and dance in his belly as he exhales storms through his nostrils. Sensations of flesh, now become wonders of *mortal* comprehension.

He steps forward, the floor caressing the soles of his feet despite Neville's sweaty, all-day-worn shoes. Deville resumes the tour, walking through the next exhibit, past dinosaurs that never get old, and casts his gaze down at the floor.

"Why did they clean up the blood? It added so much character to the place!" He skips merrily up to the storage cupboard and stares…

"It's so empty without any guests staying in the spare room!"

The tile under the door is blank, yet with an immortalised carmine hue to it.

"They even cleaned up the welcome mat."

His head rolls back, laughing.

"What a dump…"

Deville sighs wistfully. He sees to his right the door to the toilets and marches inside, onto a floor of discoloured avacado tiles, some of which are already cracked. Somehow, *this undying shithole* managed to have three cubicles squeezed into the Mens.

Deville looks into the speckled mirror, and jumps, at the sight of himself. "I'm… I'm *gorgeous!*"

He stares at the rigid red face fitted onto the fleshy, living-tissue-original and takes a curious step closer towards…

"Those eyes…"

…animated eyes moving from side to side…

"*My* eyes… This face isn't real… It isn't right."

He brings his hands up to the sculpted cheeks and slides his fingers into the hollow eyes, feeling the distinction between cheek and cheek. Mask and face… He shuts his human eyes, digs his thumbs into the sides of the mask and pushes it off from his face… It comes loose.

Neville lifts the mask off. It shrinks as he holds it further away. The inside is more of a 'skin' colour than before… Less *red pepper* and more… *toffee yogurt*.

"No more blood spill. Ever!" Neville looks up at the mirror, into the reflection of a meek, pale undertaker of a man. He slouches over this blood red, snarling, monstrous face in front of his stomach, like an expectant mother clutching her baby bump.

"This thing is not safe to leave here."

You mean, you don't want anyone else to have it.

"Can't have anyone else exposed to it. And I can't have it so close to me every day I'm here."

Neville rushes out of the toilets with the mask, at his side, to avoid seeing it. The malicious essence in his grasp elongates the trek back to his office…

He picks up a briefcase leaning against the desk and opens it. Empty, as there is only so much paperwork the museum processes. Neville places the mask inside, facing up. It appears to sneer as he shuts the case.

How sophisticated, keeping it with you at all times like a superhero!

Not justifying that input with a response, Neville flees the office, but halts before the surveillance room.

"Mike? Are you still here?"

Good job the cameras aren't recording yet…

You're in the clear, then.

"I can't leave anything to chance these days."

Neville escapes through the back of the museum, into the falling light and rain. It pursues him over darkening tarmac as he runs to his VW nearby.

Shutting himself inside the car, Neville sets the briefcase down on the passenger seat. With a sigh, he starts the car, but in the corner of his eye the case makes itself known, just by being.

It won't just burst open any time…

Yet, *it* is inside. Smiling… *Breathing?*

Neville picks up the dreaded briefcase and drops it onto the back seat.

***

Detective Inspector Lake and Detective Sergeant Tout stand outside the complex of flats as Neville parks up.

I'd recognise those creeps anywhere!

He climbs cautiously out of the car, leaving the briefcase on the backseat, and approaches. "Hello, team. You're not here for me, are you?"

"Looks like business is booming at your museum, Mr Pike," says Tout.

"It's a nice change," Neville admits.

Lake steps forward. "We have some follow-up questions for you, Mr Pike."

"I see… would you both like to come up?"

Neville shows the detectives into the building and upstairs to his door. Not a word is said, or a look exchanged.

He lets them into his flat, watching over his shoulder while their *conniving, interfering little brains* analyse the contents of his grubby, humble home. The smell of damp does not deter them from circling round to the front of the couch like sharks. The grime and dust on the coffee table further intrigues them.

"Tea?"

"Yes please…"

"No thanks," Lake answers over Tout. They look to each other. Tout breaks away from Lake's icy scowl.

Trouble in paradise?

"Just me, then?" Neville turns away with a cute grin and puts the kettle on.

Lake speaks, "We were expecting you sooner, Mr Pike. What were you up to after closing time?"

What kind of question is that?

Neville composes himself as he moves to the solitary chair and sits, followed by Lake on the couch, then Tout.

"Well," says Neville.

"Could I use your loo?" Tout interrupts.

"Yeah, just through there, opposite the bed."

Tout stands, stepping awkwardly around Lake as he enters the bedroom.

I've seen enough police stuff on telly. You won't find anything, you prick.

Tout shuts the door on his way through.

Neville restarts his tale before Lake's sharp eyes and keen ears…

"I said to Tracy – at the reception desk – that I would start organising the new exhibition pieces this evening… but I took one look at them and thought 'stuff that!' So, I went back to my office to wrap up a few other things, and then I left early after all. Why do you ask? If you don't mind my um… asking?"

Don't play too dumb.

"I wanted to see if you would lie."

What?!

"We spoke with Tracy on the phone, and she said as much, so we assumed you would be late, for one reason or another. Your whereabout would've been of greater interest if your stories didn't match."

"Bleddy hell, am *I* under suspicion?"

"This is a murder investigation, Mr Pike. Everyone is under scrutiny. We'll do whatever it takes to apprehend whoever did this. And keep people safe."

Why go through all this trouble? Do they suspect me or don't they?

"Okay, then what about privacy?" Neville looks over at his bedroom door and raises his voice, "You can tell your man in there that if he wants to use the toilet, he may as well *open* the creaky bloody door, and do so."

Lake blushes.

Oh, the context… I don't somehow think you'd be my type, anyway, madam.

She snaps out of it, back at Neville. "You seem particularly hostile today, Mr Pike. Perhaps you really do have something to hide?"

"Don't we all…?"

Lake raises an eyebrow.

All is still, until the kettle shakes as it boils…

"I would never risk prison," says Neville. "I have a family to think about."

Her blue eyes glance over Neville's shoulder, before resting upon the whites of *his* eyes.

The kettle clicks off. The bubbles settle.

The bedroom door opens. Nonchalantly, Tout trudges back into the room. He shuts the door and stands with hands behind his back, watching Neville.

The Grim Reaper, returneth, doth loometh.

"So you say, Mr Pike," he says, "but we can't rule out anyone at this stage in the investigation. No-one could vouch for your whereabouts on the night of the murder, could they?"

"I commend you on your hearing, Sergeant," Neville glares, but flinches slightly at his own tone.

Is this really me speaking?

Something strange shifts within him, slithering down his very core. Neville changes the subject, pronto. "Did you hear the kettle go on your way in, Sergeant? I'm just about to make the tea. Are you sure you don't want any?"

Do the undead drink tea?

"No," says Lake.

"Okay. Well, do you have any other questions, Detectives? Or was this just pretence to go snooping around my little flat?"

How much further do you think you can push your luck? Stop it. Now.

Lake and Tout exchange sly glances and look back at Neville.

"No, I don't suppose we do at the moment." She stands abruptly, "But if you should change your mind, feel free to call us, Mr Pike."

Lake hands him a *little card*, with her *little name* on, and her *little phone number…* Her professional number, of course.

"Don't worry, I will." Neville tries to sound more co-operative than hostile, as he stands to meet her eye-to-eye and take the card.

Tout steps towards the front door, followed by Lake, followed by Neville, as they see themselves out.

He shoves the door to. "Good fucking riddance."

Well done. If you weren't suspicious before, you are now.

Neville hops into his bedroom. He finds nothing has been *obviously* disturbed, but for the strange vibe of another entity having been around the room.

"To think that creepy bastard has been rifling through my abode…!"

What are you going to do, kill them? Losing your temper hasn't solved anything so far, but hey, why stop now?

"It's been *your* solution to everything so far, hasn't it? Why are *you* so on edge? I just want them to leave me alone."

They're the authorities. If you get caught, it'll be all for nothing. And you did kill those men, good and proper. You had fun in the process. But if you think you can get away with it…

"It was all in self-defence! I wasn't even *me* at the time!"

Will the authorities see it that way? You didn't have to follow the intruders, did you? You could have waited them out or went straight for the back door.

"I had to see what was going on. What I'd tell the police!"

But instead, you snapped! You couldn't take any more shit from your life, so you gave chase like a fucking animal and beat them until all that was left was roadkill.

"The kettle's boiled."

You can't run from what you did. You can't deny this is

what you want… Delicious freedom… of expression.

Neville marches out of his bedroom and over to the hot kettle. He takes a cup and pours into it, but he tilts the kettle too quick. "Shit!"

He pulls his hand away to shake off the scald.

Watch out, clumsy.

"Fuck this, I'm off out."

Neville gets his coat and his effects.

"I still have at least *one* friend. And there's a pint out there that's calling to me."

CHAPTER 16

Rapping at the door warms Neville's knuckles against the evening chill.

Quiet...

His agitation knocks harder.

No answer.

Bastard! Why aren't you in?

Neville steps back off the doorstep. He throws a vengeful thump at the door.

Typical. The one time I need you! Why can't we just go out and get a drink like we used to?

Still no answer.

"He's supposed to be in. He's *always* in!"

What did you expect? You simply can't rely on anyone.

Neville marches off, downhill, and into the hellish depths of town.

He finds the *damned fucking* pub, naturally quieter of a weekday.

"I swear I never used to drink so much." Neville sits at the bar and orders a double whisky and coke, like a splashy student.

The stoic barman utters no more than two words at a time while conjuring Neville's drink.

Neville pays, and then continues to mutter into his mixer-filled glass. "Who actually sits on their own at a bar and drinks neat whisky?"

His fingers wrap around the glass as if hugging an old friend. Neville takes a large sip of the cold, fizzy abyss and places the drink back down on the bar as the black, peppery sensation chases down his throat…

Warm, modest lighting would melt *anyone's* grip on time, while Neville enjoys his fourth drink, or his fifth.

He scans couples around the room. Two blokes, pint in hand, watch the football. A man and a woman sit close together as a two-headed, symbiotic organism, like any other couple.

Neville is an 'other', but not a *significant* other…

"…Not significant to anyone at all…"

You're just going to sit and stew in your misery, are you?

"Out of sight, out of mind. As far as even Gemma is concerned, I'm sure." He brings the cold glass to his lips for another swig.

Surely, you can strike up a conversation with someone who isn't the bartender… or your drink.

"Everyone else is paired up. I don't want to appear desperate. That's all…"

Too late!

"I wouldn't be here if… if I was home. With Kat. And Gemma. Is there any hope of redemption? It's always the way… You're not given a second chance. Especially if you lash out like *that*. It was only the *once*. I made the right call to leave… but then she moves on, instead of working things out between us!"

The barman, now at the other end glances over, wondering who Neville is talking to, but he finds himself fixating on the loner muttering into his glass.

"I can take care of myself, so that makes me a 'selfish bastard.' I'm a shitty provider anyway… but bringing what little you can to the table, only to be reminded that it's not good enough… Somehow that's enough to make you…"

Snap.

Neville sees the couple far opposite wrap around themselves, looking intimately into each other's eyes. They share a kiss.

"What a slap in the face, that even this *adorable* pair of slugs can look up from the dinner table to find love." He looks intimately into his drink and takes a loving sip. "See, friendship and alcohol can each make you feel better. You can pay for alcohol on demand, but you're pissing away the money, and the hours… And you can waste all the time in the world on people who convince you that you are *like* family, but when it comes down to it, you're not family… You're just another stranger. And then there's the hangover the next day."

Tentatively cautious, the barman approaches.

"Well?" Neville challenges, "Don't you have anything to say?"

"Are you alright, fella?"

Neville jumps. "Yes?"

"Who are you talking to?"

"Oh! How embarrassing… Looks like I've been left hanging. Dunno how long my mate's been gone!"

The barman is summoned to the other side of the bar. His enthusiasm to serve other customers quickly is the least of Neville's troubles.

"Friendship costs too, apparently... You give up time and energy to be with them... listen to them bitch and moan with the hope that they do the same for you. Even *liking* the fuckers is optional. You never know when they'll turn up. When they'll go... When they'll come crawling back... You won't see me crawling back to anyone again, that's for sure." Neville enjoys another, heftier, swig.

Let's be clear, Neville... this *is not a friendship!*

He jumps, nearly falling off his chair from the deafening words.

You are the one who bitches and moans. If life is so shit, do something! If you're even worth the skin that holds you together, you will prove that you deserve better.

Neville looks around. Of course, no-one else hears the voice in his head. "Why *are* you here, anyway? With me?"

He drains the rest of his drink, sets the glass on the bar with a knock, and looks to his new best friend, Barman. "Excuse me, same again, please."

"Make that two," adds a voice, the silky vibrations of a woman's, indeed.

Neville looks to his right at the dark-dressed redhead now resting her leather jacketed elbows against the bar. "Is that on *my* tab?"

"Why? Are you offering?" she teases, smiling.

He stifles a grin as he plays with his chalice.

Barman takes a new glass and pushes it against the lever under the bottle.

Avoiding me*, the bastard.*

He takes another glass and does the same.

Should I engage with the tasty lady?

Neville turns to her. He turns away.

No, of course I can't…

However, something *else* turns *up…*

"Well, what if I was?" he asks her anyway.

She looks back at him, surprised. He watches her eyes wander around the room, considering her options, before she faces him at last with a closed, naughty smile. *Good at those…*

"Looks like I've got some time to kill." She sits upon the stool.

Barman returns with two drinks, places one in front of Neville, and the other in front of *her.* He plucks up the money from Neville's hot palm.

I'm stirred. And *shaken.*

Neville turns to the redhead again, still in character. "Do I have to get you another, before you tell me your name?"

"Eager, aren't you? It's Tabitha." Coy, she glances up, into his eyes.

"Really? You don't usually get many 'Tabithas'."

"Who knows? Maybe you *will.*" She claims her drink, and savours her cool, wet wit.

A silly schoolboy smirk slips from Neville.

"Well?" She holds back a chuckle. "Are you going to tell me yours?"

"Why? Could you do with a laugh?"

"Come on, now I *really* need to know!"

"Brace yourself… 'Neville…'"

"'*Neville…*'" she faces ahead, locking her lips.

If you can't say anything nice, don't say anything at all, right?

"Or…" he saves the day, "'*Nev,*' for short."

Tabitha smirks, "Still doesn't do you much justice, does it?"

"No." He enjoys a medicinal sip for the thirty-nine-year trauma.

Hail Mary, full of booze. Hail Mary, full of booze.

"It still gets a laugh to this day," he says. "If I have to reference the other odd kid in *Harry Potter*, I'm already clutching at straws."

"Well, why not change it?"

"It's supposed to be a family name. It can't have continued out of honour. Probably more because the father was spiteful at being lumbered with it. So, when I produce a son, I shall name *him* Neville, so *he* can suffer as I have."

"That's so cruel!"

"So, you *do* think it's that bad!"

They snigger away from each other and pick up their drinks and sip again.

What on earth's a gorgeous creature like this doing, talking to such a 'rough diamond,' like me?

He must not spoil this. Not now…

"So," she struggles to contain herself, "your father… your father's father, and more besides, were all called 'Neville'?"

"I would assume so."

"You don't know for certain?"

"It was my father's parting gift, not long after I was born."

Tabitha's face sobers up. "You mean he… died?"

"No. He left. And my mother kept her maiden name, which is my second name today." Neville sips. "By the time the family realised my bastard father was gone for good, I wouldn't answer to anything else. What an innocent child I was…"

"I'm sorry…"

"I make the most of it. It can be quite handy, to tell you the truth."

"What do you mean?"

"Whenever I introduce myself with my funny name, I can gauge people by their response to it. If they're about to laugh in my face, I can tell that they're honest. If they scoff, it tells me that they're disrespectful. But, if I get no reaction from them at all, I know they mean business."

"Wow… scary." She takes a large gulp of her own black, sparkly drink.

"But I know that *you're* okay. Because you're an *honest* person."

"Oh, I'm *okay,* am I?"

"Sorry, poor choice of words. You're *more* than okay. You are *stunning.*"

Don't gush, you fool, you'll scare her off!

Neville catches the barman wincing.

Tabitha blushes and sips her drink.

Another handy gauge of her is whether she'll still be sticking around for the booze… paid for by 'yours truly stupid'.

"Steady on, darling," she says.

"May have been a bit presumptuous there… Only a bit, though. So, what've you come from today?"

"Me? Today I've been…"

Neville jumps at the demonic visage behind the shelf of drinks. From the mirror behind the bottles, the face of the Devil glares in place of his own.

The beast in the reflection bares teeth at Tabitha, with

intentions more carnivorous than carnal.

"Are you *okay*?" She worries.

"Hey, Tabby." An arrogant male appears at the bar, "found someone better to hang out with, did you?"

Tabitha turns to face a tanned, *blue-eyed angel* male model, taking the piss. "That's what happens when you turn up late."

The guy stands behind her and Neville. "I'll take it from here, mate."

"See you around... *Neville*." Tabitha is led off the stool by the guy's hand.

"Bye," he stares, then sinks...

"'*Neville?*'" scoffs the guy, pulling Tabitha towards a table.

Neville sighs hopelessly, breathing despair.

He looks again into the mirror behind the bar and sees his face. Human. Pale, with no demonic features protruding from his skin...

He shuffles off the stool to stray over to, and into the Gents.

Well, if you like peeing in solitude, then 'urine' for a treat...

He smirks and goes over to relieve himself.

You know, more than 'two shakes' is playing with yourself.

"Well, maybe I like to have fun," he chuckles.

"You what, mate?"

Neville tidies himself up quick and looks around the empty Gents, but one of the cubicles is shut.

Talking to strangers while on the toilet? In the Gents? Weirdo...

He washes his hands and forgets about drying them. As

126

long as he gets out before *Mr Shitter* can interact with him, fantastic!

I could stop for one more drink, maybe two… more…

Finally, without looking back, he staggers outside the pub. Spots of luminous yellow streetlight pool over the pavements and onto the road. The wind is frozen, with no cover from the row of cars parked end-to-end…

"Which way's shhhhhithole home?"

Wandering left, Neville wavers from side-to-side over his imaginary straight white line, marking the middle of the night. Hostile voices echo from up ahead.

Who the fuck's out at this hour?

Some bloke shouts at a glaring woman. "It looked like you were a bit too friendly towards Chaz, didn't it?"

"He's just an old friend, Luke! Who are *you* to be judging me when…?"

"*Excuse* me, pleez…" Neville stumbles towards the *silly buggers* in the way of his imaginary white line.

'Luke' looks up and down at him and steps back. The two go quiet as Neville plods on. And then they are at it again, behind.

Off she *goes now...*

"Who are you to be judging me, when you were chatting up that tart Carly?"

"*What?* She's my cousin!"

"Yeah, well, I bet that wouldn't stop you!"

She yelps against a smack…

"Let go of me!"

Neville looks back at Luke, pinning against the wall. He leans into her. "How fucking dare you…!"

Tabitha? And that dickhead with her earlier…?

Double vision, dim streetlights… who knows? Neville walks back towards *the four of them*, "Oi!" he raises a wobbly, authoritative finger. "Whaddya think you're doing with that *woman*?!"

Luke turns his head towards him with those slight, chilling blue eyes. It *is* the same guy he saw before. He bears a flicker of recognition before Neville. "Walk on, mate. Piss off."

"Not until *you* do, and she's safe, *mate,*" declares Neville.

"Oh really?" Luke steps away from her and struts up to him. A quick fist collides with Neville's face, and he falls to the floor like a knocked-over shop mannequin. Luke walks around to his side, kicks him. And then once more.

Neville grunts, and shrinks like a dazed insect.

"Yeah, I think she's safe now, *mate*." Luke walks off, but not before calling back at Tabitha, "You can make your own way home. Or to wherever the fuck you think you're sleeping tonight. I'm getting a taxi back."

Tabitha steps gingerly over to Neville, lying on the ground. Her wavy red hair envelops his periphery, rays of midnight sun under streetlight…

You look nice. Are you coming home with me?

"Are you alright?" she asks, or so he thinks. Her voice is too *far away* for Neville to tell. All sounds seem far away… Neville finds himself almost at peace.

Stupid question anyway…

Tabitha crouches beside him, talking at him, but not a word penetrates Neville's drunken ears.

What you still doing down on the ground?!

Tabitha looks to call after Luke. Her voice finally drips into Neville's ears, "What did you do that for, you bastard?! He doesn't look right…"

You're going to let that creep get away with what he just

128

did? It's people like him who get in the way. People like him who get women in trouble and leave innocent boys to grow up broken. Missing pieces... Just like Daddy dearest... People like him deserve to be... punished.

It is like a lizard shedding skin... Neville, worn down, battered, sits up and breathes in the universe around him. Everything becomes one... The woman beside him just part of the background... He stands, with bones crackling all the way up, like a creaking ship steady at sea. Muscles tense all over, absorbing all the strength in the world... The line is thin between a dull, hopeless reality... and the *need*... digging claws into his flesh to peel off his old self and start anew. He exhales venom. His weak mortal persona evaporates as he steps forward, a bolder, more daring beast. Hungry... It marches off to seek revenge upon its prey.

A woman's shout fails to reach his ears. Worry? Rage? Mere sounds. A furious *Deville* sprints forward, under and out of the streetlights. Dark, light, dark, light, dark, light, dark, light, as he nears the **bastard pretty boy** from behind...

Luke turns to face a tight bunch of fives, hitting him full in the face. He stumbles forward and looks up to see Deville, throwing another fast punch. Luke is sent flying into an alleyway.

There is no trace of light.

Luke struggles to his feet, panting, putting up his meaty dukes, as if he has a fighting chance.

The silhouette of Deville steps closer and closer.

Like somersaulting underwater when he was a boy, Luke's sinuses flood with pain from the force that hit him in the nose.

He throws a punch at the man-shaped, shadowy beast... and misses. His fist... passes right through? Luke falls onto his arse. He looks up at calm, cold Deville stepping closer.

Luke coughs, shuffling back along the ground... but the shadow pounces. It straddles his stomach.

Raising a closed right fist, Deville brings it down into Luke's hot, red-wet cheek. Lifting a steady left fist, he slams his knuckles into the other side of the man's face, turning his head.

Deville brings up his right fist again, but it hovers in the air.

"What am I doing here...? I can't do this," Neville's eyes tear up, "I have people to think about."

"Go on, kill him! *Kill* that pig!"

Neville looks over his shoulder, at a female silhouette standing in the way of the light.

"*Do* it!" Tabitha closes in. "Do it for me, *Nev.*"

'Nev.' Like Kat used to call me...

"...Used to? She still does!"

...Even after she decided to divorce you. She doesn't even want you! What does it matter?

A cold wave pumps through Neville's body.

"I would do anything *for her...*"

Burning heat runs under his skin, boiling through his veins. A magnetic force pulls his fist down over Luke at last. *Deville* feels the bone under Luke's face shift inward, with each impact against his knuckles, as he pummels him into something deep red and unrecognizable...

He stops to marvel at what remains of Luke.

A faceless, twitching body. Clockwork flesh breaking down, like a broken *automaton*. But...

The world hasn't stopped turning with him... Maybe 'Luke' wasn't real after all. He was already dead behind the eyes...

CHAPTER 17

Strange dreams, lately. All… bloody.

Neville sits up. "This isn't *my* couch…"

Did I pull last night?

Here he is, thinking someone has moved his furniture around… He looks around at the warm yellow walls, the red and purple throw, the coffee-coloured couch, and the blue blanket flopped over his legs…

This is definitely a woman's place, minus any colour co-ordination…

The white, fluffy rug in the middle of the room dazzles his eyes for a split second. A flat screen telly is situated in the opposite corner to the one at Neville's.

In tight jeans, Tabitha walks through an open door, pulling on a black top. Her belly button winks at Neville as he admires, briefly, her smooth her pale stomach cradled by her hips.

She catches sight of Neville on her way to the kitchen cupboards. "Oh, you're finally awake, then."

Neville turns to put his feet to the floor. "Morning- *Aah!*" He claps hands over the *ripping* at his sides.

"Don't move too quickly. I suppose it *is* still morning. It's eleven-thirty…"

"What? I'm already late!" He stands, *groans*… and falls back into the couch.

"What did I just say?" She clatters around in the kitchen, plonking a mug onto the counter…

There's nothing like a nice hot beverage after a bloody good slaughter.

"What the hell happened last night?"

"Last night? Well," Tabitha walks over to crouch down before him, "we made it back here… and we did *everything*. You were such an animal! It was amazing…"

Confusion holds Neville's face.

Her laugh slips out. "I'm joking. Believe me, if we had, you wouldn't *forget*."

I believe it… What bleddy stopped you, then?

…no doubt the unconsciousness from your injuries.

"You were hammered." Tabitha sits back, onto the rug, disappearing her hands into the thicket of white fur. "I wasn't much better… but I basically carried you back here and dropped you onto the couch, where you so thoughtfully fell asleep… So, then I got a bowl of water to wash all the blood off your hands."

"Wait, blood? What?" He looks at his hands, shifting from the one propping himself up, to the other, but they feel fine…

"Mhmm. It was… something really special, actually." She glazes over.

"You… you were arguing with that guy, outside. Luke? That smug prick that came over to us before…"

"You *intervened* when he hit me. He ended up kicking you about…"

Neville notices her left cheek redder than the rest of her

face. "I remember that- *ow*. But the rest is… *hazy*."

Bloody…

"Things got… heated." She puts a hand over Neville's knee, somehow knowing under the blanket exactly where to find it.

Bet she knows her way around to other things, too…

"You got up. You just *got up*… chased after Luke, and then beat the living shit out of him!"

Bloody good…

"And then", she continues.

Why, oh why, does she continue? This is terrible. It can't be true!

"…you finished him off. You killed him." Fascination rings through, like the wonder of a child.

Neville says not a word. This is no prank. What are the chances, after the incident with the break-in? The walls sway to one side, closing in on him…

I'm going to be sick…

His entire being goes cold. He can only sit and check what is real. The air is stale.

Think of something else…

The soft leather pressed under his palms.

…Like the blood on your hands.

The warm fluffy blanket over his itchy legs…

Warm, sticky…

Tabitha's grip over his knee…

What fun!

Her hand slides up his thigh as she purrs, "No-one's ever

done anything like that for me before..." Her hand slides down, splaying out her fingers to ensnare his knee, like talons seizing prey.

Neville lies paralyzed, trying to resurrect the hope that he is still dreaming...

I am not a killer. I am not being accosted by this twisted woman...

What a great excuse to justify post-homicidal sex.

Tabitha stands and brings one leg over Neville's other thigh. Her stiff jeans scrape against the back of the couch and most of his leg. Her fingers curl into the waistband of his trousers. Soft, alien skin touches Neville's... He shivers as her warmth slithers under his belly, and coils around his already keen, rising mast.

With Tabitha's modest weight over his legs, her knees sink into the couch leather, creaking and moaning... She wraps her other pale hand around the back of Neville's neck and lurches forward, pressing her lips onto his, the way a snake lunges, bites, and pumps venom into its prey.

She sucks his face, and the breath from his lungs, while her other tightly wrapped hand squeezes, and pumps the rest of the venom out of him, at an increasingly rapid pace.

The early bird does gets the worm...

***

Static. He has not moved, or even twitched for a whole hour... *Or has it been two?*

Neville, spruced up in a fresh suit, sits immobile in the chair at his desk. Somehow, after a quick trip home, he made it to the museum.

However, his *temple* is void of mind altogether. He stares ahead, never daring to look down and confirm the reality of blood on his hands, which have been all over Tabitha this morning, as he endured, or rather enjoyed, the quality time.

How base, that all romantic desire boils down to one

thing…

But Neville's mind is so distant even the voice cannot reach him. On a whole other plane, Neville spends the rest of the morning stripping Tabitha of her clothes, sculpting with his hands the lines and shapes of features yet uncharted. It is so much more lovely to think of anything but murder. Naturally he spends the time *savouring* the feel of skin he has not yet touched…

The office door opens, *reality doesn't knock first!*

"Oh! I didn't see you earlier," Tracy barges in, "how long've you been here?"

"Um, I've not kept track of time…"

How long have *I been here? I can't have lost control* again…

"Anyway," Neville looks up at the clock: noon, "did you need something?"

"No, nothing. It's fine as you're already here. I'll just… head back to the front lines." She leaves, inconspicuous as can be, shutting the door after her.

"It's '*fine* as I'm already here,' is it? Who does she think she is?"

Funny how she scarpered, isn't it?

"What did she really want?"

She still has eyes on this hopeless joint.

"I'm pretty sure I have bigger fish to fry."

How so?

"'How so?' I have to make sure I'm not gonna get done for several counts of *murder*, never mind looking out for this shithole!"

You shouldn't worry about all that…

"Why not? Why shouldn't I worry?"

If the police had found your snuff films, they would've

charged in to arrest you, already.

"So, now I have to worry about someone who's already found them?!"

Nothing else from the voice.

Neville is alone again. With the rest of the afternoon to get through, he ponders lunch and comfort-eating, but after chewing over recent grim events, his appetite must have left with the voice. Carnivorous thoughts turn carnal again as Neville's mind pans from the texture of a ham and cheese sandwich at his lips, to Tabitha's curves and pale skin under his fingertips. And curling up with her...

Curling up... in my bed... Maybe I could sneak out. Just for today.

Realising the wish to share this comfort, Neville remembers Kat and recalls her disrobing in advance of his desires in times gone by. Neville studies her shape next to his and looks back up to see *Tabitha's* face.

Yes, I could go back home... Just for today...

He resumes his exploration south and notices her belly – a different colour, a different shape from before... It is not her body at all.

Neville scans over the expensively dressed man, from designer shoes to jeans, to low-cut top and jacket... to the imploded mass of flesh and bone that fail to make up *Luke's* face.

The body sits up and turns its head towards Neville. Muffled squirms and moans echo from the head in attempt to speak, spouting blood instead of words from the cavern where its mouth should be.

Neville shuffles away, but a cold hand, and another... and another... and *another*, grip his arms and legs. And then the *weight*...

Oh god. It's crushing me!

He looks down again at Luke's body... Straddling Neville is the medley of merged, dead, grey-skinned men. Deville's victims crawl together as one in the shape a spider, now at the base of Luke's torso. The beast with its different heads, more animated than before, moan and drool, and pin Neville down, as the half-man, half-corpse-spider, clambers onto him...

The faceless man leans forward, dribbling hot *red* over Neville's stomach, and reaches out, placing both hands over Neville's face.

The limbs of the other bodies press such intense weight upon him, as the beast's fingernails dig into his forehead beneath his hairline. Neville feels its other stray hand slide down his torso, over his belly, under his pants. The hard, chilly fingers coil around Neville's shrunken fruit, ready to pluck...

Neville shouts himself awake and sits up, in bed.

Cold sweat soaks his bed clothes. He looks at the clock: 4.13 *AM.*

Neville steps out of bed, onto the bumpy, cheap woven carpet, shivering through to the bathroom door, and then puts the light on. He turns on the tap, to splash some water onto his face...

He sees his anxious little fizzog in the mirror.

"Nothing droll to say? No cameo appearances?"

Silence. He stares at himself, and his now furious, glowing eyes. "It wasn't my fault about that prick Luke."

So you say...

He and his reflection jump...

But it felt right, didn't it?

"It doesn't right now. Why... why, *why* won't you leave me in peace?"

Neville's reflection snaps back at him an angry, toothy smile. The *unhingedness* makes him shudder.

You can sleep long enough when you're dead!

Neville stumbles back, losing sight of the reflection... that *thing* inside him. Hell, it *is* him.

The voice speaks softly, seductively, as ever...

No-one's stopping you from sleeping. Except yourself...

"I never wanted to kill anyone!"

You keep telling yourself that, but just remember how every other person you know – hell – everyone gets in your way. It's worse still when they cross you and expect to get away... with 'murder.'

"But *I* don't expect to get away with it! And now I'm acting so *weirdly*! What – *why* – is this *happening* to me?!"

Not too loud, think of the neighbours! This is all you, you know.

With those self-indulgent, obnoxious words, practically at the point of orgasm as ever, Neville can feel the *other* enjoying itself. It does have a will of its own. It *is* a will of its own. "And why are you here?"

No response.

"What *are* you?!"

God-like, the voice remains silent.

Neville backs away from the mirror, and crawls into bed for a sleepless age.

The souls of the damned could secrete their way into his room at any time.

His eyes shut. If he cannot see *them*, they cannot see *him*...

CHAPTER 18

A flashing red light nags at the crack of dawn.

Neville must answer to the answer phone.

Of course, it would ring yesterday…

There was only one woman on his mind at the time. Now, there is another, with a message…

Only one, thank fuck.

Kat's voice breaks through. "Hi Nev. I had to get a bloody letter from the school, before Gemma would tell me, that she's in this play that's coming up. Typical, she would leave it to the last minute before saying anything! The thing's next week, Wednesday evening. It would mean a lot if you came to watch her. Let me know, okay?"

Neville pushes the button to save this… but his finger loiters. It releases.

I'll call back later. It would be fabulous to wake Kat so early just to tell her, 'Yes, I'll come.' There's enough bad feeling between us as it is.

Carrying more knots than empty space in his stomach, Neville skips breakfast and goes back into his room to get ready to go out. Yet the pressure, the very density of the air inside, makes him hesitate. He cannot even approach the confining bathroom to ablute in case the clawing fingers and gnawing teeth of re-animated battered corpses burst out to greet him.

Ever since the night of the break-in, the hours separating consciousness from sleep become less of a barrier between reality and nightmare.

Before 8am, early enough, Neville makes it outside fully equipped with his suit – his armour – and goes for a walk. A nice, innocent walk, *not* to the park on the other side of town… just *anywhere* to avoid getting to the museum any earlier. Or staying home, closer to the mask.

I can't risk being seen that way… let alone the potential bloodbath!

Neville stops halfway between the street corner and the ugly truth. "What?"

The sign outside the newsagents shows the front cover of today's paper:

MAN FOUND MURDERED IN ALLEY

"He was just left there?"

You clearly had 'better' things to do… with Tabitha.

Neville goes into the shop and picks up a copy of the same newspaper.

Don't go looking conspicuous, now…

He clutches the thick paper tight in his fist. It denies his fingernails the breaking of skin of his palm as he doubles back for the dreaded flat.

At last, he crosses the white, grey, and beige inter-dimensional plane between the outside world and his flat… and makes it through the door.

Neville opens the paper as he circles around to the taupe couch and sits. His scowl fixes in disbelief, in advance of the print on the pages. He finds the article, but Neville already knows – first-hand – of his repeated blows to Luke's face. According to the article, 'the victim' was identified by the contents of his wallet. 'No arrests have been made at this time.'

"Yeah, for *now*…" Neville collapses on the couch and drops the newspaper onto the coffee table in front of him, hoping the weight of his strain is carried with it, like the tedious supplement. He smooths his palms over his temples. His hair tufts along his fingers as he cradles his weary skull. "I can't go on like this."

Sure you can.

"I'll hurt someone who matters at this rate."

Matters to you, you mean. Don't you get it? Nobody matters. Not really. What you need to realise is that this is 'kill or be killed.'

"I didn't have to kill anyone. Even with the break-in, I could've just scarpered, called the police and avoided all this… pressure."

How were you to know what **those intruders would do? What you did, you did in self-defence…**

"It was *overkill*. In that footage I was so… angry. And then dancing around afterwards like a lunatic? That was madness. Surely…"

Surely *you can enjoy yourself from time to time. It's not every day you get to win a fight against three people.*

"And execute them? And what about that Luke? I could've let him walk away, but instead I went after him. I was under the radar before that… happened."

So sometimes it can be 'kill, or let people walk all over you for the rest of your life…' but you have to take responsibility for your actions. It was your fists that knocked that smug face of his to the back of his stupid head!

"But I didn't *want* this!"

Part of you always has. A surprisingly large part. People can be such obstacles. Just because there are certain laws

against how you 'clear' them, you hesitate, but it's so much better this way. And you haven't been caught by the police, have you?

"Yet…"

Did the burglars manage to steal anything from the museum that night? No… Would a woman have shown any interest in you, if you had kept your passions so deeply buried inside, Mr Look-but-don't-touch? No! These inhibitions of yours are inhibiting you from living a better life!

Neville jumps to his feet and struts to the door, entertaining the delusion that he might leave the voice behind.

Even now you still march into the slaughterhouse of humdrum life. You could be so much more…

"I just have to keep my head down till it all blows over. Actions have consequences, dammit!"

So does doing nothing.

Escaping the flat, Neville ventures again into the sharp light of the outside world, and the harsh growling of cars that pass nearby. Two women in trackies on the other side of the road chatter side by side, each with a pushchair. As Neville pulls the front door shut, one of the women snaps a glance at the haggard man, before carrying on.

With the voice silent once more, Neville gets into his grey VW, wary of the invisible company that keeps him. He puts the radio on for desperate distraction as he drives to work. This guitar intro would massage some ears, but not Neville's.

The 'voice' is a passenger. And it rides and it rides… until journey's end.

***

Like a nervous sundial, Neville's shadow casts midmorning over the desk, as he sits in his office, deciphering papers of vague importance, when a slight *creak* at the desk stops play…

Neville drops everything to look around, but his eyes are

drawn to the empty chair opposite, as the weight of an invisible force *rests its feet* on the desk.

The phone, the plastic, sun-faded *baby having a tantrum*, wails for attention. Neville starts before he picks it up, for once 'glad', to receive Tracy's voice, "I've got Mr Mosley on the line for you. Are you able to speak with him right now?"

"Yeah... Yes! Put him through please, Tracy."

Will I get any answers from him right now?

A rusty, well-spoken male voice booms through. "Hello. Mr Pike... *Junior*?"

"Yes, Mr Mosley! Hi..."

"I'm terribly sorry about your grandfather... I can't stay on the line for long. I'm still in Cannes! But what is it you want to talk with me about?"

"Well, it isn't... *urgent* I suppose... I have some new stock in for you to look over... but I'm curious about one of these masks we already have on display."

"Oh, really? Which... which would that be?"

"It's the *Face of the Devil* that... caught my eye."

Is it the real deal? Is it making me into a cold-blooded killer?

"Well, I'd need to have more of a look at it first..." says Mosely. "Just please... don't *touch* it."

"I beg your pardon?"

"...You didn't put it on, did you... Mr Pike?"

"Well... supposing I *did*...?"

Silence.

"Mr Mosley? Is this a bad line?"

"I'll be on the next flight to Exeter, Mr Pike. You can expect to meet me soon." Mosley hangs up.

"Mr Mosley!"

What was that about?

Resonant silence surrounds Neville. He puts the phone down.

"Is there really something about the mask? What does Mosley know?"

But Neville is alone again in his office. His *other* offers no input. No insight.

He tries to sense the space around him, as if he could chart what is between the filing cabinet, the planter, the bin, and the printer on its little table, from their respective corners…

But no-one else, nothing else, loiters in or outside the office. He looks down at his desk, contemplating its dimensions, how he could have Tabitha right there, with all this privacy… He remembers having Kat in some unusual places too…

Have I done the right thing? Taking over this place? I mean, I was right to move out after the incident with Kat but, I still want to redeem myself, yet she's out looking for someone else… Is it right to just let that go?

As Neville smoulders with doubt, a deep sigh fans the flames.

I don't know what's right anymore. I don't know what's wrong, but whatever I do, something bad happens anyway, and everything just gets worse! It's hell. Am I in Hell? There's no-one for me. Hell really is other people…

"Ha. 'Can't live with 'em, can't… live at all…'"

The resounding silence, Neville's only company, offers no response.

"Well, what's the point of living at all, then…? Nobody talks to nobody… Not even *nobody* talks to a nobody like me."

CHAPTER 19

There is no light at the end of the corridor.

The end of time, the end of the *day after day after day*, muscle-memory carries Neville out of the *arse-end* of the museum, going into the dying light.

A job is hell. Confined to a space by the demands of the powers-that-be… Left with a pittance of time to live one's life, while your body withers away…

He is 'one of them' now, the 8.45-ers who metamorphose into the 5.05-ers, who then hibernate overnight and devolve back into the morning people.

After too long complying with the regime, they stop rushing home to preserve what little time they have left, if there is any point living in-between… so long spent dead inside…

If the voice is speaking at all, Neville does not hear it.

Nobody talks to 'nobody.'

Neville locks the door, leaving behind the remaining spark of his soul within, when a hand grabs his shoulder and whips him around.

Nick White shoves him against the door and grabs Neville's shirt, "Listen, I've been chasing you up for long enough, but I just can't stick the 'suspense' anymore. Do you have that latest batch in, or not?"

Maybe I'm not a nobody after all!

"I don't know…" says Neville.

"You don't *know*?!"

"…what you're on about."

Nick stares, with the leer of a prehistoric predator. He might just *eat* Neville.

"Since my grandad passed, I've taken over the museum… but I don't know the full extent of his affairs. So, I can't help you if I don't know *what you want*."

A flicker of fear chills Neville's body little by little. Maybe the warmth of the thrill makes him aware of how cold he is.

Nick releases his grip, throwing Neville back against the door. "The materials the old man was selling to us made good business… and then for some fucking reason our stock stopped coming in."

The rich, rosy sun sinks steadily, drawing dark curtains on the world. Whatever cold that slithered under Neville's clothes drains and drains away, awakening his blood. Enjoying the rush, he almost loses touch with curiosity.

"What materials? What was Grandad tied up with here? If it's this shady, was it *this* that killed him?"

"Aw, bless, you think we're breaking the law? Nothing here is even listed as *illegal…* but they do the job. Very well, in fact. Mr Pike *Senior* had a deal with us, ordered the stuff in with roots, herbs, spices, and shit, and sold it to us… in bulk. Simple. But currently we're out of stock. And *that…* is not good for business."

"So, what you paid him… kept him afloat?"

"Yeah. It did."

The museum is going down the drain. This is necessary. "I

don't know what to look for. How do I order it?"

"Work it out! I've only been trying to tell you this whole time, that you've been missing out on a lucrative opportunity." Nick pockets his hands and turns...

"Wait," says Neville, "how do I contact you?"

"Make the order. If you do it now, it'll be here by tomorrow." Nick asserts his way away.

Neville had better not move, yet. He waits until Nick's white shoes have carried him out of sight.

No-one else's insignificant little lives are met with such danger...

***

Reaching into the lion's mouth, Neville snatches up the papers inside the desk drawer...

It does not take off his hand.

Silence roars over the stillness as he sits in his office. Grandad's old office, which had quietly *digested* the old man over one weekend like a Venus fly trap, before he was found... the following hot Monday...

The museum had already tasted blood...

Neville closes the drawer before it traps his hand like said carnivorous plant. The dark chocolate brown desk is made of wood, after all – once a living tree. It would not be the first time the bitter dead came back to *devil* Neville.

Was the blood of the three strangers enough to sate it since?

He lays out the papers over the desk. Receipts at last, listing strange herbs and spices and whatnot, dating back long before Neville left that bureaucratic fortress, to work in this affected *disaffected* warehouse.

Is it really better to serve in heaven than to reign in hell?

But that is blood and piss under the bridge. It will take discipline and ingenuity for Neville to better himself, and, *whatever* kept Grandad afloat.

I must find how he made his profit before I lose this place. And before that bastard, shady Nick, comes back to 'persuade' me further.

Neville shuffles through each white sheet, eyeing the dates going back months… a whole year…

Around the time I moved out. When my marriage took a turn for the worst.

Soaps by the dozen. Quite a few dozen… Teas, Pot Pourri…

He can't have sold this much!

They do not appear too costly. It would not take much to fire up the computer and place a new order online for whatever is amongst this lot.

Is this necessary? Is it even what I want? I could throw away any chance at following my dreams for the sake of easy money. At least, it looks *easy…*

Easier than anything his whole life… so far…

If only I could overwrite my past… Just to make my life a little bit better – I'm not greedy…

…At school I could break away from the playground football, to give that busty maid in my science class a good seeing to, or actually listen in class and do the work… I could be popular. Likeable!

But instead, his present day surrounds him with the erect tastebuds of magnolia textured walls, musty, plastic air, and the confines of his suit…

"*This* is how my life has unfolded. No second chances for me…"

I certainly couldn't do much about my bastard father leaving as soon as I left the womb… Was staying with my grandparents after Mum died, beyond my control? I was only seven… Living by their rules, making their mistakes… It's all me. My life is so fucked up because "I shouldn't even have been born!"

His fist flies up and hammers on the desk.

Shut up.

"What?" He jumps in his seat. Was that Neville's own temper, or…?

I hear nothing but 'I wish I had an easier life', 'Why is everything so shit?' Boohoo, Neville! You should be living in the present! That's all you should ever have been doing. Not doing so has been your biggest mistake.

"Living in the present? What present do I have to live for now? I'm nearly halfway through my lifespan, I have no wife, a daughter who will grow up to reject me… no proper home… what could I possibly do to make my life worthwhile?"

Get out. Take what is rightfully yours. Make up for lost time…

"Am I not too old to just go out and do that? I'm sure said *thrills* would reject me, as they always have."

No. Age has nothing to do with it. The only one who has ever done the rejecting, is you. Every opportunity, every chance at having a good time, you throw a spanner in the works to provoke rejection from the other side. You have a job, of sorts. You have been married. And, you have produced… an 'heir.' You've done your bit. What could you possibly have to lose now?

"The life I *know*…"

What life?! You said it yourself, the life you have now is shit! You want to commit to your mistakes because you spent so much time making them? You may as well be committing to suicide. You're not as hopeless as the rest of the cattle out there, you know how people work. You have an insight that no-one else has. Don't waste it. You're… special.

"'Special,' yeah right…"

You can do as you please. To Hell **with the consequences! If there is something you want to do, do it. If there is something you want to eat, eat it. If there is someone you want to fuck, fuck them. If someone is in your way,** remove them… **If there is something you want to do… Do it.**

The paper in Neville's other hand crumples in his grasp.

***

The truck drives off, now empty.

Neville rolls the shutter down. He looks over the wooden boxes on the floor, shaking his head. "I don't know if I've done the right thing."

Remember, a weak man has doubts before a decision. A strong man has them after.

"Who else said that? I've heard it before…"

Tap-*tap* at the shutter.

Neville stares. It could be someone knocking at his head….

Harder, faster, raps again.

Neville steps toward the shutter. With both hands he drags it up, releasing one hand, ready for self-defence.

Cold chattering aluminium unveils white shoes, grey trouser legs, and the *will* of someone wanting 'in,' as Nick waits for the rest of the shutter to come up. He steps inside from the dusk at last, like *he* owns the place. "Who were you talking to?"

"No-one", says Neville, "just my voice… mail."

How rude…

Nick scans the space. "Now this brings back happy memories…"

"Your last order wasn't that long ago, was it?"

"It wasn't. I'm just surprised you went through with this. And set it up exactly the way the old man did."

"He kept his old receipts. I just placed the same order with the museum, and here we are. How long were you and Grandad doing this?"

Is it weird to refer to 'Grandad' to this thug? I'm letting a stranger in…

"We'd been doing business for years," says Nick, "until he 'died', obviously."

"Obviously…" says Neville. "I don't know what's special about what I ordered. I was hoping you'd know what to look for if I just re-ordered the same…"

"Fortunately…" Nick steps awkwardly over one of the boxes. "…I do know what to look for." Nick approaches a crate, crouches beside it, and then turns to face the one behind. He stands. Keeping his eyes on that one side, he stretches out an arm and open hand towards Neville.

Now he wants to shake hands?

"Crowbar," Nick monotones. Expectant. A surgeon requesting a scalpel.

Neville agitates a look around.

Sod's law, going through all this trouble, letting this creep in, when we can't even get anything open…

He faces the corner where Nick's arm indicates, and there it is. Dull blue paint flaked away from the dark grey metal, scratched-up under the surface. Neville reaches down for the crowbar. It whispers a dense, tinny scrape against the floor as he picks it up.

As he stands to hand it over, he sees Nick's head and eyes already turned, watching for the heavy blunt object Neville is about to place into his hands. Either Neville's arm slows, or the flow of time itself, as he holds out the crowbar. Their eyes lock onto each other as metal settles in Nick's palm, and fingers curl around it. All Neville has to do is let go…

And he does.

Nick, staring back at him, wraps his other hand around the crowbar... jams its teeth into the side of the crate, and then pries the side off. The square lands flat in front of him, as the wood fell once before in its original, natural form... at the hands of another man, with another merciless metal weapon...

Nick tries to hide a playful grin, "Paper covers Rock. Rock breaks Scissors."

One way or another, Scissors always cuts...

Nick drops the crowbar onto the wood, with a thud, and reaches into the crate. He pulls out one plastic transparent pouch.

Isn't that just 'weed'?

Bright green, under Neville's eye, *luminous*... "Is that it?"

"Yeah," Nick holds up the pouch the way Hamlet holds up a skull, "that's it." He looks over his shoulder out of the garage and whistles. Two strapping henchmen stomp inside, taller, if not twice the size of Neville and Nick.

One of them carries a metal briefcase and hands it to Nick, who takes it and opens it up to Neville.

Holy fuck!

Wads of notes stacked neatly from side-to-side and front-to-back.

Just like you see on screen, but never in real life, if you're not wealthy or a crook. Well, maybe I am just a crook...

"That's ten thou," says Nick. "For two months' supply. Happy with that?"

"Yeah..." the shock hits Neville. "That'll do."

Nick nods, and then to the henchmen who push other crates out of their way surprisingly delicately. Nick shuts the case and hands it to Neville, who takes it as carefully as he dares, resisting the urge to swing it back and forth like a child skipping home from the sweet shop.

"Backs straight, boys." Nick looks over to the men as they stoop down to the crate. "Remember, lift with the knees…"

In front and behind the great cumbersome crate, the *Backstraight Boys* lift it from underneath. The front man faces away with his hands behind him, holding the base, while the other guy follows, supporting the back.

"Do you use this stuff, yourself?" Neville asks.

No doubt he is definitely a 'user'.

Nick answers Neville, not just modest, but composed. "Me? No. I'm actually more of a health freak. Unusual, in my line of work."

"You mean as a… chemist?"

"Yeah, that's right. A *chemist*."

"You usually… Make the stuff, then?"

"No, I… *prescribe*." Nick looks to the boys already out of the garage. Turning back to Neville, he puts his hand out, towered by a distinctly tall thumb. "It's been a pleasure, sir."

"Likewise." Neville grips it. One firm, abrupt shake and they release.

Nick turns away and follows the men out in confident strides, not looking back. "Place the order again for a couple months' time."

Neville *rests his case* on one of the crates and clicks it open. The money is no hallucination. It smells… rich. It is real, laid out… Compact.

"Just waiting to be spent by…"

Lesser, impulsive minds.

"What do you mean?"

An engine starts nearby. Neville walks out of the garage, resisting the urge to wave at the van, which drives off with Nick in the passenger seat, like a commanding officer being escorted back to base.

It's a business to them. A serious one. You need to be careful how you spend that money. That glorious, handy, untaxed money... You need to treat it just as seriously or you will raise suspicion. What were you thinking of doing with it? Throwing a party? With booze, drugs, whores? Would you even know how to organise something like that? Do you have enough friends to share it with? Can you even tell anyone the truth about...?

"I get the point. I'll hang onto it..." He steps back inside and stands over the sacred papers. "Well, what would *you* do with it?"

Me? The booze, drugs and whores do sound tempting. But I'm talking about spending the money wisely. You can treat yourself. Go out for a nice, bloody steak. Go and buy yourself a new suit, or ten. Look for a new car. A new place...

"So that's what *you* would do?"

Money... well spent. You can piss it all away, or you can invest it... in yourself... Better your life, for a long-lasting good time.

"I was actually thinking about a little trip away, a proper holiday." Neville places his hand over the side of the case. And the other over the corner of the lid, fondling it... like a former lover's cold hard breast... "Maybe with Kat... And especially for Gemma."

Leaving town is out of the question, remember, Killer? Besides, it's too little, too late with Kat. She has already made it plain she's moved on.

"Even my marriage is just another victim. It should never've happened!"

It was necessary, Neville. Now, you are unbound. You can even operate around the law. Why stop? Now would be the worst time to leave! You don't need to look guilty, so stop feeling like it, stop acting like it! Think! You have a 'business' to run. If you leave now, Tracy will have found a way to take over the museum – don't think she's just forgotten about that!

And you can't afford to rouse the police, leaving your castle unattended. See, you still need to get your affairs in order.

Neville slams the case shut. "So, 'don't spend it all at once.'"

Exactly! See how that Nick looks after himself. Quite rare for a drug dealer, apparently, but he's got the right idea. Money conquers all.

"Paper covers Rock."

CHAPTER 20

It's a new dawn, a new day, a new life… for… me… And I'm feeling-

"Adequate!" Neville switches off the ignition and gets out of the car less reluctant than usual.

Things could be on the up and up.

He skips just as quickly up the steps for the museum's front doors.

Can't be complacent. If my guard is down, something else bad will happen!

The walk to the front desk appears so much smaller than Neville's first visit. He finds Tracy, the sentinel, at the computer. "Morning, Tracy."

"Morning, Nev."

She must be in a good mood too, then. Nothing's stopping me today…

"You know, I notice in the storage…" *No, not the storage cupboard, God forbid!* "That 'garagey' space, there's a lot of stock I don't see going anywhere very quickly. I was just thinking we could perhaps try to expand the business online…"

"Ah! I'm actually way ahead of you. I was gonna show you this later, but…"

She turns the monitor his way. "Double-u-double-u-double-u-dot-Pikes-Museum-dot-com. 'Dot *com*', Nev. But we could go global if instead we use *this* site..." She clicks and summons another website: 'Pandora's Box'.

Neville can hardly contain himself in the face of this whirlwind pitch. Oblivious, merciless, Tracy keeps on whirling.

"...somewhat *independent* of the museum. We can sell the excess stock Mr Pike used to bring in for the gift shop, if we give it a different name!"

Unfortunately, that's a no-brainer. That's her way in. She's burrowing deeper. She's trying to take the wheel!

"Yeah," he says. "*Pike's Museum of General History and Antiquities* doesn't exactly exude sex appeal, does it? This looks great, Tracy."

She already knows it's great. She's not just talking about the site. She's talking about how great she is. Tracy knows she's great. And that's what makes her dangerous...

She continues as if he had not said a word.

"Just when I finally managed to persuade him to let me do this, his health went downhill so it stalled. But this is what I've been working on for some time. And I've nearly finished. I've been setting up profiles on social networks, uploading pictures, writing a little about each exhibit..."

And making yourself even more indispensable in the process...

"...I might even set up a blog."

'For us', say 'for us'...

"That way, we can give the business a voice. Some credibility."

'We'... The business under what name? It needs to be Pike's for a little longer, so I can be the one to rename it. This business was Grandad's baby, it's mine now! But she's the evil stepmother. She wants to find a way to push me out and make it

hers. I won't let her claim custody over my child. My only other child…

"I should've known…" says Neville, "that you'd take the initiative. Keep up the good work!"

What else can I say? What else can I do but show my 'full support?'

"I'll let you know when I'm done," a smile plays around her pink, pasty lips. And a sinister twinkle dances in her eye.

I'm sure you will…

He leaves her to it and waltzes wilfully into the corridor, around the corner…

And… release…

"That cunning bitch," he hisses, to suppress the eruption. If only she knew…

Or maybe she does know…

Neville continues into the privacy of his office, slamming the door. He turns and launches a running kick into the desk. "This is not what I wanted!"

He somewhat finds sedation in the numbing chill of his big toe.

It's what happens when you go through the motions of a leadership position. Your subordinates start to think for themselves.

"Tracy is no subordinate. She's smart. Probably smarter than me…" He paces up and down to each side of the desk. "I was just starting to do something different, finally take up the fucking reins! And now she's gone one up on me."

You know, she's only as smart as you are angry.

"Then she must be a fucking *genius*!"

You just took too long figuring out what you wanted to

do. All you have to do is keep calm and-

"Carry on?"

Play her game... On her level. Better yet, above her level.

Neville slows by the middle of the desk. He faces the door and inhales...

The tide comes in. Waves crash against the stone harbour wall... The tide goes out...

"If we- 'we...' Damn it, she's indoctrinating me already. It won't work!" He sits on the desk. "If *I* can change the business, move it away from failing as a tacky museum, we... *I...!* can get rid of the shit Grandad has been exhibiting all these years... and do things *my* way."

Your commitment to this dump is admirable.

"Tracy's moving ahead with *my* ideas. She just plucked them right out of my head! *Pandora's Box* has deliberately been given a more elegant design... It's going to grow. It's going to swallow up Pike's Museum like a cancer. She's going to eclipse me and keep it all for herself... I can't just fire her for thinking of the company's best interest, not while she's on that bleddy contract with that weird bleddy arrangement. I can't stop her... Thank you, Grandad!"

There may be only one thing for it.

"No. I couldn't! Not again..."

Everyone needs to toe the company line.

"What the hell happened to 'playing the game on her level'? No... No more blood spill!"

You could've fooled me. You're the one who keeps jumping to violent conclusions... Have you not considered actually using your dusty creative skills for once? Why don't you try writing something on this blog?

Sometimes the voice speaks sense. Neville hops off his

desk and circles around to sit in the chair. He ignites the computer, with the plastic surrounding the switch nibbling affectionately at his fingertip. It is sluggish, but the idea finally dawns on it to switch on, alongside Neville's wits.

"But has she put it up yet? And more importantly, has she made me an admin? This epiphany will mean bugger all if I can't access the site or change it in any way."

Stillness surrounds him waiting for the computer to resurrect. Motes sink and settle like microscopic snow, a slow storm of passing time. But the internet is a dustless place. What Neville has to put out there must be timeless.

***

I couldn't kill her. Tracy is catching the public eye… so write I must. It's the best way I can start taking back control. Now… flex those old muscles…

…They creak. They churn. Like the old leather chair cradling his numb buttocks. Creative grit rattles, shaken loose by desperate tremors of frustration.

You won't get anything done like this.

"Well, what would *you* write?" snaps Neville, leaning back in his chair.

Lies, mostly. Singing seductive false praises about the museum and what the place has to offer… What do you want to write?

"I want to write about the waste of space this place is… How these shitty exhibitions constitute a museum by Grandad's standards. What was he thinking? Both my Grandparents held me back and ruined my life. One time, when Grandad was supposed to pick me up from a school trip, I was the last one to be collected. But as he came round, thinking he was early, he turned and left the school premises. One of the teachers chased the car, calling after him. About an hour later he finally pulled up with a milk churn he just bought in the backseat of the car. A fucking *milk-churn!* Little things like that add up and quash a child's ego."

Silence.

Neville looks up from the computer. He glances over his shoulder for any sense of where his invisible *other* might be...

Pardon me. I just had to let you stew in your self-pity for a moment. Do you know... how pathetic you sound?

"Yes!"

It's all very well, Neville, but the truth is, no-one cares. No-one wants to hear it. Mull those ideas over, think about what you really want the museum to be. See how you can appeal to these lesser minds.

"I'm powerless. I can't engage. I can't knuckle down to what I'm supposed to do. There's so much else I would rather do..." He slouches, shrinking in the chair. "The world doesn't have any mercy. 'It doesn't stop just for you. No-one cares about *your* sensibilities.'"

That's what your grandad used to say, wasn't it?

"Yeah... It could be I've turned out as bitter as him. But the man was right."

The world doesn't stop just for you...

The tune is in his head. Neville sits up and plays a symphony of chattering plastic on the computer keys.

'Pike's Museum. Where history stops for you.'

"This is more like it!"

A knock rattles the door...

"Yes?"

The door opens. Tabitha strolls in, scanning the bland, drab room before resting her eyes on the gaffer himself. "Well, hello you."

Lost for words, Neville freezes. His jaw does not even drop. What to say...

'Hi, Tabby! How have you been since I beat your boyfriend

to death? I hope I left you satisfied the morning after…'

In that eternal second, different personas fight for control. Even 'James Bond' is hard pushed to quell 'The Hunchback of Notre Dame…'

The second has passed.

"The scenery just got a whole lot better," says 'Mr Bond.'

Thank fuck he *made it through. For now.*

Tabitha slinks around to one side of the desk. *Her* move… "I do like to bring… a touch of colour."

"To my cheeks, for sure," says Neville. "This is an unexpected pleasure. What brings you here, honey?"

Tabitha glances to a picture on the wall beside her, of a bare tree off centre on a grassy bank, under a cloudy sky. She reaches out and slides her fingertips over the glass which denies her the feel of dried brushstrokes.

Not bad for a print, is it? Cheapest to the last, that was Grandad.

"I was just curious about where you work," she says. "And… it's hard to get in touch without a means to reach you."

Neville stands gracefully, slipping his hands into his pockets as he steps around the desk to face her. "That's a problem, isn't it?"

I'm not going to be clingy and go to her. I'll see where this is going and let her come to me…

"So, what do you think of this place?"

"Well, it's not *my* cup of tea," she moves away, running her fingers along the front edge of the desk, "but then, I'm not a big fan of history. It's a little depressing to see things so still, so dead, on display behind glass."

"I know. It's only been mine a while but, believe me, there's going to be some changes around here…"

"You're gonna turn this place into an aquarium?" she guesses, sarcastically.

Neville takes a step closer to her after all. "Let's just say, I *will* be bringing some life into it."

Makes a change from taking it, eh?

The voice does not penetrate Neville.

Tabitha takes two shrewd steps closer, just short of him. "So, about your phone number…"

He holds out a hand, "I'll give it to you right now."

Instead of giving him her mobile, she takes his hand and pulls him in, wrapping his arm around her waist, while her other arm slips around his back. Her hand slithers down to one of his cheeks. Neville and Tabitha's lips hover just inches from each other's.

"You do know I meant my number, right?"

"Yeah," she whispers.

CHAPTER 21

Getting away with murder, hope for the business at last, a possible new woman…

Smaller problems appear bigger. A sure sign that everything is much closer now to how it should be, such as finding a decent dessert in this half-dead shop.

Something bittersweet will be appropriate for this evening… but made to be a guest in my own home? Having to bring an offering? It must be so strange for Gemma to see me like this.

Neville should not get anything too fancy, but he should not cheap out either. "Ah, a tiramisu will do," he mutters, smirking at the tenuous rhyme.

Nothing like a bit of trauma to make you enjoy the little things in life.

He takes out the box from the fridge cabinet and then goes searching for cream. A little bit of light in case the darkness is too much for them. But it is *just dessert*. Now to pay…

Service with a 'smile'…

…from Neville's side of the counter, anyway.

The blue polo-shirted cashier scans the goods one by one, like the end of his shift depends on it. Yet no words are exchanged.

There's no pleasing humanity. You're told to be happy, but then when you actually are, nobody likes it!

"Keep the change." Neville turns to walk out.

You can choke on my happiness if I don't first.

***

The main attraction, the prize for whoever can get there first... The tiramisu sits prominently at the centre of the dinner table. Aptly chosen. Neville, Kat and Gemma tuck into homemade chicken, cheese, and tomato pasta bake.

Italian night could be my way back in.

Neville suppresses a contented sigh, as a sigh of any kind at this point could be misread.

Working so hard to survive so long without my family, I think I deserve this slice of mediocrity.

Happiness in a brief scene of normal life as it should be.

Not as a killer *at the table.*

Sitting beside him, Gemma cuts her food with surgical precision and devours daintily each piece of pasta. Neville's little girl of six moves like a woman of sixty-six. More like a sadistic hag, carving...

She sees Daddy looking at her and smiles. Still a child. Still his daughter.

No need to call for an exorcist just yet. Not for her, *anyway.*

A nice, simple meal. Together. They chew in silence, but at least not in awkward silence. Neville looks up at Kat, opposite him, tucking in with a more enthusiastic use of knife and fork.

Say something. Please... lest I put my foot in it! Every day the world offers a hundred new ways for a man to ruin his life. Or, to end it.

Neville's mouth is already full... But rather than take any

unnecessary risks, he sits and enjoys this picture. This meal, the aroma of oven grease, and the warming symphony of chewing amongst cutlery, scratching at their plates. He looks forward to dessert.

Out of the corner of his eye, Gemma slows the dissection of her food. Neville glances cautiously to find her staring at the tiramisu. He bites back a smile and looks to Kat, also staring with the same vacant yet animalistic expression. She catches him looking at her. Neville's smile tries to prise its way out of his mouth as he nods towards their daughter.

Gemma looks up at the sudden stillness. And at her hungry parents.

Epic silence, as they all realise what they are really thinking about; they laugh heartily, innocently, together.

***

Swirling patterns fade and drift from the dishes soaking in the washing-up bowl.

On the settee in the living room, Neville sits with a dinosaur book on his lap, while cuddling a sleepy Gemma.

"Come on, munchkin." Kat holds out her hand.

Gemma tightens her grip on Neville, and then releases. Kat picks her up.

"Night-night, Gem," says Neville.

"Night-night, Daddy," she is surprisingly abrupt.

'Pleasure doing business with you,' Gem…

Neville snickers as Kat carries her out of the room, leaving him alone with thuds that mark vaguely her ascent of the stairs.

He scans from right to left of the couch to see what has changed. His chair, for one, is now pushed from the telly and left in the corner by the window.

The walls could do with a new coat… Should I offer? How

much do I want to be 'back in', anyway? If she's that serious about moving on, she should probably do it herself. I can't be going out of my way to make it easier for her. She can't have the satisfaction of me being wrapped round her little finger, in spite of all this.

On the shelves left of the telly, above the hi-fi, one picture, with a happy Neville holding a littler happy Gem, has been restored to its rightful place.

Maybe there's hope after all. There's only six more Pike-tures to go...

"She's all tucked in," says Kat.

Neville turns. He must have zoned out, and not heard her come back down.

Black lingerie, scantily cladding Kat as she leans casually against the doorframe... is a sight Neville used to relish this time in the evening.

Kat is, in fact, dressed as she was when she took Gemma up the stairs.

But at least he was welcomed back for dinner. Two steps back. One step forward... "I didn't hear you come down."

"Thank you for tea," says Kat.

"You're very welcome." He only dares to look modestly happy as he gets up. "I'd best be off. Thanks for having me, love."

He winces. Luckily, a second is all he needs before he faces Kat.

"Are you sure?" she asks. "Just one more cuppa?"

"I don't want to impose..."

Just bend her over the couch and see to her, for fuck's sake!

"Just stay for one more," she says.

"Yeah. Alright."

Kat practically glides into the kitchen, leaving Neville with a glowing smirk.

Traditional foreplay is much more fun than this 'Sunday best' bullshit. Makes me sick.

Neville *does* feel sick, having enjoyed too much of a good thing. Too much anxiety, too much tension… Too much tiramisu… but the Deville in him has enjoyed a good 'meal', too…

This is your house, isn't it? Your family. If you're going to dwell on this sorry lot, you might as well just take it back.

A breathy roar from the kettle follows Kat out of the kitchen.

Neville sits on the couch again, cautious of the unwelcome voice in his ear.

"Well," Kat sits back down beside him. "That's the most tired-out she's been for a while."

Now it's your turn to be tired out…

Neville hisses at the voice, "Not here!"

Kat looks up. "You what?"

"I… s'pose it's because… I'm not… you *know*…"

"Yeah, it has been harder without you, Nev. In that respect…"

"But Gem is happy, isn't she? In spite of…"

Who cares? Disrobe your wife and assert yourself!

Neville feels the heat, his blood, warming with the kettle. Boiling over.

"Yes, of course she's happy," says Kat. "I'm trying, but it's bound to be confusing for her."

Even the cushions cook Neville where he sits. Hugging his back, the heat bites down, threatening to overcome him.

Please, release me from this couch!

The embarrassment, of leaving the most epic sweat patch, pushes him closer to the edge.

"Though I have to admit," Kat continues, "it's a bit confusing for me as well, after an evening like this…"

The material smothering Neville's oddly humid back threatens to release an ungodly odour. A petty, diabolical intervention to disrupt the mood between him and Kat. Tension rises within him, leaking out through his foot dancing up and down. He allows it to ease the pressure, so the dam does not burst.

"It reminds me that sometimes… what we had was great."

Neville's foot settles.

She misses you. Wonderful. Now, pounce!

"Well, Kat, it's only natural for us to miss each other. We do have plenty of good memories. But we still don't know whether that's good enough to give 'us' another chance."

What?! Where is this coming from?!

Kat stares at Neville. Her hand moves from her lap to grip Neville's hand. She brings it to her lips. And then bites him.

"Ahhhh!" cries Neville, "the fuck was that for?!"

Kat does not break her gaze. "So, after all that profound drivel… you were really just a fortune cookie all along."

A spark of a laugh escapes Neville, setting off an explosive fit. A sputtering round of machine gun laughter, swiftly accompanied by Kat cackling with an exhausting giggle. Their sides feel the pinch, getting tighter and tighter, as their lungs fight to draw breath again. Kat and Neville clutch their stomachs while embers of their chuckling tumble out of them, and fade to silent cinders.

Neville looks to Kat, finding her chuckles have turned into sobs, as she brings a hand to her mouth. He wraps his arms around her. The stillness of the room surrounds them as he rests his chin on her head.

"It's okay," Neville soothes.

"No, it's not."

"Look, I'm not going to fly the flag for calling off the divorce. It would be nice if things could work out again, but maybe we really do need more time before we can settle on a decision. Yeah?"

Kat pushes free of him and wipes her face. "I dunno, Nev. It'll take a clear head. I can't think about it right now."

"That's okay… Shall I go?"

"No, don't go. I'm not letting you leave just because I spoilt this evening… Oh my god, look at me. *Don't* look at me."

"You didn't spoil the evening."

I'll *say*…

"What's probably spoilt it," Neville continues, "is that I still haven't had my bleddy cuppa."

Kat chuckles. "I feel stupid. But better now, thanks… You may leave…"

"Charming… Anyway, we're doing okay with Gemma. Considering… It's obviously going to take a bit longer for us to work out what *we're* doing."

Kat sighs.

"I've said enough profound tripe for one evening. I'm heading back to the flat before I say any more…" He gets up, and then watches her face settle. "You want me to stay?"

"I do. But I don't think we should confuse Gem." She stands. "Besides, you have work tomorrow, so…"

"You're right… I'll be off then." Neville faces the hall and walks out of the living room, followed steadily by Kat to the front door. He opens it and steps out into the stagnant chill of night. Neville turns to peck her on the cheek… when instead, their lips connect. With their eyes open, Neville closes his and returns the kiss. Kat pulls away and watches him come to his senses, looking at her.

"Goodnight, Nev." She retreats inside, waiting for him to turn around before shutting the door softly.

He faces the door again, certain that Kat is on the other side, listening for the crunching stones under his every step. Neville lifts his foot and brings it down gently, to whisper over the gravel. He takes his time with the next step, and then the next, uneasy that his still-wife will have moved away from the door.

Instinctively keen to keep her in suspense, he wonders whether he has left her with an urge to open the door and call him back before he gets to his car.

But the door does not open.

CHAPTER 22

Another door opens… in the half-dead of night.

Neville gets into his car and *shuts* it, on-

My *home.* My *wife and* my *child…*

As *his* gravel churns under the tyres… Neville drives out.

Warm, fuzzy memories of the evening die down, like sleepy embers in the hearth, snuffed out by gales roaring down the chimney as wind rushes into the car. Neville's sense of self burns down to a glimmer, on the dark cold road to nowhere.

I can understand why people kill themselves… She closed the door on me, and I get to go on my merry way back to my little hidey hole. I'm all alone, what do I have to live for? 'Turning my life around'? Watching Gemma grow up from the other side of town? By then Kat would've turned her against me… I'm sure she wouldn't let years of adequate marriage get in the way of that.

"She might cut me out of their lives on a whim. One meal does not make a mended fence… I can't expect she'll do the decent thing and let Gemma keep her daddy. Not when, saint that I am, I'll make some glorious mistake and suddenly become the worst person in the world… I'm just waiting for the axe to fall."

Get over yourself!

Jumping, Neville barely keeps control of the car, and swerves back into the left lane. He just about gets his breath back.

"You certainly changed your tune from wanting to jump my wife's bones!"

What can I say? I'm an opportunist.

"My family is off limits to you."

Your world is bigger than them, damn it! You already think they're not your family anymore.

"That's not what I…"

You're letting yourself get sucked in. Now it's 'back to reality,' again! There's no certainty of family. Instead of wasting your time chasing after them, you should be pursuing your own goals. Then you'll get to see how much they want you back… the minute you become successful…

"They're not gonna want me for my money!"

They will.

"At least I'll be able to provide for them. At least they'll want me!"

But not for you they won't, will they?

"Nobody wants me for *me*. Nobody wants *me*…"

The car drifts further left…

"I don't know myself anymore."

Now, now…

"I don't know anything…"

Neville.

"I just want to…"

Neville!

He swerves right. The low growl ceasing tells Neville he is back on the road.

"*What do you want?!*"

Are you really giving up? Now? When your business is growing?

"It's pointless. Nobody wants *me*..."

Everybody will want you when you're done.

"Done? Working with low lives? I don't care how much money they give me. It's dirty. And I can't share that with Kat and Gemma... can I?"

Yes, done! You are better than them. You're better than them all... You've always known, haven't you, Neville? Why share your accumulating fortune with one woman and child when you can share it with so many women? The whole world, you altruist, you...

But not in that grotty place you live in now. No, no... They wouldn't let you drag them back to that place... Though I'm sure any number of people, rich, glamorous, tasty, willing people, will want to follow you back to... the Mayoral Suite...

"What the fuck are you talking about?"

You could be somebody, Neville. You've done your bit with family. You can tick that off the list... But now, you can be a success! And what better time to do it! With Kat grasping at independence, and possession of your daughter, you'll have next to no ties to hold you back...

Of course, you'll be working with low lives, Neville, but with the right *low lives,* the right *business transactions, the* right *palms greased, favours owed, you can build yourself an empire. Why not? The whole country in your hand... Why not the world? Neville Pike, survivor, museum owner, mayor, MP, Prime Minister, ruler... Victor... You could beat everyone. Conquer the world. Why not? What do you* really *have to lose?*

The lord of the manor arrives in his silver chariot. He steps onto the ground and, with head held high, glides majestically towards his palace, garments adorning him dance as he makes his way, ignoring that this is where 'his old flat used to be.' He ascends to his throne room and enters the grand hall while serfs close the doors behind him. Lord Neville sits upon the highest seat above all. His loyal, most trusted, cunning advisor appears from behind… Both hands reach above, to place the crown on Neville's royal head…when the phone rings.

Neville snaps back to reality *in his flat*, with his arms over his head, holding the devilish mask aloft. It was about to cover his face… to *consume* his face…

The phone reaches its last ring as Neville sits frozen, with the mask suspended over him.

Si's voice booms from the answer phone. "Alright, Nev? It's Si. Me and the boys are looking to do the pub quiz tonight. Wondering if you wanna join? Catch up with everyone? Hope to see you later." The machine rings off.

Does Neville join the lowly mortals?

He lowers his arms… the mask covers his face. It *is* his face, horns, and all. Neville stands. He strides out of his throne room, red and snarling.

CHAPTER 23

So grand that they threaten to pierce the ceiling if not the heavens, Neville's horns protrude from his head.

Hapless patrons engage in civilised revelry at the tavern. A cacophony of chatter. Single voices drown under a sea of groans.

A hand floats above the greying and balding human craniums to wave. It is Si, from Neville's mortal life, seated at a table between two so-called comrades and one empty chair.

The heads of Neville's subjects all turn, as the once and future king approaches and takes his seat at the round table.

"Whey! Alright, Nev? It's good to see ya." Mark is already halfway there… and *living on a prayer…* "You still a Thatcher's man? We've got you a pint."

What's this? Why do they talk to me so boldly? Can't they see my face? They should respect me! They should be cowering…

Neville looks down, aghast, at the glass tower of sour golden nectar. "You're damn right I am." *These mortals have appeased me… for now…*

He scoops up the pint glass and takes a sip, a gulp, and then one more lustful swallow.

"Bleddy hell, he's on it tonight!" calls Kit. On it himself, with his obnoxious one-liners. Like the good old days…

I never much cared for you, Kit. Obnoxious creep… I shall end you tonight.

"Does something displease you, O mighty one?" Si asks.

"Hm?" Neville is puzzled.

"I said, *'are you alright?'*"

"Yeah, you?" Neville expects his devilish snarl will break Si to his very core. *See my face!*

"Yeah… You're looking a bit… spaced out."

"I'm fine." *You accept me as I am? Well, I suppose with friends like Si there's hope yet.*

"What have you all been up to?" Neville asks.

"I got a new job," says Mark.

Again? You do surprise me!

"…Oh, so you're waiting for me to ask, 'what as'?" Teases Neville. "You're not a hitman, then?"

Mark's shotgun-laugh bursts out. "No, I'm with this cleaning company now. Driving up and down, and from coast to coast with my company van. I'm shit at it actually, but they just keep paying me."

Kit pipes up. "You must be doing something right then, otherwise you'll *have* to try the hitman thing!"

Shut up, Kit.

"Well," says Si, "you're all caught up with *me*…"

Neville looks over to Kit. "So, what are you up to now, *mate?*"

Si and Mark turn to him as well.

"I got a new house, didn't I?"

Of course, you did, you bastard.

"Well done, mate," says Mark, "is it nice?"

Of course, it's nice, you moron! Kit *wouldn't go buying a place that doesn't meet his high standards. Don't you dare 'well done' him…*

"Yeah, it's not bad," says Kit, "me and Colin moved in last month."

Yeah, I bet it's 'not bad,' you prick.

"What does Colin make of it?" Si asks.

I always preferred your boyfriend over you, mate.

"He's settling in alright. It's him doing most of the decorating, I've just been doing most of the heavy lifting."

The things I'd do to get a proper place of my own again…

"Okay!" a microphone booms with the voice of the pub landlord. "It's nine-ish! Which means it's time for the Pickled Egghead's quiz night. Get your pens and answer sheets ready, it's time to start. And for the first round, question one…"

"…What's this I hear about you and this museum, Nev?" Kit asks.

"What?" says Neville, "You've heard this from Si, then?"

"And now…" the landlord announces. The light dims all around Neville. Si shuffles closer to Mark, who picks up his pen to scribe for the team.

Magically Kit appears to be the landlord, now wearing a tacky gameshow host's sparkling pink suit. He sneers into the microphone in his hand, "What's this about you taking on this museum, *Neville*?"

"Oh. Well, my grandad died," Neville sweats, "and he left me his business."

The spotlight on Neville warms him. Cooks him. A bead of

moisture from his brow tickles his cheek on its way down.

No! Why don't I have the mask on? Did I arrive just as human as the rest?!

Question two… Kit asks, "And you left your job for it?"

Eyes of a hundred spectators, a forest of silhouettes, bore into Neville, stalking him as he tries to duck and dive through questions with frantically codged-up answers. "I was optimistic. No. I… really just wanted to get out of the office!"

Question three… "Is it worth it?" Kit enquires. "Are you really that much better off?"

"I feel great, believe it or not," says Neville. "Really. It's taken a bit of work, but I've had a breakthrough. Money is rolling in at last…"

Question four. "Even," Kit pries, "if it means you're in fact a budding drug baron on the side?"

"What?"

Question five. Kit leers, *"Was* it worth it?"

"I've already had that question!"

"Was it worth killing all those people… just so you could feel so *big…* and so *powerful?"*

"…Yeah," Si interrupts, "the worth of a shilling before decimation, *decimalisation* sorry, was… five pence, wasn't it?"

The room is lit up again. The landlord continues quizzing, and Kit is wearing casual clothing. Back to reality… or whatever constitutes reality this evening.

"Wow…" Mark adds. "Opportunities like that don't come around very often. Sorry about your grandad."

How much did I tell them? "Well, he was a miserable sod but being in his shoes now, I think I understand why. How on earth did he get into the trades he did? I also wonder now, actually, what he really wanted to be."

Mark, Kit and Si all look around at each other.

What? Why have you all gone quiet? Am I the oddball again?

"Well, I wanted to be a musician," says Mark, "but I can't play anything. I can't even carry a tune!"

Throwing their heads back, Si and Kit laugh. Neville manages only a faint, hollow chuckle.

That's right Mark, make some inane joke and move on. This is why I didn't kill myself keeping in touch with you bastards. You never take me seriously… You never take anything seriously but yourselves. And even then, it's a competition to be the smartest, funniest, most successful, betterest bastard in the room!

The boys do not stop laughing. The space goes dark again.

They never stopped laughing. Ever since…

Neville sweats. A familiar grubbiness, from the suffocation of a school shirt and tie. A blazer weighing down on his shoulders, trapping the intense heat.

They always laughed at me. "Neville, Neville, dirty devil…"

…the resounding chant of a dozen or more greasy, spotty students. Neville is sweatier, dirtier, as the tamping power of obnoxious, noxious chanting, sucks the perspiration out of him…

"You gonna sit down, or what?" Mark sounds off.

Hang on- What am I doing? Where have I been?

The pub table stretches before Neville. Kit, Mark, and Si, seated at the other end of the table, drift further and further and further away…

"You've already missed the rest of the first round because you went out for a conveniently long tinkle."

So, I've been then, have I? Back to reality once more… Fleeting reality…

"Wanna come and suffer the next round with us or what?"

"I wouldn't let you sorry sods lose on your own, would I?" Neville retorts.

"That's the spirit," Si chuckles.

Neville sits. He tries to put his loose grip on reality to the back of what is left of his mind. Tonight, he is a normal man again.

Could've have been worse. I might not have made *it to the loo!*

Scribbling onto scruffling paper, the intense muttering of answers doomed to be wrong, and spontaneous laughter in the face of being in last place at the quiz, is washed down with a couple more pints...

***

A round of applause for a quiz well done... Second-to-last place is cause for celebration among Neville and his old comrades.

"Whey! We're not total losers!" calls Mark.

Kit slaps his hand over his eyes.

"Speak for yourself!" says Neville.

"Oi," calls Si, "Can one of you able-bodied buggers come over here and help carry these?"

"I've got it." Neville stands up and approaches the bar.

Si observes him delicately huddling three full pint glasses together. "You... getting on alright?"

"Yeah, fine," says Neville.

"You seemed on edge earlier."

"It's just been a while since I've seen those two. We're good. Have you got yours there? I'm not made of hands." Neville lifts the three pints and carries them over to the table. Si hobbles behind with his hand clawed over the top of his own glass. They are met with a cheer and indeed a chuckle, as Si's pint lands daintily on the table, like a butterfly on slowed-down documentary footage.

"I think I might head home after this one," says Mark.

"What?" Neville carries a faint echo of Deville, "Just end the night there? Do you not want to *live*?"

"Eh? *Yeah*, but I've got work tomorrow."

"Same," adds Kit.

"But *chaps*, we don't have to remain *losers* tonight," Neville rallies.

"What do you mean?" Mark's eyebrows reach for each other.

"Of all the nights we've come and lost this bloody quiz," Neville continues, "we've not once gone into the casino up the road to try our luck there."

Si, Kit, and Mark all look to each other with joy, trepidation, and intrigue.

See no evil, hear no evil, speak no evil…

"You what?" says Mark.

"The casino," says *Do no evil*. "Catching up has been all good and nice, chaps, but right now, why *don't* we try our luck up the road? 'You only live once…' The night is young, hot, and ready. More importantly, it's yours for the taking."

Blank expressions glaze over from Neville's ten o'clock, his twelve o'clock and his two o'clock. Silence is broken by Mark, "Eh?"

I'm wasting my breath on these fools…

"You've used too many syllables, mate," says Kit, "he was lost at 'casino'."

Bang, Mark laughs. "Fuck off!"

I'll end you all tonight…!

"I'm game." The spotlight is on Si. Silence against the white noise of crowd.

Naturally, Kit is the first to pipe up. "Haven't you got work tomorrow? If you're late back, you'll be out like a light the next day."

"So? I work from home," says Si. "Nev's right. You only live once."

Yes, heed my wisdom.

"Well, I'll live to play another day," says Kit. "Goodnight!"

"It's an early start for me anyway," Mark adds. "I couldn't join you if I wanted to. Have a good night, lads. Let me know how it goes."

Kit heads sluggishly for the door, followed by Mark, who stumbles into him.

"Oi!" Kit fusses. "Watch out, you bleddy great pudding!"

Bang. Mark's laugh erupts, "Sorry, mate. Don't wanna make *Colin* jealous!"

As the door shuts on their way out. Neville glares after them. "Goodnight, you boring pillocks!"

Si looks to him. "Just us, then."

"Right, down *that*. Then we're gone."

Both bring their glasses to their lips and drink the rest of their pints dry. Slammed to the table, the glasses jiggle close to tipping as the men totter out.

CHAPTER 24

Spirits entice with their fragrance… victory – and desperation – hang in the air. Stale drinks escape from glasses atom by atom to caress newcomers' noses.

Neville is not to be enticed tonight. He knows what he wants. To take a risk, to roll the dice, to win. He has already tempted *Si* down that road and through the door. They cross a sea of red at their feet enroute to the bar, onto solid black floor.

Their elbows rest on the glass counter as the buttoned-up bartendress glides over to them. Half-drunk, the boys are half-amazed at the sight of her breasts *not* breaching the security of her tight blouse.

"What can I get you?" She asks. "The…"

"Double JD and coke for me," Si jumps ahead, "Nev?"

"The same."

'The usual'? Was she about to say, 'the usual?'

The bartendress seizes two stocky glasses and whirls towards the spirits to conjure… their *drinks*.

Si looks to Neville. Despite the apparent lack of custom in the building, there is still the low hum of crowd, generated by patrons dotted here and there. Souls of the damned heard, but not seen, have long been absorbed into the building, along with their cash.

Si tries to raise his monotonous voice above it, "So, where should we start?"

"The fact that you have to ask kind of undermines the point, Si."

However, Neville's almost romantic perception of this casino world is dispelled upon seeing the dearth of custom. Yet sweaty saps on stools slump in front of the huge, alien touchscreens, which loom inanimately around the perimeter of the bar area.

The wonders of modern technology. Why even approach the roulette table when you can just finger-blast a screen? Even James Bond need no longer leave the bar to waste government money...

Delicate, efficient hands place two black-filled glasses on the bar.

Thank fuck for that.

Neville scoops one up before him and lifts it to his lips for a swig.

Si digs out a note to pay, along with the exact coinage to cover the two drinks. Not a word is exchanged between him and the tasty bartender.

"Spot on!" Neville smirks at the little victory, "Nothing's stopping us tonight!"

Having just tucked away his wallet, Si nurses a long sip from his drink.

"You've got that okay?"

"Yeah," Si holds his glass steady for the coming walk, "I've got it."

Neville carries his drink from the bar, over to a seat in front of a screen.

Si follows awkwardly. "Five quid to play."

Hang on, you couldn't have read that from all the way back there...

Neville pulls out his wallet and opens it up, studying the surprisingly bountiful fruits of his labour inside. He plucks a five-pound note from its leather maw and offers it to the thin lips of the hungry machine. Its mechanical avarice sucks the note from his fingertips. A novelty for Neville. A wonder for Si?

Neville pushes his fingertips against the numbered tiles on the screen. Seven and thirteen. Both black. 'Lucky seven' and 'lucky for some'.

"Let's try the best of both."

The screen shows footage of the roulette table dancing its hypnotic whirl clockwise. It *cuts* to the ball hopscotching over the metal wire between red and black until it stops, landing on eight... *red*.

"Typical. I really should've known." Neville taps on the numbers again, but the screen ignores his touch.

"That's your money gone," says Si.

"Eh? Bung on a fiver and then 'gone'? Are you serious? Is that it?"

"Let me try..." Si fishes for a fiver, rather like his life depends on it, but Neville beats him to the punch.

"Here." Neville plucks one from the rapidly thinning contents of his own wallet. The boon of taking a ridiculous amount of money for some exotic leaves and grasses. But, for now at least, *that* weed is legal.

He offers up this note to the machine again, feeling the pull from his fingers as this second one gets swallowed up.

Stepping in front of the machine, Si sits, forgetting Neville as he shoves him off. Neville remains curious to see the knack to this.

Si taps the numbers thirty-six and thirty-eight in red.

They wait for the wheel to begin its rapid whirling dance again. The ball begins its mocking jig over the blurry ring of red and black.

The roulette slows to a halt. It catches the ball in the number nineteen. Red. The wheel spins round, carrying the ball through its victory lap.

The house always wins…

Neville throws his hands up. "Well, fuck this!"

"Maybe it doesn't like your notes." Si looks to haul out his wallet.

"Na, let's look for something that's not rigged, shall we?" Neville swigs his drink and strolls out of the bar area, once again onto the *red*, flowing everywhere.

Si stalks behind, pulling his eyes away from the screen, forgetting his drink on the nearby table.

"What else is there, anyway?" Neville asks.

"There's the slots. I think there are craps tables… and definitely poker."

"Have you been here before?"

"Yeah, but not for a good while…" The hum of the damned resounds. Si's eyes glaze over; his silence is not the casino's silence. But he does not quite lose himself in his daze. "The slots won't be any good. Unless you have the odd bit of change and the odd bit of luck. The trick is *not* to spend your winnings when that works out."

"That's from experience, is it?"

"We're here to have fun, now, aren't we? That's why we're here."

"We are not losers here, tonight, Simon." Neville, or perhaps Deville, looks to imbue his friend with the power of victory, to help him throw caution to the wind. Never mind risking his money… or his very soul…

"Right," *Simon says,* "poker tables are this way."

They chart a course onward across the red sea, and turn at a corner into another realm, a separate room marked by black carpet, where money is spent, claimed, sometimes claimed back… sometimes taken with a *vengeance*. A long green island grows larger as they approach. A bright green table, almost luminous. Behind it is another, and another, and another… *more*…

The groans of the damned have faces now, fully formed avatars projecting their mumbling voices.

Along three sides of each green felt arena, thugs, townies, a few men in suits and, even fewer women, sit around each table. Each croupier at the end – an objective demon – is a different shape from the others, but all dressed the same. A waistcoat over a white shirt, or blouse, and no calculatedly avaricious incubi, or succubi, is complete without a red bow tie, the cherry on the cake. A touch of colour. These *people* are literally more in the black, than in the red.

One smooth creature gripping the vast green table, releases a right hand and gestures to Neville and Si. The simple open hand welcomes… Beckons…

Si steps forward, not looking back, or to Neville at his side… enthralled by the silent siren song, and the bright grass green. Not a dark, jealous green, but the vivid magnetic colour of greed; a shade not quite as yellow as fear.

"We have to get chips first," says Si.

A rumble thunders from Neville's belly. *If only…*

Si, as if in a strangely familiar trance, takes unsteady steps to the kiosk left of this space. A solid plastic screen holds one of the casino's *demons*, strangely captive. Perhaps it is everyone on *this* side of the screen who is imprisoned, while the innocuous devil enjoys the show from his little counter…

"Five hundred pounds, please."

Neville catches up to Si, whose nonchalant request can easily be mistaken for confidence. *Are you alright to be taking out quite that much, mate? I'm really up for getting some 'chips'-chips at this point.*

The plastic barrier between them is reminiscent of a post office, bringing an almost human touch, which brings a stranger comfort to Neville. Almost human indeed, as the cashier speaks. "If you'd like to just pop your card in..."

And just like that, the deed is done. Si retrieves his card. The cashier slips a small plastic packet under the screen, with chips inside. A small variety of red, green, black, blue... flowered with white. Values in multiples of five, or twenty-five.

And just like that, 'pop your card in', and piss away five hundred pounds...

Despite Neville's recent deals with good ol' Nick... old habits die hard, as access to his laundered cash is limited. *Do you really have that much money to throw away on poker, Si?*

Si steps away from the kiosk, turning to face inwards at the poker tables. A bead of excitement appears to trickle down his cheek as he passes Neville, who approaches the kiosk, and performs the exact same ritual, uttering the exact same words as Si. At last, they both greet the great green table.

Limping towards the empty seat at the end, Si grips tightly as he lifts his weaker leg, and sits in favour of his stronger side.

Neville watches him with hazy-eyed fascination.

Si's unwavering stare fixates on the cards and chips, which seem to have magically appeared stacked before the dealer.

Those were here the entire time... haven't *they?*

Halfway up the table, Neville sits between two other players who seem oblivious to the spell of the deceptively timeless space. There is no clock to be seen, only one's pulse to judge time. The room is red, dark-as-night black, and green, with other sad souls dotted around each table. The cattle spread out, look indifferently at one another like shifting animals.

Hungry Hippos, given half a chance...

As if the very floor opens up to speak, if not to devour, a voice announces to the players at the table, "Buy-in is fifty pounds." Strangely, the moving mouth of the suave dealer appears to articulate *after* speech. It is just the *poison on the rocks* pumping through Neville's body, distorting the flow of time.

We're covered for ten games of breaking even, aren't we? Or maybe a couple of games that really swallow your funds.

Chips tower in various accomplished stacks in front of players around the table, who fidget with their crowning token, or simply tap at the table.

The dealer's voice resounds. "Bets, please."

The first player, sitting left of the dealer, throws down the first chip onto the felt for the Small Blind bet.

The second picks up a twenty-five, and then another, and throws them down to *double* – for the Big Blind.

The betting continues with Si, Under the Gun... he stares ahead, practically tossing his chips at the growing pile in the middle of the epic green.

The next fellow matches Si's bid.

Neville picks up the matching chips and throws them in.

The woman beside Neville looks him right in the eye as she throws in hers.

The dealer turns to the first player.

As does everyone else.

The first player throws in one more chip.

Suddenly, the dealer's hands shuffle cards, separating them, bending them, making them dance and work up the appetite to swallow money like every other game in this realm. After one more shuffle the dealer slides a card to each being at the table. A straight flightpath each time, and then once again.

The players all sneak a peek under their cards.

Si snatches a look at his own cards before Neville, under the cover of his own hand, peels a Jack of Spades and a Nine of Spades.

The dealer nods to the player left of himself, who once again, throws down.

Each player plucks chips from their own collections to drop in front. A mindless action, like an instinctive handshake, or to recoil from the threat of a hug.

Si, more animated than alive, is not mindless behind those wide-open eyes. Watching. Waiting, he doubles down.

As the first player completes his bet, all have matched.

The dealer pulls a card from the deck, and then another, and then one more, laying each on the luminous green felt for all to see: the King of Diamonds, the Ten of Spades… and the Ace of Hearts.

A slight sigh escapes Neville, perhaps most of the other players as well.

Well, that's someone else's *lucky night sorted!*

"Bets please." The dealer is indifferent.

Fuck. Someone else will gain with this. Come on, Firsty. What ya gonna do?

Firsty is thirsty for more. He blinds.

The second fellow raises it.

Si sweats. He matches.

The next gent matches.

Neville also matches.

Not acknowledging Neville this time, the dolled-up woman matches.

The dealer flips… a Queen of Spades onto the green.

Face cards counting up to victory, this is more like it!

Neville fights to hide grinning teeth when a look at the other players sobers him. They stand, *sit*, in the way of his incredible first win.

The first player lifts one end of his cards with his thumb and then releases with a flick. He throws a chip onto the green for the blind.

The second player peeks under his cards, and then raises.

Si, without looking at his cards, immediately picks up two chips and throws them down to match the previous bid.

The next bloke looks under his cards, and then matches.

Neville remembers his cards. He matches. His lips purse together, to fight against a smile. If only he could stop suspecting the better cards around the table. Yet he senses, two seats over, a bead of sweat chasing down Si's neck.

Relax, mate, it's just one game.

The dealer nods to Firsty, who throws down another two chips.

Of course, you did… Fine.

Second's eyes lift and dart from side to side. He matches.

Come on Si, worst case, I hope you get it!

Si peeks beneath his cards. Matches.

What about you? Don't go getting ambitious.

The next guy matches.

Yes! Now let's seal the deal…

Neville doubles down.

All surrounding eyes flare at him.

And what do you have to say about that, madam? I hope

you see sense.

She matches Neville.

Fuck! It might not be so bad. It could be a bluff.

The dealer nods at Firsty. He peeks beneath his cards, shakes his head… and folds.

Yes!

Second folds too.

Fucking marvellous! Now Si, if you bow out, we can win this round…

Si breathes heavily, peeks at his cards, glances at Neville… Si matches.

What, do you have a hand?

Si does not meet Neville's glare. He merely stares at the ever-growing pile of chips in the middle of the table.

The following chap peeks at his cards. He looks around at the other players and back at the chips in the centre… and folds.

Sternly, Neville doubles down. He watches the woman beside him… match.

Fuck!

The dealer nods at Si, who is entranced… as he doubles down.

What the hell are you doing, you shit?!

Neville picks out the chips to match him. Glaring at Si, he throws them down and then turns to the determined woman, but in his fluster, *Deville* turns to his prey. Meeting her gaze, he winks…

The vixen's lips part in awe. She smacks her lips… and folds.

The dealer nods again to Si.

Neville faces him, with burning eyes.

Don't you dare do anything else!

Si double-takes towards Neville, who watches with his fingers pattering up and down on his cards, like cat's tails flicking in temper.

Si's sweaty hand hovers steadily over his chips.

Neville's eyes widen, letting loose his fury through only the whites of them.

Si matches.

Neville restrains a sigh. He faces the dealer, who finally flips onto the felt... a King of Spades.

Si gasps. He doubles down...

And then Neville matches...

The moment of reckoning is nigh. It is suddenly time to reveal.

Si drips with anticipation. He turns over his cards... A King of Clubs. And a King of Hearts.

"*Four of a kind,*" declares the dealer, dispelling the void of sound. The wet and raspy response is lapped up, as if the first glorious reverberation in all time nourishes the thirsty souls around the table. The flow of time begins again...

The jewelled white jellies of eyes swivel to Neville, the centre of attention. The centre of all tension...

Neville savours the eternal moment of truth. The feel of cards under his fingertips. The soft green felt against his hand as he reveals his cards...

The Nine of Spades and the Jack of Spades...

Against the Ten of Spades, the Queen of Spades, and the King of Spades...

"A *Straight Flush*," declares the dealer. "Well played, sir."

Neville is almost certain he can hear the vixen's lips, like fine tape peeling from a precious package, before a clap calls his attention from across the table.

Firsty, of all people, applauds beat by beat, spurring a modest, sophisticated round from the rest of the table.

I won with the second-best possible hand! For once, I can happily settle for second best!

Si's hands collapse over his chips. His sweaty palms kiss plastic in a desperate embrace for hollow comfort.

Tropical moisture from Neville's sweaty palms does not warm him as much as his achievement. His charisma is in full bloom. He is the *best man*... No, the best *person* in the world. The whole world is his, starting with this sign that the fates are on his side ...but not Si.

His seat at the end of the table is now empty. *Judas* has claimed some chips for his own. Stolen... along with Neville's thunder.

The applause dies deafeningly quiet, but the irregular steps of Si's attempted run, echoing the rapid tattoo of Neville's heart.

CHAPTER 25

"Si? You alright? Where've you gone?"

The game's stupor is dispelled. Neville turns away from the green expanse of table, verging on the half-hearted, in two minds…

Forget him. He's weak. He'll only drag you down, hold you back. You've just won a lot of money… Why don't you play another game?

Another gamble, either way.

Pale faces stare at the epic pile of poker chips in front of him after his *first game*. The game Si taught him years before…

Two of these faces bear more of a scowl, as Neville's closest friend has stolen their chips, too.

"Look, he's with me. I dunno what's wrong with him, but I'll get him back!"

No, you don't have to do that… the staff will take care of him…

"I'll look after your chips, mate," creeps the 'stealee' beside Neville.

"Na, you're alright, pal."

"Well, you can't cash *them* in and *still* expect to catch up with your thieving 'mate', can you? I wouldn't mind splitting these with this gentleman opposite me. We're *both* missing our chips, you know. We can forget about your friend if you play just one more round. You won't fluke this a second time, do you?"

Just take these chips and cash them in. Forget everyone.

A sinking feeling weighs upon Neville's stomach, surely under Deville's fist.

"Fine," Neville turns away from his chips, "Choke on 'em..."

He leaves the vultures to snatch at his winnings as he marches out of the dark realm. Neville is oblivious to the souls of the desperate damned turning their heads, following his every step.

What are you doing?! That money is yours!

Despite having a good thing going with his new 'business,' Neville's first win as a 'respectable' citizen is lost to his effort to be a respectable friend. Hopefully, the only *red* will be the carpet between worlds within the casino... not Si's blood...

"I'll make that money back up," Neville retorts, "but I'm still short on friends."

Who needs friends?

The bar is still scarcely populated. Deadbeats and empty seats, but no Si.

You should try the Gents. While you insist on looking everywhere...

Opposite the bar, the stainless-steel sign for the toilets blinks in the warm light. Neville approaches and pushes the door wide open, breaching the privacy of any potentially piddling fellows.

No one inside. Brighter in here than in the rest of the casino, it is the light at the end of the tunnel.

Don't go into the light...

Neville ignores the voice as the door squeals closed. The

Gents is empty, but one of the cubicles is shut.

"Si? Are you in there, mate?"

Silence.

Neville peeks, confirming pigeon-toed feet and knock-kneed legs under the door. "It's just me, mate."

"Shh!" Si shuffles on the toilet seat. A poker chip drops to the floor and dances around, rouletting unpredictably until it spins out. "Fuck! They were about to chase me..."

"Can't say I blame them."

"Yeah, well I'm here now."

Neville leans against the side of the cubicle. "I don't think they'd be too forgiving even if you gave those chips back."

"I know!"

"Then what the bleddy hell did you do this for, you daft bugger?!"

Si is short for silent tonight.

"You've got a problem, Si, and I don't just mean this situation! But you already know that, don't you?"

"Shut up!"

Neville stands square on his feet, continuing his inquisition with the door between them. "Did Mark and Kit know?"

The Gents door opens. A hapless chap wanders in and strolls up to a urinal.

Neville approaches one himself, blending in two units down. Ready, aim... quiet, draining drizzle.

Cheerfully, the other man shakes his whole body for good measure, zips up, and then goes right out the door.

Neville sighs. He zips up and approaches the sink to wash his hands, like the respectable, well-adjusted fellow he so is. "He's gone."

"Don't judge me," Si snaps.

"I'm the last person who gets to judge you right now, mate." Neville rips out some paper towels.

"Oh yeah? What've *you* done that's so bad?"

You've only done what's within your nature.

"I've just… let myself go, I guess," Neville confesses, wringing his hands dry, "and there've been consequences. Or at least there will be."

"That's right, steer the attention back onto you…"

"Oi! Where's this coming from?!"

"Get all philosophical on me, why don't you… Now of all times…"

Neville screws up the paper towels. "Why are you being such a prick? Tell me that."

"Says you! Disappearing for months on end… Or is it years? I lose track. Of time *and* money…"

"You're saying that because *my* marriage turned to shit, *you* lost the plot? Now who's attention-seeking?"

"Fuck off. At least you've still got your health!" *Thump.* The cubicle rattles with Si's fist.

"What are you on about?"

"You know… The Obvious."

"You've managed all these years, haven't you? A proper job despite all odds, your own house, a partner…"

"Yeah, if only! I'm falling apart, Nev. I'm struggling. Not just my walking. *Moving.* And eating, too. I've a pharmacy's worth of meds to chug, and everything just knackers me. I can't work. I can't hang on to anyone. I can't keep up."

"Fuck…" Neville throws a balled-up paper towel into the bin. "Why didn't you say something?"

"You've had your own shit to deal with. You seemed to be too wrapped up in that to come to me… You could've, you know."

"Well, you certainly seemed to keep *your* distance. I was only trying to fix my marriage. Sorry, I'm not a talker."

"Well, I had other problems *too*," Si squirms, "but you wouldn't know."

What a pair of whiny schoolgirls…

Another chip falls to Si's feet. "Bollocks!"

Is this the chip from his shoulder?

"What do we do now?"

"I don't know!"

"Look," says Neville, "just leave those. Those muppets probably stopped to follow you on CCTV and are waiting outside that door."

"But I've got the chips now. I just wanted to get ahead again."

"Out of the question! Fuck's sake, just leave them, and face it like a man!"

Clack. Si's door snaps unlocked. He opens it, sweaty, teary eyed, "Like I can match up as a man…"

"Come off it, you know what I mean!"

"Fine." Si teeters forward, turns, and chucks the poker chips at the toilet. A high-pitched round of applause patters onto the floor, and into the bowl. "Let's go."

As Si stumbles past for the door, Neville catches sight of his own very *human* face in the mirror. "Did I really leave without that thing on?"

Si opens the Gents door and stomps out. Neville follows before the voice can respond. If only he could just leave *it* behind.

As the door slams into Neville's arse, he bumps into Si.

Lo and behold! As the prophet Neville hath spoken…!

Two men and one butch woman, bouncers with incalculable bulk under shirts and coats, spread out to surround them.

The middle man, a larger identical triplet, opens his mouth with a thinly veiled leer directed at Si, "You alright there, mate? You'd better come with us…"

Si turns to Neville, looking *through* him for the door back into the toilets…

But another bouncer with a tattoo growing up his neck, shoulders his way behind and shoves them away from the Gents.

Si barely keeps his balance, and looks up at Neville with a bitter glare, badly hiding his fear.

As they find their feet, Neville assures, "It's alright, just stay calm. Be cool."

"Fuck off," says Si.

"*Okay!*" Neville puts an arm tightly around him, leading the way in-between the bouncers, "We'd best be going now…"

The bouncers do not budge. Nor do their cold, steely gaze.

Si wrestles free of Neville, letting loose a rogue punch at him in the process. It just so happens to miss… A *happy accident* Si would merrily claim.

The middle bouncer's eyebrows launch upwards as he speaks again. "You're gonna *have* to come with us."

"Look," Neville raises desperate pacifying hands, looking more like a creeping Nosferatu, "he's got *problems*. We don't want to take up any more of your time…"

Not even a twitch from the alpha. Not even those annoyingly

thin eyebrows of his, *pretty* eyebrows on such a chubby face, like little axes poised to fall. "Yeah. *Sad.* We've all got problems. You're coming with us. *Both* of you."

Neville stares, irritated. A malice in his gaze sharpens under the light... "Those are some pretty eyebrows you've got there..."

Butch and the *Troll* each side of *Eyebrows* look to each other, befuddled.

As Eyebrows recoils, the little axes fall.

A fist flies up, colliding with his stupid fat nose. Now red and wet in the face, as sudden and silent as a leaky fountain pen, he falls back. Butch and Troll turn to tend to their alpha as he hits the floor.

No time to contemplate how much those knuckles were Neville and how much were Deville. *Neville* lurches into a sprint, knocking Troll over, *bouncing*...

Running unsurely forward, Neville recalls the way he and Si came in earlier. He runs the opposite direction, left for the door, hoping Si will follow... and keep up.

Staff were at that door too. Maybe more were called down.

No time for paranoia... to overthink, or to think at all. A curiously incurious instinct guides Neville right around a corner, as luck would have it, to a fire exit.

He rushes for the door. Reality chills Neville to his fingertips as he pushes the cold metal release bar.

His heart leaps ahead, but somehow an irregular rhythm catches up to him, calling out, "Hold the fucking door!"

Si has just caught up. Even he can ride the adrenalin.

Already out in the drizzly dark, Neville had all but forgotten him... "Come *on,* then!" He holds the door for Si, just like in school when they were late for class...

Si springs out. Neville slams the door shut. They run further into the dark and wet alley, away from both the traffic, and the main entrance…

"Why did I do that why did I do that why did I do that why…?" Neville panics. His clapping shoes on the tarmac is shadowed by Si limping offbeat hastily behind. Another round of applause for a successful escape… so far…

Neville does not look back. "Fucking idiot…"

"What?!" Si is more focused on keeping pace… Keeping his balance…

Neville curses himself, his darker self, and *Si* for going to the casino in the first place, knowing full well they had demons that could not be *checked*.

The road opens out to them, but they are still far from civilisation in the middle of town… but the fire exit door bursts open, slamming against the wall.

"Hurry up!" Neville calls.

So considerate…

"I'm trying!" Si struggles. "I can't keep up…"

Three apes, *men* in the right light, rush from the fire exit in pursuit.

Si lags so far behind, permitting them the idea that they can catch up.

"Come on!" calls Neville… but Si slows more and more.

Poor fucker hasn't 'run' for years…

Fatigue hits Si harder.

He could die tonight from the strain alone!

The steady beating of shoes on the ground gets louder, catching up to Si…

"Got ya, you cunt!"

Si tries to lurch forward, but *Tattoo* grips onto his shirt, lifting him off of the ground as he pounces.

Si falls onto his face, pinned under the weight of bone, fat, and muscle.

I've got to go back.

Neville stops, expecting them to pursue him, but he turns to see Butch and Troll slow before their prey. Each lift a heel behind for a kick…

"No…" Neville rushes towards them… but freezes.

Their boots hit Si, kicking agonised grunts out of him as he curls up.

What can I do against these three?

Neville clutches at his face. "I can't do anything. I don't have the mask!"

It's not about the mask… You've got yourself this far, defended yourself, and a woman's honour, in the space of a fortnight… without putting on 'your face.' Oh Dumbo, you had the feather to fly all along…

Neville runs at them. "Get off him, you pricks!"

One more kick for luck from the bouncers.

Si utters not a word, or a grunt. Or perhaps even a breath.

"You dickheads owe us money." The first thug lowers his foot, knowing that Si will not be getting up. "Plus, interest, for embarrassing us. Or we'll beat the cripple back into shape!"

"You'll have to!" shouts Neville, "because he's flat now, after *your* rancid fat arse landed on him!"

Si's whole body coughs up a chuckle.

Tattoo kicks him quiet.

"We don't owe you *anything*." Neville runs forward with his right, tightly balled-up fist. He throws a punch, expecting the momentum to carry his knuckles through to Tattoo's fat ugly face…

But the thug catches the telegraphed punch with his left hand and nonchalantly slings a right hook into Neville's cheek.

At least the tarmac is there to brace Neville's arse as he falls back…

I've done this before, haven't I? What's different? What's wrong?

He sits up – sore – and nearly falls forward with the weight of his head.

Tired after all that running, I suppose…

"Stay the fuck down," Tattoo points. A gold ring winks on his left hand. He turns back towards Si.

Neville looks up, rubbing his raw cheek. Pain and shame rile his disgust… "Now I know how your *missus* feels…"

Tattoo stops. He faces Neville with a glare… and charges.

Neville stumbles to his knees before the distance closes between them.

Tattoo swings his foot back for a running kick…

Neville throws a mighty punch. His arm, straight. A hard fist hits Tattoo square in the groin. Tender meats squish against knuckle. A pathetic groan escapes the hulking man before he falls, clutching between his thighs.

Neville stands, and raises his foot to *crack a nut*.

Through all his wincing, Tattoo does not see Neville bring his foot down. One fell stamp, and Tattoo's head hits the ground. A dreaded *thud* like the sound of a rock falling from a great height.

The bouncer does not bounce. He lies prostrate and unconscious.

Neville looks towards Troll and Butch.

They step back in caution. The man now approaching them should be the one who is afraid. They are not used to this opposition. If this *weed* got lucky, knocking out their comrade, surely, they can take him… "You'll pay for that!"

Neville vaguely hears Troll as he approaches. Walking steadily, each deep breath gathers steam. Neville straightens his back, crackling with rumbles of thunder. Some poor soul will be struck again, but not by lightning…

The gobby one charges, launching a punch that collides with Neville's jowl, turning his head… but Neville does not go down. Troll throws another.

Neville ducks… and punches him in the square in the teeth.

Troll stumbles. His shirt is clawed at, grabbed, by Neville's hand, while his other fist meets Troll's face enthusiastically, again, again… and again…

The remaining bouncer, Butch, pushes Neville, who releases his prey in favour of throwing another punch. The nimble Butch ducks, when, a hand rests over her head… and a knee shoots up into her face. *Crunch,* as Butch's nose sinks inwards. She goes strangely limp and falls to the ground. She could be dead.

It's all about confidence…

Neville looks around at his latest work, uncertain any or all of these 'men' still have a pulse. Uncertain it would be a good thing if they did…

Si lies on his back with laboured breaths. Eyelids swollen, like plums. Cheeks inflated. *Red,* runs from his nose, and more on his teeth. His hands rest feebly over his stomach…

Neville reaches for Si's collar, the rage of a ruined night clutches at it. "All this fuss… over you and your pathetic greed, you… fucking *wretch!*"

The disappointment of a ruined friendship released… its hand hovers over Si's throat, rests over his neck… Neville's fingers wrap around and squeeze…

The eyes of his best friend open before Neville's unbridled rage, marking lines and creases in his face.

Si's weak hands reaches over Neville's, clasping in a struggle as they share a bitter grimace...

"You got us into this...!"

A tear flees down Neville's cheek... He releases his grip on Si, who gasps, and coughs, and chokes.

What have I done?

Neville pulls his mobile phone out from his pocket and dials for an ambulance. He turns away from the horror in best friend's eyes...

CHAPTER 26

Behind buildings, the bright sunrise develops in chocolate-brown sepia photographs, rippling in puddles on old tarmac.

A thick, red reflection of Detective Inspector Christina Lake dances under the light drizzle.

Wrapped in a navy coat, she stands in the middle of the long, narrow crime scene. Blue and white police tape is fixed at both ends of the alley, a pathetically thin barrier between the public and a bloody fight… from the night before. Carmine echoes, painted on the floor, scream *red*.

Forensics pass in hooded white onesies. Their eyes, adorned with bags and crow's feet, care too little to look up at Christina. Yet, one voice reverberates from a passing phantom. A human voice. Male. "This isn't your case is it, Chrissy?"

Without looking around she acknowledges, "Just passing through, Sam."

Sam has fallen behind the other hoods. "Surely you have better things to do. Like… have *breakfast?*"

Sensing this is more an offer than idle curiosity, Christina shies away. "I'm an early riser, so I like to keep busy… The bouncers came from this casino, right?"

No answer, as Sam's befuddled eyebrows converge over

his nose. Not that she notices… He walks away, following the rest of the white-clad squad into the police van.

Brick and mortar, grey grubby walls, are each marked with yellow and blue loopy graffiti, a good five feet apart each side of Christina. A tight arena.

As if a mechanical throat clears, an engine starts. The police van drives off.

"This is *not* my case."

…But three strapping thugs losing a fight against *one*? She has seen this before. Recently. But *those* three were *killed*… crammed into a ridiculously small space… an impromptu effort to hide the bodies. Desperate? Careless… Juvenile, even. When a parent demands her son tidies his room, and the boy settles for shoving toys under the bed, to make the place *look* tidy. Or… stuffing them into the cupboard. All three victims.

Yet *here*, out in the open… *restraint*. All three were left alive.

"Why?" Christina asks, as if the blood could talk.

The rain whispers white noise… too many answers from the elements rush down onto Christina, running down her cheek.

Remorse?

Three pools scream redder than the rest.

"How did you get *here*?" She looks around… up to the green and white sign, over the nearest point of entry into the alley. "Yeah, through the fire exit. Whoever they were chasing wouldn't need to run if it were such a winnable fight…"

Downhearted, Christina shakes her head.

"It was simply three rogue bouncers taking things too far. This is *not* my case." She turns to leave, but her boot stops short of another dull red stain, more *modest* than the *loud red three*. The bullies chased after a disadvantaged man and beat him down. "So… was it some bystander who stepped in to defend him?"

Christina looks up at the busying street beyond the alley.

And around the corner, there is the casino entrance. "No harm in asking around, is there…?"

***

"Thanks very much."

The staff nod as Christina's steps out of the foyer and into the main street, her thoughtful gaze is displaced by a glowing smile. "And thank *you*, CCTV."

Pike's museum was where the last freakish brawl occurred. And the surveillance tapes are still missing, but this time…

Christina pulls out her phone. One call is but a few taps away… Just as Mickey picks up, "Guess who was at the casino last night, right before that fight."

Her wizened partner's voice moans through. "You alright, Chris?"

She rolls her eyes. "Wanna know something *interesting*?"

"Dogs can't look up?"

"What? No, of course they can. Listen, Mickey, I've just stumbled onto something *really* interesting. At the casino, the bouncers beat someone up. And guess who they were chasing…"

"Pffft…"

"Fuck's sake, Mickey…"

"Ooh, *Christina*… What would your father say?"

So far nothing has disappointed her father more than her being born a daughter. Christina faces yet another boy who has not grown up.

"*Neville Pike*," she stresses, "our man, that weedy man, was right there at another fight where three whopping great bouncers got beaten down. *Just* like…"

"…in the *museum*." Mickey is suddenly solemn. Somehow his change of tone echoes her father's disappointment.

210

"And even better," she continues, "someone else was there. So, we have a witness who can confirm whether Pike was the one who fought off these bouncers, and if he was, he would've been involved with the killing at the museum!"

A blowing car horn mosquitos past, just missing her as she crosses the road... she gasps.

"Calm yourself, Chris." Mickey's concern virtually leaps out of the phone to grab Christina. The one occasion he takes her seriously is more real than a car almost hitting her.

"There are no guarantees, I know," she says, "but the coincidence would be insane! We stared him right in the face after that first incident..."

"The only incident we can link him to, so *far*."

Christina finds herself before her car, gagging to spit the fire from within. "I should've just waited till I got to the station to tell you."

"You can tell me anything, anytime, Chris. Just don't ever get too emotionally involved in an investigation."

"You don't have to tell *me*." She hangs up, snatching the car door handle just shy of breaking it off.

CHAPTER 27

Disinfectant tangos with the smell of illness and imminent death.

The bovine nurse leads Neville across the jaundiced rubber floor. They pass bed-ridden old men to the end of the ward, where a bed *supposedly* lies beyond the curtains. *Nursey* parts them to patronise the stranger lying beyond. *"You've* got a *visitor."*

He's not a child. Don't talk to him like that.

His features are distorted by bruises and cuts. Hills of purple risen on planes of light olive skin. A face unrecognisable as Si's.

"Thanks," says Neville.

The man's eyes open. One of them is still half-covered by a plum eyelid. Their blink hides the shift of Si's gaze.

"I'll leave you to it," Nursey turns and does just that, without a second look.

"About fucking time," says Neville. "How are they treating you, buddy?"

Si's nostrils flare.

Neville tries once again to dispel the simmering quiet… "I'm sorry, mate."

Si spasms… a flicker of rage.

Neville softens, cautious of listening ears. "What went down last night… It shouldn't have happened. I'm so *sorry!*"

His quiet apology only screams guilt. It fails to pacify Si in-between his hot deep breathing. An eruption is long overdue…

"I can't expect you to let it slide, just like that," says Neville.

A pained grunt struggles out of Si. Words manage to follow. "S-stay… the fuck away… from me."

"Hey," says Neville, "it's alright. You're safe."

"I *never*… want… to see you again."

A chill strikes Neville right in the chest, and courses through his entire body.

Nobody wants me…

"Alright, mate," He stumbles back, "I'll leave you to it. Just… go steady…"

Si's faces away.

Cold rejection closes in on Neville, running dark in his veins. Pitch blackness eclipses him within…

He claws the curtain back and walks hastily out of the ward. Stark lights hurt. Neville averts his eyes from the gaze of other people's. The rattling and chattering of hospital wards and corridors cling to his ears. Surely, he can find some oasis from the buzzing chaos, in this towering limbo of life and health and sanity. A desperate voiceless search for a sign carries Neville forward, left, right, up, down… and inside-out…

"Thank God." Ironically, he lurches for the double-doors to his salvation. The 'Chapel' sign overhead appears to darken before Neville.

Somehow humbly majestic inside. The warm light here does not impose on Neville's eyes. The almost natural wood colour of treated pine soothes him, draws him away from busy mortals, and closer to tranquillity. Closer to God… or at least, the idea that there might *be* a God.

But most of all, the divine quiet at the centre of a tower of sound, the eye of the storm, brings him closest to peace…

"It's a wonder I don't burst into flames right here and now."

Neville ambles down the aisle, brushing a hand over the end of each row until he sits on a pew in the right side at last.

What makes you think you won't?

The creeping silky voice is in no danger of being confused with the weary tones of a frustrated creator, yet Neville's own mortal voice breaks out in a whisper… "Well, I haven't, yet. So there."

With that blood on your hands, you'll always be… highly flammable.

"*You* did this."

Did I? Your pathetic self has been in charge the entire time…

"No, I… that wasn't *me*…"

And here it was looking like it was your better self… That you were literally of one mind…

"No!"

Dusty coughs burst out from an old man in the front row.

If you want to wear the crown, your head must be able to take the weight of it.

"I don't want any fucking crown." Neville catches sight of the stained-glass martyred messiah fixed to a cross. The pale background, the red, the green, the skin, somehow even the black borders, seem to glow at the end of the chapel.

Holding that delightful mask aloft before placing it over your face would suggest otherwise…

"It's a mask. A Devil's face, no less. No good was going to come of that thing… especially if it had any real power."

So, it has never occurred to you that in playing with such an artefact, in wearing the face of the Devil, you had invited him in, conversed with him… shared a body, all this time?

"What? No… That couldn't be true." Neville gazes up again at the crucified Jesus, almost looking for any sign of care in the still sullen face hanging down, but only finds himself mirroring the immortalised woe.

Why not? If there is no such a thing as God, or a Devil, then there's nothing to worry about. In which case, maybe you are just 'a bit mad…' But then, everyone is their own Devil, aren't they?

Neville lifts his head to look at the Jesus once more, but his gaze stops at the torso. A sinking feeling. He is afraid to look up and find the expression has changed, into one of malicious rage at Neville and his offensive mistakes, or an expression of mocking smugness, taking joy in Neville's suffering. Worse still, that he might see his own face etched on the body, and never able to leave… with his own hands and feet nailed to the cross…

Neville stands and marches for the door. This greater fear motivates him to brave the abrasive world outside the chapel once more.

His fingers stretch out to the handle… when the door opens on its own.

Neville recoils as it swings open before the Grim Reaper himself. Detective Sergeant Tout's bony hand holds the door, as he leers into the chapel with a smirk. A predatory stare fixed upon Neville.

The other door is pushed open by Detective Inspector Christina Lake. Both look to each other, surprised to recognise Neville.

Can they cross the threshold, onto hallowed ground?

"Neville Pike…" Her voice cuts through to his very bones…

***

Expecting handcuffs with a ravenous taste for Pike, none are clasped around Neville's wrists to bite into his flesh and bone.

He sits back on his seat in the interview room, restraint-free.

Why bother? I'm already in a cage, one way or another…

Bleak, officious walls surround him. The dark glass to his left reflects Neville's solitary self, sitting forward, resting his hands on the table.

Neville turns to his reflection as it turns to face him, smug, leering, mocking… It smiles, baring teeth that resemble those of a predator. Teeth, like a shark's that could render flesh into pulled *long pig.*

If I request a solicitor, I look guilty. Just co-operate… Look co-operative. I'm not worried. I am not worried…

Having mostly blended into the wall on the furthest side of the glass, the door opens. DI Lake asserts her way in.

Neville glimpses a ghost of her smile, as she pulls out a chair and sits opposite, not looking him in the eye.

Lake sits up, ready for battle, and arms the recorder to capture Neville's voice. "Detective Inspector Christina Lake, conducting the interview with Mr Neville Pike. The date is the thirtieth of October, and the time is ten twenty-one am… Now Mr Pike, footage has been found recently…"

Oh god, no, not that *footage!*

"Of you," she continues, "fleeing the casino with your friend Mr Simon Breward while being pursued by three security staff members, shortly before they were all assaulted. This occurred around one-twenty am last night. We can confirm by the footage that you first assaulted one of the security team before running out of the casino, and from what we understand, the staff who followed you both outside then proceeded to assault Mr Breward…"

Of course, you can… What the fuck did you tell her, Si?

"From 'what you understand'?" Neville agitates, "Was there not… another camera? Outside… around the alley?"

"It just so happened to be out of commission, which is why I would like to know *your* account of the events of last night."

"Okay… the whole evening, including before we got to the casino, right?"

"If you could start from there, please, yes."

Neville's first and greatest performance on record yet, as he breathes calmly into character… "We met up at the pub down the road from the casino, to do the quiz with a couple of mates…"

"The Red Lion?"

"Yeah."

"When was this?"

"About… quarter-to-nine."

Lake nods steadily, holding eye contact while the recorder's unblinking red light maintains its own void stare. "And the quiz started at nine, did it?" she echoes disappointment at the mundanity of the story.

"Yeah," says Neville, "and we were all drinking there until about midnight."

'Of course, you were' is written all over Lake's face, as unamused as a wary cat. "But the quiz didn't finish that late, did it?"

"No. More like eleven-ish. We came second-to-last. We usually come *last*."

See? Nice guys really do finish last…

Lake's glacial eyes permit only a steady blink before Neville's endearing display of hapless humanity. "And then you and Mr Breward left for the casino?"

Neville nods, steadying a nervous tremor. "Yes."

"Why didn't your other friends go with you both?"

"Kit had work in the morning. So did Mark, I think." *Those rat bastards. They knew about Si's problem. They had to. Wouldn't check with me before I led him astray, but they knew...*

"So," she says, "why did you two go to the casino last night?"

"'Why?' What does 'why' matter?"

"Every detail matters."

Neville remembers evoking the voice of his darker self, leading an expedition in pursuit of pleasure... "Just fancied a change from staying until lock-in. That's all."

"So, you got to the casino around midnight..."

"Just before, I think..."

"And you made it past the door staff."

"Yes."

"Did you or Mr Breward do anything to cause a disturbance, or upset someone at the casino?"

"No, not that I know of."

"Nothing that would get the attention of the security staff?"

Si was twitchy ever since the mere mention of the casino!

"He was just enjoying being at the casino," says Neville. "We got to the poker tables, and I won the first game – I never win *anything*! I looked to Si... but he'd gone."

Do I tell her? Do I drop Si in it?

Lake's face remains unmoved, ice cold.

Your so-called friend already dropped himself in it when he ran off with those chips...

"Well," Neville sighs, "he did run off with the chips from the table. Before that, he was constantly playing to win, until he saw sense and folded."

"Did you know? About Mr Breward's supposed gambling

addiction?"

"No. It's been hell of a while since I saw him. We caught up only recently. But he and our so-called mates neglected to tell me about any addiction of his. And they all knew where we were going!" Neville's pleads with his eyes before the glacial Lake, for her humanity to thaw out and engage with him.

She's only playing ball on her terms. I'm gonna keep hold of it until the bitch finally reacts!

"Then I found him," Neville resumes, "I got to talk with him in the gents…"

"What exactly did you talk about?"

"Everything that went on before we last saw each other. Bad luck, and life getting us down."

"More specifically?"

"It was really more of a heart-to-heart. I'd rather keep that private if you don't mind."

Lake watches him. Static.

Please buy it. I don't want to go into that again…

"Anyway," Neville continues, "Si was in a hell of a state. And by the time I got him to come out with me, the Gents was surrounded. The bouncers were looking to… *punch first* and ask questions later."

Lake sits forward slightly, forgetting herself as she practically salivates at the juicy bit of the story. "So, that's when you proceeded to punch Mr Hamley?"

"Who? Yeah, I hit *someone*… Never done anything like that in my life… but it was self-defence. The bouncers kept closing in on us and Si's health is in a bad way, he couldn't have coped with being roughed up by these louts. I surprised myself when I hit the one in front of me, so I got Si to run and somehow we both made it outside into the alley."

Lake blinks, registering the story. "What happened next?"

That's all you've got to say, is it? There's me trying nobly to defend my friend, and you just want to know, 'what happened next?'

Neville smooths a quick hand over his hair, as if in to attempt coax the answers out his head.

"We kept running. Or so I thought. Like I said, Si's health isn't what it used to be, and it wasn't great even backalong. He was falling behind when the bouncers followed us out."

"How many?"

"Three."

"Are you sure?"

"Yes."

"There wasn't anyone else in the alley?"

"No," says Neville, "not yet, anyway…"

"So, there *was* someone else?"

I wasn't exactly myself at the time, so…

"Yes," he says, "yes, there was."

"Did this person assault the security staff?"

"When they all started ganging up on Si, yeah… he intervened."

"Can you describe this man?"

"No."

Lake rolls her eyes so hard she recoils in the chair. She brings her hand to her face to stifle an itch.

An itch to throttle me right here…

"Why not?" she asks, "it wasn't that dark. There was a streetlight. You must've had the chance to look at this man at some point."

"It... *it all happened so fast...*"

"Can you try to describe him? Anything at all?"

"Well... he was shorter than all the bouncers. And thin."

Just like me...

Lake's eyes glance down and then up at Neville, sizing him up.

"But a bit bigger than me," he says. "He had no problem taking them on."

"When did you see him?"

"As soon as they started beating up Si."

"Where did he come from?"

"He... must've been having a fag. He came out of nowhere."

"So, this man who was already there, appeared from nowhere? Did you call out for help? Or were you still trying to run from them? What about your friend?"

What are you going to tell her? You could own what you did and admit that it was you who took down those thugs, whether you were trying so 'nobly' to protect your feeble friend, or you just wanted to prove your worth and make them suffer in the process. What would she say to any of that?

"Well, Mr Pike?"

Of course, you could admit to your cowardice, that you continued to run ahead at first, that you were even too cowardly with your conscience to leave him behind. Decisions, decisions... Sooner or later, Nev, you're going to have to choose who you want to be, or the choice will be made for you!

"I froze," he says. "I was already further ahead. Maybe I *could've* grabbed someone to help. Maybe I *could've* just let them rough him up a bit, teach him a lesson... I couldn't have done anything else myself. There were three of them, and they were bigger than me. I thought about it, I thought about everything! But

Si was taking a beating, and in that time, I was thinking, someone else took over…"

"And this man took on these three by himself?" Lake asks, "You didn't fight them as well?"

Neville shakes his head, nearly sobbing. "No. I did what I had to. I… hid."

"What about after the fight? Did this man hang around at all?"

"He left, he… He scarpered out the other end of the alley."

What a dishonest man you are, Mr Pike…

"That's when you called the ambulance?"

"Yes," he says.

"But not the police, right away?"

"No… The beating was already occurring. I… I froze…"

All in the interview room has likewise frozen still. Silence echoes Neville's pathetic state having confessed… a most convenient lie, before clear blue eyes that long to confirm the transparency of his story.

That must be everything, surely! Is she satisfied? Please let this be over.

"Thank you, Mr Pike," says Lake. "Interview concluded at ten fifty-three am."

Neville catches a sigh of relief behind his lips before it can escape. "What about the bouncers? Have they identified the man?"

"It just so happens that they are… unable to recall anything *at all* about their attacker." Lake gathers herself and stands, with no indication of relief, no sense of tension permeating through.

Yet Neville's heart races under controlled breaths.

Of course, this is not her *first rodeo.*

"The case regarding the break-in to your museum is still very much open," she says, "especially when, on two occasions now, you have been present while a number of attackers were beaten down, three-on-one…"

"I don't know what to tell you, inspector. I just hope I don't find myself in a situation like this again…"

"You must've had a guardian angel watching over you each time."

Neville stands as well, at just about the same height. Their eyes meet.

You have no idea how right, and how wrong, you are…

CHAPTER 28

She looks long into the abyss of Pike's dark eyes… which look back into Christina's crystal blues.

His mouth opens. Another abyss which she cannot help but sense is little more than a pit of lies, writhing tales that turn under and around his tongue. Everyone else seems to choke on every word…

"I just feel relieved, inspector, that *you* are working on this."

He seems so human. Too human. It is too convenient that the man at the centre of everything is *not* behind these violent incidents. Yet his voice charms her skin into a crawl.

"Thank you for your cooperation, Mr Pike, we'll be in touch." Christina approaches the door and opens it for Pike to head out first. There will be no shaking hands with this man. Not this time. Not ever.

He nods and half smiles like an awkward stranger making accidental eye contact. This man – more strange than awkward – steps around the table. He looks towards her again with eyes lingering as he passes her, before crossing over the threshold to the other side…

Christina follows him out, slamming the door shut.

Pike looks over his shoulder as if a shot had been fired.

She overtakes to escort him out, checking over *her* shoulder to make sure Pike follows. His meek smile is fixed, as if to protest kindness and compliance.

They pass an office window, but as Christina faces forward, she sees his reflection in the glass. His smile extends like a cat that got the cream. His lips part, revealing teeth that could render her flesh from bone. A face resembling more *shark* than Pike. More monster than man...

She reaches for the door to the foyer, snatches it open and rushes through, so she can look back at Pike to confirm...

"Thanks," he says. Human. Unimposing. His calm face and eyes pass her by, merely inches away, not baring teeth. Pike walks steadily, perfectly, as a civilised man, a respectable citizen more confident than the blubbering wreck, who stuttered and stammered through the conversation with her just minutes before.

Christina stands in the doorway, gripping the handle tightly as she watches Pike walk out through the main entrance... and not look back.

"How can it *not* be him?" she mutters to herself.

"Evidence, perhaps?"

"Jesus!" Christina turns sharply, raising her fists.

Mickey jumps too at her reaction. "Alright! *Jumpy*..."

"No," she collects herself, "but sometimes you *know*, don't you? That you're dealing with a *bad 'un?*"

"Too bad we don't work like that. When we've got any evidence, we'll know if the bugger killed anyone." He holds up a green apple, and then takes an irritatingly loud bite.

"You should listen to the interview," she says. "It's all too... convenient, too plausible. He..."

"...sounds like a bloody good liar." Mouth full, Mickey wanders back down the corridor.

Christina catches up to walk beside him. "And if he is?"

225

"Well," he gulps, "we won't know without any trace evidence, or any other witnesses, will we?"

"We can't just wait for another body to turn up."

"Calm down. You're not a bleddy robot! It's just procedure… *my 'ansum.* All we can do is station a couple of units outside his flat and perhaps the museum to keep an eye on him if, God forbid, we don't do it ourselves."

So wise. So unhelpful.

Christina paces ahead to the interview room. She lurches in, takes the recorder off of the table and whips out again to keep up with Mickey.

"Humour me and listen to this interview. See what you think."

"May as well," he says. "Nothin' else better to do, is there?"

A likely murderer has been let loose, but everyone must adhere to procedure. Nothing else better to do indeed…

CHAPTER 29

Frosted glass chills Neville's knuckles as he knocks at high noon.

A blurry figure takes shape behind the door. Tabitha opens it all the way, looking Neville up and down. "Hello you..."

Neville steps over the threshold, placing a hand on her neck, his thumb under her jaw, and pulls her face towards his own. Their lips collide and dance a wet rumba.

Tabitha releases the handle and looks to grab *another.*

As Neville presses against her, into the wall, his foot hooks the door shut. Heat-seeker fully loaded... he locks on target.

Her arms wrap around him. One hand squeezes his shoulder. The other slides down his side, over a buttock. Her leg rubs up against his, lifting until her calf rests over his other cheek.

Neville pulls his lips away to come up for air. As he presses them against her neck, his teeth brush against her skin as he kisses. His hand slides down over her breasts... *over the hills and far away, he'll be coming round the mountain* before he comes...

His hand squeezes and Tabitha gasps on command. Her foot goes down. She grabs his hand and pulls him around the corner, into her bedroom.

He snatches the door handle, and lurches after her, pulling

the door shut on the otherwise empty flat, and on the rest of the world out to get him. His new private place, with Tabitha all to himself. He is just a mere man again. A man with desires, unwrapping her like a present, he clings to her soft skin against his.

And *she* wraps herself around *him*…

***

Lying still, under the covers, two of its eyes threaten to open, and dispel the state of slumber. Its two remaining eyes stay tightly shut.

All four arms, and legs, coil around each other. They shift, and uncoil, stirring sighs with thighs and the gentle friction of skin. Two of its eyes peel open…

Neville stares into Tabitha's face. Sweet. Still. Innocence restored only in the stasis of unconsciousness. Paralyzed by his gaze upon her, he is unable to pull away. Unable to think. There is only instinct… A question of whether he should wake her, or if he really *wants* to pull away.

He savours the power of being first awake. He gets to watch and enjoy her for longer. Oblivious. Peacefully asleep. So much trust, so much *risk*, behind the impulses that led to this. Neville is a fickle predator, and Tabitha, his willing prey.

Morning, like *Neville*, is broken. The clock facing the bed ticks by, staring off with Neville long enough for him to see its hands turn as slowly as the Earth.

His skin warms with irritating heat under the sheets. Tension, dread, threatens to dribble out of Neville's pores. Dare he move? Dare he even scratch?

A wave of reality comes up fast. What might wash up on the shore and splash over him, as the tide comes in and goes out, with Tabitha's every oblivious breath? The monster reaches out from the deep and wraps its arms around Neville again. A spoilt child, clutching her teddy bear of flesh… She need not be conscious to control this cursed fool.

Neville lifts his arm and rests it over her naked shoulder. His hand slides down her smooth back and traces down her spine, to soothe the beast. He charts the map of Tabitha, having conquered her. He looks down… at *Tracy*…

And jumps awake.

It is still Tabitha. Still asleep, unfazed.

Neville exhales relief. Of course he finds it hard to tell these fierce, controlling women apart. He is still just a simple man, after all…

One of his legs hangs over the bed. He prolongs the touching of toe to cool floor, but once again, sooner or later, he will have to face the reality that has washed up before him.

I'm a murder suspect.

His echo answers back from the dark.

Oh, you know you're more than just a suspect, Neville.

He turns over to shut his eyes from this cruel waking world.

You can't sleep off the blood on your hands.

"But I wasn't myself," Neville whispers.

And yet you called upon the strength to defend yourself time after time… Face it, Neville, you're the one responsible for bringing pain to others.

The clock ticks inevitably out of time with Tabitha's breath… and her pulse.

How dare she be so carefree.

Neville looks up to see the quarter-hour bites that the hungry face of time has chewed away.

Seven… 'ate' nine indeed! What gets her *up in the morning? What do you actually* do *for a living?*

He untangles himself, pulling steadily away from the grip of his concubine, and sits up, ready to step down from Heaven… His foot finally reaches the Earth.

"Where are *you* off to?"

Neville looks back at her dreamy get-back-into-bed eyes. She stirs, hugging the pillow under her head, while wrapped in a white fluffy cloud of duvet. Her comfort strikes him as tedious in his hurry.

"I've got to get to work." He finds his boxers and pulls them on.

"I thought you owned the place," she groans sleepily.

"If I want to keep it that way, I've got to make sure I'm there to run it. How about you? Do *you* have to be anywhere today?"

She yawns. "Nope."

"Do I *want* to know what you do for a living?" He snatches his trousers from the floor and slips them on.

"Stick around and you might find out…" she smirks.

The squeeze is put on Neville's stomach.

She could be anything…

"I can't believe I hadn't asked you yet," he jitters. "You could be *anything*…"

"Aw, *thank you*," she turns flat onto her back. "That's the nicest thing anyone's ever said to me."

"You know what I mean." In the hope of finding his shirt, he looks around the bed which takes up most of the room.

"Would it change anything?" she asks.

"No. But can I have a clue?"

"Okay. I… sell stuff."

Oh. Thank fuck… I took off my shirt here last night…

"Good," he smiles. "I'll be thinking about my guesses all day."

"I'm sure that's not all you'll be thinking about..."

Tracy will be at the museum. Typing. Digging... Nesting...
But it's mine!

"You know it." He dashes out of the room for his shirt.

If I let her take over, I'll lose everything...

Neville smells the stress on his shirt before he threads his arms through and buttons it up. He looks around for his blazer... but finds Tabitha stepping nakedly towards him.

She brings her hands up to his neck and pulls him in to kiss.

I've got places to be...

But Neville succumbs, wrapping his arms around, pulling her in. Tight, against her many textures.

Decisions, decisions...

His hand slides down to her cheek for a hard squeeze, surprising her into a pause, parting lips.

"I'd best be off." Neville keeps a tight grip.

"If you insist..." Tabitha pecks him once more on the lips.

Neville relinquishes the warmth of her buttock to face the door. And his jacket on the floor. He scoops it up and slings it over his shoulder, looking back at the view of naked *her* on his way out, as she stands with her hands on her hips.

"See you dreckly." He pulls the door shut on her pale, smirking face, and body... ever... so... slowly...

CHAPTER 30

The chilling autumn air tickles and teases Neville as he ascends the steps to the museum. A shiver runs through him.

Such innocent thoughts, observing the weather while being investigated for assault, and probably murder… while the stress is still leached into yesterday's clothes.

But what a 'treat' to be distracted by Tabitha, in time for Halloween…

Neville's palm finds the wavy grain of wood. Another chill hits him as he pushes open one of the knob-less doors.

Maybe it's Tracy's mood that burns so cold.

He approaches the desk, and the officious gargoyle herself typing away. A sound Neville could mistake for the bones of her *victims* cracking between her teeth… But Tracy's mouth does not move. Her fierce glare is fixed on the monitor.

"Morning," Neville strides past.

"Morning," she *monotonates*.

He slows to a halt. "You… writing up more content for the site?"

"Of course."

"Great. I'll look forward to reading it."

The typing stops. Tracy's eyes swivel to glance at him, just as Neville marches out of the foyer. Her gaze falls onto the screen again.

Put that in your pipe and choke on it.

He walks the *green mile*, with as much foreboding oozing from his desk as an electric chair.

One way or another, I'll die in an office chair... Like Grandad...

He turns the corner, pressing on towards his wood-furnished cell, and the rest of his sentence... He sighs, and inhales, pulling him... towards the office. The door is already open, but not by the push of his breath...

Is that how I left it?

He steps in, grabs the handle, and pulls the door shut.

"You're spending a lot of time in contact with the police." Nick emerges from the corner of the room behind the door.

"Not that much," Neville jumps, slightly. "Why are you so worried? It didn't concern you."

Nick steps towards Neville, with his brow stretching up like a cobra's markings to terrify prey. "Did it not? My... *business associate...* gets called in by the police, and 'it does not concern me?'"

"It's cute that you care." Neville sits on the desk, scared, *thrilled* for his life.

Maybe it's not all bad. I won't be bored!

"I care about our business," Nick states. "I care about what you could be saying to the police that puts it under scrutiny... but I *don't* care about *you.*"

"Thanks, *Nick...* but you don't have anything to worry about."

Nick chuckles, on the verge of mania. "But that's just it, Neville. You can't tell me whether I should be worried. The fact remains that you've been in touch with the police, and I don't know what's being said… And *that* makes me worried." His sober, deathly glare attempts to scare some sense into Neville, or some answers out of him.

Neville is mesmerised, on the verge of beaming a child-like smile. Cornwall's 'most wanted man' would never have felt so alive, but for that damned Devil's face. The mask of fear he bears now is just as exhilarating, but *Devilishness* becomes him… "I was out, with a mate, if you must know. He got into trouble with the casino."

"Oh, *did* he?"

"Yes. We got chased out and the bouncers were beating the shit out of him. They went too far and… they got what was coming to them… That's all."

"So… You were out with a *mate*, who got into trouble with the casino… Do you see… how that fails to fill me with confidence? The company you keep does *not* reflect well on your integrity."

Neville stands his ground, unsmiling. "You can trust me."

"Again… it's not about what *you* tell *me*. Either I trust you, or I don't. And I don't think I do, especially, when I have it on good authority that it was *certainly* not 'all' that happened that night."

Neville savours the thrill of the exchange, but the danger is real. The joy and the anxiety converge beneath a veneer of chilling calm. "Whose authority?"

"'Beaten to within an inch of their lives', much like how three others, *more respectable fellas*, were beaten way beyond that… right here, in this very dump."

"Those were *your* men who broke in?!"

I'm cursed beyond belief, because of you*?!*

Neville holds his gaze, hiding the fear, and his darkest secret.

"The police," Nick continues, "may need evidence to make

234

a connection between two events – in such a small world – but sometimes… you just *know*."

He paces from one side of the office to the other, gesticulating like a lecturer giving a talk.

"Now, assuming I do happen to be working with such a *freak…* what do I do about it? I don't like leaving things to chance… He *might* have things under control – all well and good – but I can't make any guarantees that it won't jeopardise the business. If I were to *dissolve* him, and his involvement in this deal, that's even more mess to clean up. So, perhaps I could offer some… incentive…"

Neville feels his face shifting second by second into a savage, hateful glare.

"…to remind him that he is trying to provide for his family… and, to encourage better behaviour in and *out* of the workplace."

Nick musters a glance at Neville before turning to him again. "I take it you-"

Neville's fist collides with Nick's face. The smack sends him into the door with a *knock.*

Nick flails against the wall each side, with his hands to steady his near fall.

Neville's arm drops to his side. He stands in awe… of the most extraordinary peace… with warm, glowing knuckles.

Nick stumbles to his feet and clasps a hand over his jaw, uttering a deep grunt against either the pain or the audacity to hit him. "Well, that settles it…"

He lets go of his face and flexes his jaw. "Maybe I'll wait till you get yourself locked up. Or killed. Then I'll see if that good woman at the front desk will contribute to this enterprise. Now *there's* a good idea. *There's* a great business partner. Someone with whom I might mix business and *pleasure…*"

"You won't live to fucking dare."

Neville *Devilles* towards Nick, whose eyes widen like a rabbit before headlights. With a wrathful lurch, Deville is on him.

Nick's head catches the door on his way down.

"You bastard…" Deville's malice dominates the quiet struggle. He slings a punch into Nick's head, **"Coming in here…"** he throws a punch to the other side of Nick, **"threatening *my* family…"** another punch, **"And *my* business…?"**

But the words do not seem to faze Nick. Disbelief, scrawled all over his face, is erased before each blow, reducing him to a bloody rag doll. He lies, arms spread out, like a mobster martyr…

Neville recoils… paces….

"Fuck, what have I done?"

Why, you stood up for yourself! Bravo!

"It's not happened again. I can't have another body staring me in the face!"

One less scumbag in the world. Can't grumble…

"But there are consequences. Every time! Something else will go wrong…"

Oh, keep calm and carry on, old chap. You don't know he's dead until you've checked his pulse…

Neville stops pacing. "Okay. Okay, maybe it's not the end of the world just yet." He crouches, reaching under Nick's stubbly chin to rest his fingers.

But sharks don't sleep…

Neville snatches his hand away and stands up quick.

"I can't tell!"

If there's no pulse, he's dead. End of…

"What do I do?"

You could let me take over. You need a cool head in these situations.

"You've done enough!"

And here you are with another body on your hands.

Neville paces again. His other *cleaner* hand finds its way over his own stubbly face, palm over mouth, as if to stop the panic from getting out. "I can't leave him here..."

He reaches down, grabs Nick's ankles, and pulls. The hoarse whisper of body across floor perversely soothes Neville. He could be ahead of the game, just slightly, for once. "He could just be comatose."

Please. That would bring a whole other set of problems. They're a spiteful lot, these dealers and gang members. Just make the most of him being dead and go from there!

Neville kicks the chair out the way and drags Nick around to behind the desk. With his fancy white shoes before the edge, as Neville drops him. *Thud.* "Now what? I can't just keep him here all day... Can I?"

Why not? If you leave like nothing happened, who's to say you had anything to do with it?

"Well, there is a fucking *body* lying in my fucking *office!*"

Silence.

"Shit. Could she have heard that?"

Only one way to find out...

"I can't hear her." Neville steps around the desk and over Nick's feet, to creep towards the door. He grabs the handle and pulls it ajar for a peek outside...

No-one there, in the corridor.

Pulling the door shut with a click, Neville turns around and lies back against it, deflating with an epic sigh. His eyes fall to the desk, and Nick's pretentious white shoes sticking out at the side... as if, in spite of Neville's stress, the shady man is merely enjoying a nap right there.

Neville gets up, stomps over to that side of the desk, to stand over Nick and kicks the stupid shoes. He kicks them again, and

Nick's knees bend as he rolls over, now conveniently totally obscured by the desk. Neville stares at the still man curled up before him.

Nick's grey tailored attire is all scuffed up. Red dashes colour his white shirt, like an under-topped strawberry cheesecake. Blood glistens over his face, his nose, a split in his cheek, and a small red trickle from his mouth …

Neville sees the damage. He *is* capable… but not of controlling it. He forgets how to breathe. His lungs pump into panic. "I can't leave him here."

Of course you can.

"It's not like I can get him out of here with *Tracy* stuck out there…"

Unless you go through with killing her. Now that would solve a few of your problems…

"I'm not going to kill anyone else!"

Yes, but you already have, haven't you? You say this every time…

"Shut up, *shut up!*" Neville paces again before the desk – the side *sans* the dead dealer lying alongside it. "I have to at least make sure nobody enters the office… That no-one sees this… *All day*… Yes, I can do that…"

In that case, you had better get comfortable…

CHAPTER 31

The hours pass into noon, but Neville's appetite has died with the *drug dealer*...

Or whatever *the hell he is – 'was'*...

Pins and needles stab at Neville's buttocks as he sits on the desk, facing the door... afraid to move in case, *Tracy* comes through it... and just as afraid to turn away and find Nick's bruised and battered face... glaring. One glance back might spark a consciousness in the vengeful corpse lying behind the desk. Right behind Neville...

A bead of sweat caresses his cheek on the way down. Maybe it is Nick's fingertip stroking his victim before seizing him...

Neville swallows his fear, but it is more than he can chew. He licks his lips, but not enough moisture there to wash it down.

There's a bottle of water in the bottom drawer, isn't there?

Would he risk seeing dead Nick's face, merely for the sake of hydration?

No...

But... for Grandad's leftover scotch?

Maybe...

"I can't get drunk right now."

Who says anything about getting drunk? Just have... enough to calm your nerves.

"I can't in front of... *him*..."

I'm sure he won't object...

Sensing no movement, Neville shuffles off of the desk to stand upright – uptight... He looks up at the door again to confirm that no-one will disturb him... or his guest.

Neville stomps around the desk, avoiding Nick's smart white shoes which are poised, as if spitefully, to trip him up.

I wonder when rigor mortis sets in...

He glances over to Nick's bloody face. The *fixer* fixed to gaze forever under the desk until he is *moved...* elsewhere.

Neville clenches a fist. He stoops, and with his other hand opens the bottom drawer to find... only more stationery.

"Fuck!" he growls. Nerves set in, "It's in the other bottom drawer, isn't it?"

Right by his face, yes...

Neville steps around *the corpse* and stoops again. His arm hovers over Nick until finally Neville snatches the drawer open. He pulls out a bottle and stands before Nick can stir to grab him...

But the body has not stirred. Nor has it even remotely exhibited the urge to do so. Neville looks through the bottle and can see as much, "the damned thing's nearly empty."

I swear this had more in it... Is this Tracy's dirty little secret? Has she only been sneaking into the office for the odd swig?

"I know *I* haven't been tucking into this..."

The voice is silent.

Neville grips the cap and twists it off. He brings the rim to his lips and kisses the glass as he tips the bottle up. The maple-coloured fire-water chases over his tongue and down his throat, a burning chill all the way down to his stomach...

"It's fucking empty."

As Neville drops his arm, the bottle slips from his fingers, hitting the floor with a fluting grunt as if it is hurt.

"Sorry... That was the last of it..."

Nick lies still, facing away from him.

"It wouldn't do you any good now, would it?!"

But it's always nice to be asked.

Neville jumps. It was not Nick answering...

Jumpy, aren't we?

"Of course I am!" Neville snaps a look up again at the door.

Silence...

If you kept quiet, you wouldn't have to worry about being heard!

"Forgive me for panicking," Neville whispers, "there's only a fucking body lying in my fucking office!"

And who's fault is that?

"The jury's out on that one..."

You'd better hope there's no jury involved.

Neville paces from one end of the desk to the other. "It should never've come to this!"

Oh, but it has, Neville, and you're going to have to man up if you want to get out of this mess...

"Yes... got to keep my head together for a few hours," Neville looks up at the clock showing 12.15, "and make sure no-one else comes in and sees *this*. Sticking around seemed like a good idea earlier…"

Well, at least you won't be on your own…

Neville stops and peers around the desk to see Nick. The remote possibility he is still alive appeals, soothing Neville. "It's not funny. I can't sit still… with _him…_ stuck there."

Clearly! But we're just going around in circles now, aren't we?

"I've got to get out of here." He faces the door. "That's it; I'm off to get food!"

But can you chance it? It's already been half a day. You can wait for a bit longer.

Neville stares at two inches of wood between him and the outside world… yet somehow the corpse blocks the door.

It must already be contaminating the air!

He leaps for the metal doorknob and grips it tight, chilling his palm, and snatches the door open.

Air rushes inside. Fresh air… as if _pulled_ in… by an intake of breath into _many_ gaping mouths…

Neville freezes.

Sighs rush out from behind him and brush at the back of his neck. Soles stomp heavily, the way a bull prepares to charge. Gasp after gasp suck in more air behind Neville, as steps accumulate towards him with the moans and groans of dead men.

Neville lurches out the door and turns back to confirm the worst…

Nick, grey and still in his suit, now sits leering upon a familiar 'steed,' made up of all who were killed at Neville's hand…

No… this thing?! Now?!

Two arms slam fists onto the desk. The torso they belong to rises, as the beaten faceless, previous victim, _Luke_ 'sits' up, peering over Nick's shoulder…

Neville whirls round, barely feeling the floor as he sprints out of the office.

Before he turns a corner, he glances back at the arachnoid corpse chimera and its riders, seeping their way through the office door…

"Defeated by a mere *door*, you disgusting bastards?! How about you fuck off and leave me be!"

The beast's hands and feet, now amounting to ten of each, curl around the door frame and push against the wall.

Neville stands his ground, resisting the urge to dash beyond the end of the corridor, afraid to lose sight of… *it*.

Nick sitting atop this steed, presses both his hands against the wall as two more 'feet' stagger through the threshold. The vengeful hands of Luke and Nick flex to claw at Neville. All the front-facing faces lock eyes with him. Each opens its mouth and screams a piercing, whistling *roar*.

Run!

But Neville watches as hands and feet stomp heavily, pushing the beast of bodies forward. The floor shakes with Neville's reality… He sprints away, into the foyer, past the desk and up to the front doors.

Where's Tracy, gone for lunch? Lucky her!

His hands collide with the solid doors… but they do not budge.

The panting, growling, and stomping gets louder, *closer*, quaking even the concrete floor.

Neville runs back to the desk, putting it between him and the grotesque corpse beast as it emerges into the foyer. Their *elaborinth* game of cat and mouse continues in this vast, a-*maze*-ing arena that is the museum.

As the beast attempts to circle the desk, it takes a greedy

gasp, a large bite of musty atmosphere... while from around the corner at knee-level, an upside-down head pokes out to see Neville, and snaps at air.

"Of course, you can do that, you omni-headed fucker!"

Neville retreats and then runs the other way around the counter.

Stranded, the beast shudders in frustration. Nick, and the *faceless*, snap their heads towards Neville, flexing their hands as if already tearing at his throat.

With a crackle, Luke sinks behind Nick. Pale fingers grip the edge of the counter. With bobbing, drooling heads, it straddles the desk and crawls *in-Neville-tably,* to its prey...

The beast's rancid respiration hits him. He stumbles back as a smelling salts effect shocks Neville to his senses. The heavy pitter-patter of claws and paws behind Neville inspires him to rush towards the exhibits, and through Arts History... until he sees the mask display.

"Wait, *you* can't be *here!*"

A row of grotesque faces sits on the silver rods before Neville. A full row... including the Face of the Devil.

It's supposed to be back at my flat!

Growls and huffs catch up to Neville's neck, when a cold claw shaves at his back... He lurches forward with a chill that reverberates through his spine.

Flight over fight carries his legs into a sprint. Neville wraps his talons around the familiar devilish mask to grab it and run... but it does not give.

The beast lunges.

Neville leaps aside.

As Neville evades a vicious swipe, he finds himself behind the display...

He grabs for the mask again. The whole rig shakes with his mortal struggle to pull it free, if not with anger from an offended deity.

The beast raises a thick, monstrous arm. Its rotten breath all but puts Neville under a deathly slumber when, like Excalibur from The Stone, he pulls the mask free.

Neville falls back, nearly onto the floor but for a quick foot to steady himself, as another breeze of decay blusters at his face.

The silver rod now protrudes from Luke's forearm, not that *he* bats an eye.

No use crying over dead flesh.

The beast tears its arm away from the metal rod, leaving the remaining sinews to hiss, and evaporate into nothing…

Neville clutches the mask to his chest and runs. The first time he ran this circuit he was the predator, but *this* time, he charges through the next exhibit, in and out of model dinosaurs who have turned to snap at him.

Neville rushes out of the prehistoric exhibit.

You never know what's *around the corner! Wait… Apart from* this *corner!*

Grunts and snarls close in.

Neville reaches for the handle to his left.

No, not in there*! Anywhere but in there…*

He rips it open, leaps into the dark and hopefully empty storage cupboard, and snatches the door shut.

Neville scoops at the dark for the light. He grabs the string and pulls it down hard with a *click*.

Neville glances at each of the illuminated walls closing in on him. The most threatening presences are the mop and bucket resting against a corner behind, and the scent of bleach flooding his nose and mouth. The faint, uncleansable hint of death.

245

This is where that thing came from. Where I made *it!*

He turns the mask over in his hands. The red, snarling face stares up at Neville. Its fanged mouth and hollow eyes hunger to be filled.

"This can't be the answer…"

Can't it? There's no other choice. You're trapped.

Thud. The door shakes.

"It won't be enough! That thing's huge now!"

You are smarter than it. Faster. Now, get out there and kill it…

Boom. The beast thumps against the door, or at the ground…

You only have so long before it realises the door opens with a pull and not a push…

As the voice chuckles at its own wit, Neville turns the mask over.

The creamy underside is as tender as flesh, as warm and welcoming is his second skin… Before he knows it, Neville's face is inside. He drops his arms…

The mask is now out of his hands.

***

Deville's hands curl up into fists. He breathes in the bleach and the death, swallowing *Neville's* fear… devouring him.

He crouches, without scuffing his suit against the confining walls. On the way down one hand relaxes, opening out to take up his crowbar from the floor, expecting it to be exactly where he wants it, the way a king trusts his sword will be brought to him by his subject for a knighting… or a smiting.

And it *is* there. Weapon tightly in hand, Deville stands taller, *broader*. He sighs ahead of the tedious task to 'take care' of the beast.

Disgust tightens its grip around the crowbar. Anger kicks the door open.

The beast stumbles back, clumsy on all its many limbs. It steadies itself. The void minds and faces of Luke, Nick, and the three trespassers hunger forward for Neville…

But *Deville* comes out the closet.

Hate holds up the crowbar… and brings it down onto Nick's head, like a hammer crashing into damp wood. Nick does not wince before the head trauma. With his eyes half-shut, unanimated, he is no longer magnetised to the sum of chimeric corpses. He slumps and falls to the floor.

The mass of dead meat that remains of Luke's face expresses nothing. He stretches out his muscled arms each side. The beast is stronger and faster with one less mouth to feed…

Deville watches relaxed, *bored*, with the crowbar hanging at his side, tight in his hand.

The beast claws towards him…

The crowbar flies up and collides with Luke's chin. The flesh muffles the ringing metal upon bone.

Deville's arm is already primed for the next hit. He swings again… the crowbar flies from over his shoulder into the side of Luke's head, breaking and breaching his skull under the impact.

Suddenly, teeth sink deep into Deville's leg above the ankle.

He howls a primal roar down at the bald head of the trespasser, mindlessly gnawing at the base of his shin. With his other leg, Deville kicks into the bundle of bodies, tearing the teeth free.

A heavy blow swings into Deville, knocking him all the way back to Ancient Egypt… or at least into the exhibit, where the sands of time have long run dry.

The crowbar falls from Deville's hand, ringing out a brief

half-life of rhythmic bouncing and scraping metal.

Deville takes a stand. He steps forward, biting back against the pain around his lower leg, and stoops to scoop up the crowbar.

Luke appears dazed, an easy target, as the rest of the beast continues to scuttle across the floor towards Deville, who likewise charges ahead. Each painful step boils his blood as he holds the crowbar back for a momentous swing…

The metal meets Luke's head on the other side, even harder than before. His body falls back, onto the beast, and slides off as it moves forward.

With another backhanded swing from Deville, the weapon crashes down onto the front-most head of the remaining beast. Its skull cracks like a nut, and the body with it falls away to the floor.

The two remaining conjoined trespassers clamber to their feet but fall back down… and claw at their way forward.

As they crawl, a ghastly sound tears at Deville's ears, like sticky tape ripped violently from a dispenser.

The congealed vengeful dead… *split*… get to their feet, and face Deville.

Decay in the air once again taunts his nose. Even *he* could pass out cold… but the crowbar hot in his grip, draws out a stinging, burning sweat only the dark blood of these monsters can cool.

The two ghoulish men sway as they try to walk before they can run – before they can *chase*.

But Deville circles around them. The shadow of the blunt object darkens the face of his nearest foe, as he brings it down with one hand onto the man's head.

As Deville wrenches the tool free of the man's skull, he sees no reaction… until the soulless fool collapses to his knees and falls onto his side, laid to rest.

Holding the weapon at his waist, Deville coils both hands around the crowbar for the final ghoul to stumble into a primed upward swing… He breathes relief ahead of the last strike. The impact, the sound it will make…

The weary face before him expresses more than just hunger… An instinctive jealousy, that might only be sated by killing his killer, and taking *Neville's* life… for his own.

The reanimated man rages closer to Deville, taking one more step before sweet oblivion…

As vengeful people, *vengeful things*, see only what they want, the man trips over the legs of the other body and falls onto Deville, knocking him onto his back.

Clearly more bird than tool, the crowbar is sent flying again.

The growling man grips tight, digging fingers into Deville on the climb up.

Deville roars and pushes against him… but the tenacious man continues to grip… pinch… and break skin…

The rabid man lunges forward with his mouth open and takes a bite of air, when Deville's fist launches straight for the nose, knocking him back.

Deville shuffles away, more to preserve his dignity, than merely for his survival… The tiles cool his palms as he struggles carefully to his feet, while his *bloody* foot still aches. He looks down at his rabid foe getting up.

Anyone else would be reeling.

"Enough's enough," Deville steps steadily towards him… but it is not *mercy* that grabs the man by the collar, nor *anger* throwing punch after punch into this man's face…

The final revenant plaguing *Neville's* mind falls away from Deville's grip with one last hit.

Down to the last knockings of a game that Deville is bored with… "Time to come back to reality…"

The hungry vision made flesh writhes on its front, still trying to crawl to his feet, as if he still has a chance to kill his killer…

Deville rests his good foot over the man's back and pins him down. He brings his bad foot over the man's head, and stamps hard, feeling the burning bite around his ankle, as skull percusses repeatedly against tile… until the man stops moving… until the dead stay dead.

Finally quiet, but for steam hissing from each deceased man as they dissolve into nothingness, Deville steps off the last body.

Straightening his suit, shirt, and tie, he walks elegantly back towards the office in an orderly fashion.

The battle for Neville's mind is won. His ugly, guilty conscience is slain.

***

Deville sits back and rests his shoes onto the desk. He plants one elbow onto the arm of Neville's chair and with face in hand, cheek on palm, he reflects. Heavy is the head that wears the-

Where is it?

Neville sits up. His soles sink from the desk. His hands press against his face… a soft touch…

"Where's the fucking mask?!"

Was that a dream?!

Neville does not remember 'waking'…

But he remembers the clock above the door, which now indicates: 4.57pm.

"I can't have fallen asleep! Not through the rest of the day…"

He shifts his feet to stand… but they are obstructed by Nick, lying still before the desk.

"Fuck, I forgot about *you.*" Neville clings to the arms of the chair and lifts one dainty foot across the body… onto the floor… stands… and then finally steps over it, a slight, brisk knock raps at the door.

Neville freezes.

No! Not in this *compromising position!*

The door swings open. He jumps forward. He puts himself between his latest guest and his latest victim… whoever's which.

Tracy walks in wearing a raincoat and a bag over her shoulder. Smart, but end-of-the-day weary, she greets Neville sweetly.

"I'm just off now. Haven't seen you all afternoon, everything okay?"

"Yeah, I've just been… writing. My imagination's been running *wild*," he *franticulates* with a smile, "It's all for the cause."

"Oh. Well, I can't wait to see it. Shall I shut the door, or are you going too?"

"Uh… No. Yes! I'm sticking around." He gasps with shock, revelation, and guilt twofold. "It's my daughter Gemma's school play this evening. *That's* why I'm not heading out just yet… Saves going all the way home and then back out again!"

"Aw, what's she performing in?"

"Um, something about goblins and witches… just in time for Halloween!"

"'Witch' will *she* be, this evening?" Tracy smirks.

Just. Fucking. Go!

"I don't know yet," says Neville. "It'll be a surprise, but I have my suspicions she's a witch."

"She sounds as insubordinate as her father!" she smiles, raising *smart-arsed* eyebrows and turns to walk back out. "I'll see you tomorrow, then, Nev."

"See ya, Trace…y!"

He watches as the expanse of corridor grows between him and her bottom, until she disappears around the corner.

Hiding a lie behind a truth… Well played.

"No thanks to *you…*" Neville shoves the door closed.

Now, now, you're not exactly alone at this moment in time, are you?

He faces away from the door, receiving the message in a drastically different context from what his *other half* intended. Neville ignores the voice for just a bit longer as he sees only the desk from this side… *Thankfully*, no sight of Nick's well-dressed carcass poking out from either end.

Neville approaches, pondering the limits of plausible deniability… as to how Nick White could have ended up in the curator's office at Pike's Museum of General History and Antiquities… behind the desk… dead.

Circling the desk, Neville peers around it once more, with the hope that there is no body behind the desk… that this has all been but a dream…

But Nick's smart white shoes still shine their polished shine, glaring accusingly at his killer.

Neville sighs venom, "I don't suppose *you'll* be walking out for closing time, will you?"

CHAPTER 32

Wheels squeak a dulcet tune under the weight of Nick.

Neville marvels at the simplicity of the cargo trolley; engineered to carry many items at once with ease; ergonomically suited to get heavy objects from Alpha to Omega, the beginning, and the end... with a simple push.

This trolley already has flecks of *red* on it.

Of course, it's just paint. It can only be paint... can't it?

The wheels sing faster into the foyer. He shoves, double-time, to avoid the front entrance and any curious passers-by... any potential witnesses...

The shops are starting to close up by now, so people will be fucking off home. No-one else will have to die today... to preserve my 'innocence.'

High and low squeaks siren into the Arts History exhibit. All clear, as Neville pushes forward, unobstructed, uninterrupted, towards the back door.

Thank fuck, the car's outside.

He slows to a halt, rushing from the trolley to the door ahead, and pull it open. Cool, air floods his eyes as he peeks outside.

With no-one around, Neville drags the door wide open. He

rushes back around to the trolley handlebar when he hears a slam. He faces the now-closed door behind... "Shit!"

Neville strops back over to it.

This is what you get when you try to do things on your own...

He rips it open again, with the outside so near, yet so far.

God, I miss her. The wife...

"I can't go down that road. Where's the fucking doorstop?" He scans over the surrounding floor... but alas, no doorstop.

Tabitha would probably help me hide a body. But then, she's nuts as fuck.

Leaning against the door, Neville grabs the foot of the trolley and pulls it through, until it rests against the frame. Once again, he walks around to the back of the trolley, but it drifts steadily away by the weight of the closing door. He lurches, slamming it against the wall as he pushes the trolley through...

Frustration sighs its way out of him, "Can't you make yourself fucking useful, Nicholas?!"

Nick lies still in an uncomfortable heap with his dried *bloody* face, possibly bearing a smirk.

"It's like taking extreme measures to help a steaming mate home from a night on the piss!"

I miss Kat. The wife. The wife.

Neville pushes against the door, while his spare hand pulls the trolley through, over the threshold.

I don't know if she'd have helped me hide a body... No one ever really 'expects' to have to do such a thing, after all.

The trolley clatters on its voyage out while Nick's remains *remain* a very patient passenger...

"Oh, fucking *steps!*"

Neville claps his hands around the end of the trolley and tugs it over the bottom step. Three long flat mountains, one higher than the next.

"Okay. One *step* at a time… On my *own!*"

He drags the front pair of little rubber wheels up, over the first step.

But you're not on your own, Neville…

"Fuck!" He jumps, losing his grip on the trolley.

It rolls back down off the step…

"I keep my thoughts to myself, but when *one* thing *slips out…*"

Your thoughts are not hidden to me, Neville. I am you, after all.

Neville sighs forward, off the step, and sulks after the trolley.

"So, I'm just as good as alone, then."

Not at all! Who better to understand you than yourself?

Back where he started, just outside the door, he grabs at the end of the trolley and pulls it up again.

"*You* can't possibly want what I want."

It's always 'you' and 'I' with you, isn't it? There can be only one… and, what you want – that is to say, what I want – is what the heart really desires.

Neville hauls the wheels over the first step once more.

"I don't believe that… because I want Kat. I want her back. There. I said it. You can't possibly want her as well."

Again, with the 'you'… Of course, we- 'I'… want Kat. 'I'-You… want her, without any interference…

Neville pulls further, against the weight. Nothing will surprise him anymore.

"What does that even mean?"

'We' *want her back in the most…* ideal *possible way.*

"Of course, I do…" He grips the trolley tight, keeping it in place as he 'climbs' his way back down to the handle. "But *I'm* a realist."

Neville lifts the back wheels onto the step. "She wouldn't take me back…"

He pulls further, until the front wheels bump into the second step, for good measure. "…even if she wanted to."

He grips the sides, helping it climb gently towards the top step…

'You' *are also an optimist, underneath it all… you know exactly what you want. And you can make it happen, if only you would open yourself up to it…*

Neville makes the last step and hauls the trolley over with him. "I can only do one thing at a time!"

Clearly. In that case, disposing of Nick will **not** *be part of the drive to Gemma's school play, will it…?*

"Shit, I forgot!"

Neville drags the trolley towards the VW, and with one hand reaches into his pocket for the key to do the central locking. With the other hand, he digs his fingers under the boot and heaves it up. *Open wide…* when a metallic rattle resounds behind him.

Neville turns to see complacently-dead-Nick, unfazed by his ride on the trolley as it judders off the top step with a clang.

"*Fuck…*" Neville crescendos as he curses after him, with big steps threatening to become balletic leaps that carry him over to the fleeing unit.

His hand claps onto the hard, cold, wire at the frame's end. "Okay. Third time lucky…"

Neville roots his feet and pulls, having to drag the tiny,

uncooperative wheels over the last two steps all over again…

Only a dung beetle would work so hard to roll shit up a hill.

***

Exhausted Neville lands in the driver's seat. He shuts the door with burning arms, underarms awash with sweat, and aching legs.

"Even dead and crammed into the boot of a car, Nick's *still* more comfortable than I am!" His lungs inflate, slow to release each breath.

"What time's Gem's play? Can I ask Kat?" He wriggles his cumbersome form to slip his hand into his pocket and take out his dreaded mobile phone: 17.57.

"No, I need to look alert. It would be nice to surprise Gemma. Be there, to wave at her before the play starts. At the *very* latest…"

He looks over his shoulder, at the empty back seat of the car.

No objections from his silent passenger, lying beyond.

"It's not like I have time to drop *you* off."

Time's a-ticking… or are you going to rock up with a stiff 'plus one'?

Neville faces the front, and the buildings opposite through the windscreen. Flats and shops, with mousey brown walls of second-rate stone, reach nowhere near high enough to be called skyscrapers. More 'sky *dreamers.*'

"It's six pm, so that must allow for parents to be home by now, to put food on the table…"

Are you serious?

"…change, and then get ready to bring the kids back to school for eight…"

You're really *trying to calculate this!*

257

"I've *got* to have something to eat, clean myself up… Maybe I *can* drop Nick off somewhere on the way to the school…"

You could try letting him out of the boot so he can call a cab.

"Really? That's your serious suggestion? God, I'm so tired…"

A killer wouldn't worry about leaving a body out in the open, but because you *wouldn't, this close to the museum, doing so – the exact opposite – would go a great deal towards exonerating Neville Pike…*

"But…" Neville yawns, "that's risky! It'll still be linked with the museum, draw attention, and emphasise a connection… with the other killings…"

It's all about confidence. Neville Pike *didn't kill Nicolas White, did he?*

The driver's seat grows more and more and more comfortable… Condensation clouds the glass. Neville cannot see what is right in front of him.

You've got to act fast. There's no time to sleep on it…

"Oh, too right. I'll just rock up with Nick in the back of my car and shout," he yawns once more, "'It's okay! It wasn't *me* who killed him!'"

He blinks a long blink…

…Neville's eyes open, and the car is warmer. Yet, he does not remember starting it.

He rubs his eyes, savouring the innocuous strokes of knuckle against eyelid. Lowering his hands, Neville notices a more comfortable black suit covering his person, like *another* second skin, with a clean shirt, a waistcoat, no tie… and he is showered… Feeling clean, feeling good, but feeling dirty about it.

Through the now-clearer windscreen, he sees the buildings on the other side have changed. "Where am I?"

Goodness me, you can't fall asleep at the wheel! The doors weren't locked. Anyone could've slipped into the driver's seat and took over…

He pulls out the phone, smoothly, from his pocket. "Twenty-past seven! It starts at half-past… I'm fucking *late!*"

He texts Kat, 'Nearly there. It starts at half past, doesn't it?'

"Okay," says Neville, "Who the fuck has died since I've been 'out'?"

You know, it was written somewhere that over six thousand people die every day.

Neville tastes the cold as he breathes. "If you're me, then why don't I remember the last hour?"

Maybe it was too traumatic for you to bear the drive home, to shower and change, and then stop at a restaurant for a proper meal …

"You may as well've roofied me!"

Now that would be counterproductive!

Condensation creeps up over the windows.

"But how is it possible to do all of that and for not to remember?"

You were tired. You don't need to remember…

"I had specifically set out to do things a certain way-"

It wouldn't have worked out.

"Why not?"

You're stressed.

"*No.* Really?"

You would've been too wound-up to accomplish one *straightforward task in your… ordinary mindset. So, when you crashed out earlier, it was only natural that your 'better self'*

259

would remain, to carry out what you wanted to achieve. It's a kindness, really.

"I don't have time for this. Am I at the school or not?" Neville squeezes at the handle. The cold air embraces him as he steps out of the car and into the dusk. Standing under a dull purple sky, he is all but blinded by two bright orbs charging at him.

They slow. The driver dims the headlights.

Neville shuts his door and avoids the next car with a wide berth as it parks up. He looks to the small complex at the end of the car park and rushes to the back of his own vehicle.

"So, I made it after all."

There's no need for doubt.

"It's not reverse-parked. How I like it."

Always looking for a quick getaway, eh?

Neville strides towards the school entrance beyond…

The smart creature pushes the door open, walking in from the dark, the rushing of cars grinding tyres on tarmac, and into a hall, furnished with natural wood, plastic, and primary colours. He faces the echoes of a crowded room. Voices of all ages chatter, curiously hard to tell the adults apart from the children.

Neville advances casually. He is in his own mind this time. The one voice he is concerned about will not be flooding his head. He will not beat and kill anyone this evening…

Unless he has to. He *won't* have to… He *can't* have to.

"…but I *could.*"

Little nippers, biting at your ankles…

Each step takes Neville towards the open double doors to his right.

Who knew that around the corner there'd be a silver-topped crone standing against the door frame?

Smiling, crooning softly like a cat that got the cream, the old woman holds her hand out…

"Ten pounds, please," she holds out a ticket with her other hand.

Ten fucking pounds! No wonder you look like you're pissing in the bath and getting away with it!

"Do you take cards?" He fishes out his wallet.

Madam gasps at Neville.

"Only joking." He conjures a tenner from the leather maw and surrenders the comfort of slightly warm plastic from his fingertips to her greedy hot claws.

He chuckles. "My daughter's playing as one of the goblins."

"Enjoy your evening." She pulls up a strip of paper from a box on a small table beside her, and places it in Neville's hand. *That's the ticket…*

"You make a great old hag." He launches a walk towards the front row of plastic chairs. Her gasp chases after him.

For that price, I'm definitely framing this ticket!

The wooden platform the little cherubs will be performing on tonight has been assembled at the end of the hall.

Neville strolls along the folded-against-the-wall metal climbing frames, looking to his side for the spare seat next to Kat.

There you are… next to that mother. And beside that pretty man… who appears to be in my *seat.*

Kat turns her head of blonde-highlighted hair. Her eyebrows flinch upwards.

An awkward smile and a little wave doth butter no parsnips, my love… I see how it is.

Neville tenses his face into what might look like a smile. He drops it quickly and gazes blankly along the succeeding rows of seated, chattering families. The second row, full. Third row, full. Fourth row…

At least it's not the back row.

At the end, a round man sits back over a buckling chair, next to where Neville stands. The man's his bulging arms pinch the back of the seat with his elbows as he leans back. The man's upright neck looks wide, stiff, and uncomfortable. His belly button peaks out from under his top. His arse spills onto the chair next to him.

"Is that seat taken?" Neville enquires.

"Um… no," says the man.

"Would you mind if I…?"

"No, go ahead…" The man shuffles, struggling to tuck his legs under the chair, so Neville has just enough room to slip his way through…

It's a wonder his stink didn't need a seat of its own… Poor sod.

Neville lands delicately onto the seat, favouring the further side, to avoid the accidentally sensual thigh against thigh on his way down.

Do I make eye-contact?

He turns slightly to one side, catching the man's glance. With a slip of a smile, and a nod, they each face the front.

This is embarrassingly far back! At least I don't have to buy him a drink…

Stealthily, Neville reaches for the phone in his pocket, careful not to make any physical contact with anyone… and checks the time. Five, ten minutes over. The show will start any time, now.

I should've said 'thank you'. That would've been the polite thing to do!

Between the forest of heads, he can just about make out Kat's hair towards the front. And *that tool's* head next to hers, wiggling, fidgeting.

Not a care in the world. But he really *doesn't want to be here…*

A mousey twig of a woman in a battleship grey suit creeps to the front and centre stage.

"Good evening, everyone," her voice booms. "Thank you for being here tonight. We present to you a piece performed by the Year 3s…"

The *headmistress*, it dawns on Neville. It has been a while, after all…

What is she yammering on about now? So politically correct it hurts.

"…and now," she smirks, "presenting 'Goblins and Witches.'"

She wanders stage left off the platform. Some of the lights are then switched off. The claustrophobic awkwardness of strangers dims as well.

Hello darkness, my dear old friend…

But the speakers hum and thrum a different tune: *'If you all go down to the woods today…'*

If I go down to the woods tonight… that's where I can hide Nicholas!

Cue the marching children: goblins, dressed not unlike Christmas elves, and witches with their black cowls and pointed hats. All hold hands as they stamp ruthlessly out of time. Five minutes already feels too long a performance.

Gemma, among them, tries to keep in time with the music.

Of course, she chose to be a goblin. Why conform and be simply a witch?

A smile blooms across Neville's face.

She does a better job of blending in than me.

He gazes into the shadows that make up the audience, in attempt to make out Kat… but instead, he finds the urge to weep. She is lost to him.

Some random bastard is in my *seat next to* my *wife, and* my *daughter has to catch sight of this when she's looking for us in the audience!*

Lips part, to bare Neville's gritted teeth.

Didn't Kat have the spine to say, 'Sorry, this seat is saved'?

He sulks into his fist.

Shouldn't you have had the spine to say, 'Sorry, that's my seat'? Hell, maybe she really did invite him.

"Fuck. Off," Neville whispers to his knuckles.

This is what happens when you don't know what you want. People start making decisions without you. They move on. They don't need you. But you don't need them.

The flames of his rage grow within as they devour the air without. One by one the shadows sitting around Neville turn to face him. Gemma did not inherit her ability to 'blend in' from him…

And as another consequence of how you deal with things, you're missing your daughter's performance.

Of course, his deep angry breaths would draw attention. He takes one more, for the suspense, and coughs away the tension. The judgemental *others* face the front once more.

Almost caught out. Downright persecuted… but it wouldn't just be me under the stigma of being different… 'weird'… Gemma would suffer the most after that.

The show goes on. The goblins and the witches face each other from each side of the stage…

I've changed. I was never exactly a prize in the first place, but I'm still *different from the rest.*

All is silent for a moment. One 'goblette' stomps centre-stage and picks something up from the floor…

They're threatened by you. Even deep down, somehow, they know. They know that you're different. Stronger. Smarter. Maybe that you are in fact better than them. Great potential stands out, and ordinary people, run-of-the-mill cattle… they do not like it…

"And you can take your stupid toothpaste too," a familiar voice projects… "'Chucks a tube of toothpaste at the witches!'"

Gemma throws a large cut-out toothpaste at said witches.

What's she saying…? 'Chucks?' She's saying the stage direction!

Neville cackles amongst the chuckling audience. The surrounding shadows turn to face him again, but he laughs harder for a little longer.

"That's my daughter," he smiles with a runny eye.

Doesn't time fly when you're pretending to have fun… It won't be long before they continue to put you down… To judge and patronise you, so you won't be able to rise above the rest… so, you can't lower your guard for even a second!

Neville notices the shadows are already facing the front. All is bearable for now… but soon the show will be over.

…and then it's back to reality.

CHAPTER 33

Clucking like farmyard hens…

Parents, singles, children… complete nuclear tribes chatter as they catch and receive child-sized goblins and witches with open arms. Smiles all-round.

On the outside looking in, not as 'special' as the rest, Neville watches the pattern play out between families. He looks through the crowd for Kat, expecting – perhaps with some disappointment – that she will be doing exactly the same thing as the other families, in exactly the same way.

As chairs are picked up and stacked, the pathway between loud, obnoxious, noxious families remains narrow. Neville walks through the valley of the shadow of the daft, fearing no Deville, though he is with him. His woe and his wrath, they control him…

Neville sees Kat stand up, from what he gladly presumes is just a hug with their daughter before she turns to acknowledge Neville. He averts his gaze in favour of Gemma, half as tall as *Mummy.*

"Daddy! You saw me!" Gemma runs to Neville and wraps her arms around him, pressing her cheek against his stomach.

He returns the embrace. He sees the other parents around the room.

They don't have this… They're not being greeted like this, are they?

"Yes, I did, Gem! You look lovely in green…" His eyes find Kat again. "I just wish I'd had a closer seat, Mummy."

Kat turns with gritted teeth. "Daddy was very late."

"I'm sorry," he bluffs, "I got caught up in… roadworks."

"Daddy had plenty of notice to arrive on time and get a decent seat."

"You know," he stands up straight, "Mummy neglected to inform Daddy, that he was going to get stung on the way in."

Living the dream of family life, for but a moment… and then *this*. The dream dissolves into disappointment again. At least they can share *that*.

Gemma fascinated, watches Mummy and Daddy try to hide their upset through the façade.

The heads of surrounding parents turn, sensing that one of these families is not like the others…

Kat takes in a huge breath as if to exhale fire… but instead surrenders a sigh. Disappointment cuts deep. Quietly, she addresses the man who is still technically her husband. "Well, at least you managed to get to see the show."

"And what a show it was!" he holds Gemma's face and kisses her square on the forehead.

She giggles. Cover is maintained, and the other families resume their greeting and boasting.

"It just flew by, didn't it?" Neville stands… to acknowledge Kat. "So, where's your friend?"

"Who?" she is believably puzzled.

"That fella next to you. Now *he* looked out of place. I must've missed my seat by you by *that much*."

"He wasn't with *me*... You would've had the seat of you weren't late."

I could kill *her right now.*

Neville's blood stops cold.

"Sorry... You're right." He could cry right now. "Is there anything else we wanna see here, or is it time to shoot?"

It's always time to shoot. But who should you take out first?

"It's getting late," says Kat, "We ought to leave."

Leave no survivors...

"Sure," Neville grins, barely surviving himself.

Please, not her!

Kat takes Gemma by the hand and leads her through the shrinking crowd, with Neville following close behind.

And why not? If Katherine persists in moving forward without you, she'll leave you in the dust! She, of all people, has it coming...

"Goodnight," the hag by the door smiles... until Neville sulks past.

One of the double doors is met by Kat's spare hand, but it resists her push. Neville catches up with a helping paw.

"I've got it," she snaps.

The door gives, and the building breathes in the cool obsidian night.

Neville's palm meets cold glass as the door swings back. He catches the door for Gemma, and then steps through after her, but she, his only glowing happiness, holds *Mummy's* hand.

Kat does not look back, as she and their daughter walk further into the darkness without him.

You're supposed to be walking with your family, yet here you are straggling behind like a deranged stalker.

Red boiling rage burns black within Neville's husk. It remembers bitterly the joy and hope that now feel so behind him. It melts away his face of contentment and compliance... and follows.

Kat stops before the dull silver headlights of her dark blue car, darker than any other in the car park. She glances at the little goblin beside her and then faces Neville, Gemma's indisputable father, "Well... goodnight."

Good night... 'Nev?' 'Neville?' Nothing. See? You are nothing to her.

"Goodnight." Neville kneels beside Gemma as Kat opens the driver's side door. The light inside colours their features; Kat is warning light orange, while Gemma is warm, near crimson...

"Goodnight, Gem."

They hug. Gemma lets go first.

Neville stands and reaches for the passenger side door, holding it open as his little goblin gets in. He stretches down the seatbelt for her, stretching out the time before having to *belt up*. Neville steps back with a hand on the door, ready to *shut it*.

The car starts as efficiently as Kat turns the key.

"Love you," he lets slip.

Gemma is overjoyed and less surprised than her mother, whose jaw drops.

Kat's muscle-memory tries to say it back, but Neville shuts the door against her hesitance.

However, the window is less of a barrier against Gemma's voice. "I love you too, Daddy!"

His smile is mirrored by Kat, perhaps more than politely, as the car purrs forward out of this space.

So, she's putting her foot down.

Neville waves at Gemma, who waves back, as Kat drives off into the night. The light goes out…

And after all that, you're still alone.

He faces the school, still lit up within. Shapes of adults and children merge and then separate, morphing past each other.

"I need to be alone right now, anyway," says Neville.

But there's still someone who needs a lift. And he's already waiting… in your car…

"Where *is* my car?" He exaggerates a glance around the dimly lit lot.

Naturally. Focus on the littlest things first.

"I'll have to think back and try to retrace my steps…" Neville, winds up the voice as marches back towards the school…

At the entrance he turns to face the body… of cars before him.

How in Hell have you got away with murder thus far?

"I can't see it. Gonna have to look at each car until I see my number plate." He ventures forward as steadily as he possibly can…

You're wasting time! It is imperative that Neville Pike is specifically not linked with the killings. Nick White needs to be moved on!

"I'm not worried."

That's something. Even guilty, with enough confidence, Neville Pike can do what he likes.

A smile squirms free of Neville's lips.

Of course. What else is there to say? Speaking as you… you are the best at winding yourself up…

"No. It's clearly *two* playing at that game…"

FACE VALUE

'Two?' There is no other 'two', than body and soul! We divide... and we conquer.

"You mean for us to divide, so *you* can conquer *me!*"

Neville stumbles upon his humble grey steed under the cloak of night, and steps around to the driver's side.

He gets in, slams the door, and holds the voice captive with him...

"Ever since you've been in my head, I've been out of control... I've pushed my family further away, and put them at risk, to boot! I've not had any peace from you and your bullshit. Even acknowledging you feeds your existence, but no more! I'm my own man, and you won't utter a single word, or pull at my strings ever again! Enjoy your lonely nothingness, you parasite. Get the fuck out of my head... and *stay* out!"

Neville pulls forward from the space to drive out of the school car park.

As looks up to check the rear-view mirror, a silhouette on the back seat 'greets' him.

"Be careful what you wish for."

The car swerves as Neville loses control.

Is this real? Is this because I shut him out...? What have I done?!

He throws the interior light on and turns to lock eyes with *'Neville Pike'* sitting in the back seat.

"That's done it," Deville smirks, suddenly in the driver's seat.

Neville gasps from the back seat. The seatbelt is suddenly tight over his wrists, preventing him from slipping free.

Like the stomach of a vast predator, the car growls.

I could be eaten alive!

"**How can you shut me out?**" The vehicle lurches forward as Deville mocks, turning out of the car park for a quick getaway from normal life…

The car roars faster with the pedal to the floor.

"This isn't real," Neville declares.

"**Isn't it?!**" Deville winds down the window and sticks his head out. "**Just *feel* that breeze *rushing* through your hair!**"

The gust all but knocks *Neville's* head off his shoulders, like some kind of voodoo. The chill scrapes at his scalp. A bracing gulp of air fills his lungs.

I'm not really in the back seat – this isn't real. How is this happening?!

Deville pulls his head back into the car, leaving both he – and Neville – much less assaulted by the air.

"**Now, knowing me… well, knowing *you*… Aha… Ha!**" he laughs, as he turns and drives onto the dual carriageway, "**You're probably wondering how this could be happening… but it's simple!**"

The car slows just slightly.

"**It would appear that Neville Pike *is* of two minds…**" he bellows, "**and *mine* just so happens to be *stronger!***"

The car speeds up again. Neville's heart races, but Deville's exhilaration is winning against the fear.

"Yours *has* to be," Neville shouts, "for you to drive like a fucking *idiot!*"

"***What?!***"

The car turns onto a road going back into town.

"**I'm sorry, I can't hear myself think!**" Deville winds Neville up with the window and looks over his shoulder. "**What were you saying?**"

A queue for the red traffic light gets closer and closer.

"Eyes on the road!"

"But they *are*..."

Neville stamps on the brake pedal, and tyres screech. The car recoils... stopping short of hitting the car in front. It throws him back into the driver's seat.

Neville strokes the steering wheel, checking his grip on reality. He suppresses his relief, as he glances at the rear-view mirror. The back seat is empty. With his eyes on the rear, he puts the interior light off... and the silhouette snaps into view again.

Neville faces the road, in a desperate effort to leave *him* behind.

Focus on the drive back. Just get back home, albeit shithole home...

Green light, and the cars ahead roll onward.

As Neville follows cautiously, he glances up at the rear-view mirror for any cars behind.

None. Just open road, and no silhouette, either.

Facing ahead again, everything else is as it should be. Neville focuses wholly on driving the car and being the only one at the wheel.

Don't let your mind wander. Not again...

CHAPTER 34

Silhouetted trees carve out the valley between fields of silver.

The lonely slam of a car door barks into the starlit night.

How could I forget? How would I go home, after everything, with this…?

Neville marches away from the headlights and around to the back of the VW, oblivious of whether or not his shoes sink into the mud.

Tonight's as good as any to dispose of him. Happy fucking Halloween…

But hard is the ground he walks on, dense, like thick chocolate icing on a rich dark cake.

That deep pond should still be here. It wasn't that long ago Kat and I once pulled over to 'frolic'.

Reaching for the boot, Neville rests his shaking fingers under the handle.

It's okay… He'll decompose faster in the murky water. There shouldn't be enough left of him…

He puffs himself up with deep breaths, as if it will help, and pulls open the boot to look upon Nick lying curled-up, foetal, to be delivered into oblivion… but…

"What?!"

Shock dawns on Neville's face with the interior light, and the empty compartment staring back at him.

"Where is he?" Neville snatches himself away and shouts into the tree-laden dark. "Where, the fuck, *is* he?!"

His voice is swallowed by the sea of shade.

A speeding car on the nearby road draws close, rushing past like a behemoth insect storming a racing circuit. From the vehicle's open window, a slipstream of laughter blows over to Neville, as if in mocking response…

Turning back towards the car, Neville reaches up for the boot and drags it down, shut. He marches up to the driver's side and crouches before the wing mirror. "Was this *you*?"

The overshadowed lines of his own reflection barely move.

Neville stands with the instinctive fear of invoking *His* 'presence'. Looking into the blissfully quiet country, he whispers… "What did he *do* with him?"

Neville looks over his shoulder to confirm there is no-one behind, emerging from the woods, and grabs at the driver's side door. He rips it open, slips into the car and onto the seat. "But *when* did he do it?"

He pulls the door shut and rests his hands on the steering wheel to get a grip. "He must have when I… When I blacked out. When I *passed* out!"

I'm still not even safe to sleep!

Neville looks up into the rear-view reflection of his wide screaming eyes. "How did you deal with the body so quickly? I still made it to Gemma's play… But you were still trying to persuade me afterwards to deal with the body…"

There is no silhouette sitting on the back seat. Just the rear window, and a landscape of pine trees that pierce the night sky, holding aloft the stars.

"So, who the fuck got rid of him?!"

Afraid to relinquish breath to the chilling air, Neville watches where the headlights project their beams against sentinel tree trunks, and into the dark between others.

He pinches at the fob of a hopeful reality and turns the key in the ignition. "Maybe it's all in my head. Yes, that's it! It's a nightmare, like that... that *thing* chasing after me."

Like a child relieved to finally get going, the VW starts cheerfully.

Pulling his seatbelt on, Neville prepares to back out. With an elbow resting over the seat, he looks out of the rear window and reverses. With the release of the handbrake, the car jolts back... and something scuttles somewhere inside.

Neville slows the car's descent.

He hears the rumble again.

But it's nothing I've *left in here...*

He studies the back seat and the footwells, and then unclips his belt and feels under the passenger seat, when his fingers strike solid rubber.

Neville flinches. He reaches under the seat, grabs at leather... and pulls out a pair of shoes. Pointed, annoying, white shoes. *Nick White's* pointed, annoying, white shoes.

They slip from Neville's fingers, hitting the floor in a macabre dance...

Nick has to be dead. These are proof. Evidence!

"There goes the *lovely idea* that this isn't real..."

Words do not pour into his ear from the smug voice, but his own common sense speaks up where his wicked conscience does not.

This is a warning. He left these for me to find. He's still around...

Not absent. Just silent. Neville's own words do not echo off the walls in his mind as they should. They stick to a whirling dark column of fog, behind his eyes.

Whenever I acknowledge it, I'm feeding *it.*

The fog *twitches.* Neville's own Jiminy *Crooked* has dissolved in favour of another form, tumorously creeping over his mind like rot in a derelict house.

"What do I do?"

I need to stop this… before someone else is killed. Before I totally lose it!

He gazes into the spear-tipped, blackening landscape… and then reaches by his shoulder for the seatbelt, pulling it down over his chest. "Safety first…"

Neville puts the car in reverse once more to back out of the valley, until he can turn himself around.

Nick's shoes jive with excitement, if not the uneven terrain…

Who could've known about the mask? Who'd know what I'm going through?

Braking, Neville's foot sinks onto the pedal, the car recoils, and Nick's smug shoes roll into obscurity, upside down under the shade of the passenger seat.

Halfway down an incline at forty-five degrees, in the dark, hope glimmers before Neville. "*Mosely…*"

He said to stay away from the mask. And I wish I did!

The white, stark reverse lights glare on a lonely path heading down towards the stony horizon. The hill, thicker with stones, dry mud, and grit, is lined with trees and their shadows cast behind. And the shadows of shadows beyond…

Mosely! He's supposed to be back now. Where the hell's the old fool been?!

Neville parks the deep-purring VW and stirs in his seat to

reach for his pocket. His prying fingers claw out his mobile phone. It lights up with his urge to call, but he freezes before the clock. "Fucking midnight?!"

A phone in the hand is worth a collapse into his lap. There is no-one to call or consult, or to comfort him.

At least Halloween's done… But how do I reach him, other than via Tracy?

As Neville gives in and holds up his mobile again, it awakens with his wisdom. He brings up the keys and types… "'*Did Mr Mosely make it back to this country alright?*' There… that'll get the ball rolling for tomorrow."

He puts the phone to sleep and slides it back into his pocket. With the car poised to reverse further downhill, he releases the handbrake, when the device buzzes against his thigh.

"Fuck, *she's* up late!" Neville pulls up the handbrake and struggles the phone out of his pocket again… Light, and Tracy's words.

"'He's coming in tomorrow. You can catch up with him then.' No kisses, emojis, or signoffs… Don't strain yourself, dear!" He types back, "*Great. Cheers!*"

As Neville pockets the phone again, and goes downhill once more, the dead man's shoes jitter under the passenger seat.

CHAPTER 35

A distant door opens with footsteps beating lightly into the foyer.

His *common sense* is tingling. Neville lurks around the corner, catching a glimpse of... *this stranger, who knew my grandad... Couldn't get much stranger than that!*

Tracy's voice rings fondly off the walls of the museum, but agitation rings through. "Mr Mosely, it's nice to see you again!"

Do I wait in the office? Or do I come out to meet him now?

Neville peers around, watching Tracy get up from the desk to hug an old chap wearing a tweed suit, and matching hat, and a red bow tie.

He's at least thirty years older... Not that I'd put it past you though, dear!

"And you too, Tracy, my dear," his accent is round, well-spoken. "I'm sorry to have missed you at Maxwell's funeral."

What is it with this family and names?

They release from the hug.

"Actually, I couldn't make it." she says. "I had a family emergency..."

"Oh, that's a shame. Still, I'm sure it was... *well-attended.*"

He definitely knew Grandad…

Neville retreats back around the corner as Tracy gestures toward the office.

"His grandson, Neville, can tell you how the service went."

"So, the prodigal grandson seized the reins…"

"*Reigns* he does," Tracy retorts.

Cheeky bitch.

"Is he not doing a good job, then?"

"He's determined, I'll give him that. But then, Mr Pike *senior* set the bar pretty low."

It's not the same when someone else badmouths him…

Neville steps out of the shadows to enter the fray at last.

"And how is the… *operation*?" Mosely enquires.

No! Why'd I step around the corner at this *point?*

Mosely detects movement… "Ah, Maxwell's successor! It is good to finally meet you, Neville! In the *flesh*…"

He extends a hand.

Neville meets it, sheepishly. "You too, Mr Mosely."

"Do call me 'George.' *Both* of you. I believe I'm now the only elder left in contact with this fine establishment."

"How long *have* you been working with the museum?" Neville pries.

"Since the beginning… thirty-eight years ago."

"Really? With Grandad, all that time?"

"Yes, all that time. The museum started out as a warehouse for collectables in transit, but then Maxwell had the genius idea of opening it to the public to make more money on the side."

Tracy smiles and nods patiently.

Of course, she knows.

"How have you been coping with running the business here, Neville?" Mosely gestures. "Perhaps you two…?"

Tracy and Neville steal a quick look at each other. They share shock, while hiding distaste for considering the possibility.

I'm already competing *with her…*

"I'm sure Tracy has better taste," says Neville, "I'm actually still trying to set things straight with my wife. Maybe soon-to-be *ex*-wife – we haven't got there, yet… But business here's been steady. Tracy's been very patient with me. And all that's been going on since the break-in-slash-killing has put us in the public eye."

"Naturally! You could've paid off the police to leave the bodies where they were, for some kind of display," Mosely chuckles.

"Wouldn't have much luck," says Neville, "with the detectives on *this* case."

"The authorities are so uptight and politically correct these days – when it suits them! You can't get away with a rogue donation here and there, now… It's for the best, though," Mosely nods enthusiastically.

Neville glances at Tracy, finding her eyes have shifted towards the clock above the entrance.

"Look at that," she says, "it's already lunchtime."

"So it is!" says Mosely.

Neville catches his attention. "Where shall we continue this, um, George?"

"Why not over yonder tavern, good sir?" Mosely cheers.

Oh, great, you're one of those, are you?

"I'll put up the 'closed for lunch' sign," says Tracy, "give me a second…"

No! I can't ask about the mask while she's *there!*

As Tracy reaches under the counter for a laminated card with string knotted through it, Neville strops for the door ahead of them, relaxing his poker face.

I'll have to bide my time. Get my answers from him when she's out of it…

***

The three sit in Neville's 'favourite' pub, the *only* pub on this street.

Has some massacre already happened before I got here?

Practically deserted in the middle of the day, the pub looks considerably more anaemic, in the cold hard air of sobriety…

A long and tedious wait for their orders does not sit well, after a long and tedious walk to get to the pub. Neville would feel less claustrophobic at this corner table if he had already unleashed his inner Deville.

The day is young… If the old boy carries on talking like this, he might well peg out before the food arrives. I won't get my answers, and I'll be on my own!

"Now, Neville," says Mosely at last, "How *was* the service for Maxwell?"

"Well," says Neville, "it was a reasonable turnout. Pasty in one hand, beer in the other and everyone was satisfied. The family was tolerable… but there's nothing *there* for me now. I'm not entirely convinced there was anything there for Grandad. And it was a pity the pallbearers didn't carry him in as you'd expect. They could only *bear* to pull him in on a trolley. It wasn't tasteful at all…"

"Just nipping to the loo…" Tracy gets up and slips away towards the ladies'.

Now's my chance.

"I could hardly blame them!" Mosely laughs, "Maxwell was as fat as a fool last time I saw him! Bloody troll. I miss him dearly… it's not the same without him."

"*George*, I was hoping you might be able to fill me in a bit on what Grandad was up to before he died."

"Yes, I expect so." The chair creaks as Mosely sits back, less misty-eyed, still curiously jovial. "You certainly took up the reins quick enough, my boy. Surely you must've found you'd jumped in the deep end!"

"Yes. That's *exactly* it."

"Well, he would've been up to much the same, as always. Selling on the side, bleeding anyone dry who had the slightest interest in the most worthless trinkets! He could really turn on the charm, you know. And he had his *other* imports, of course."

Neville sits forward, with curiosity resting his elbows on the table. "'Other imports,' you say?"

"Yes, exotic medicines, herbs, minerals, and what have you."

"Only, the gentleman I was in contact with… *Mr White*…"

Mosely's mouth shuts. His eyes rest on Neville.

"…has gone missing."

"Ah…" Mosely muses, "how unfortunate. A lot of things can happen in *that* line of work."

"So, you *do* know about this side business."

"My boy, you haven't been running it as a side business all this time, have you? It's all the same business. That's what makes it a good side business."

Neville sits up straight with a hand on the table.

"I can't believe it," he mutters.

I've let a whole world slip through my fingers.

A door bangs as Tracy exits the ladies.

Fuck! I haven't even got round to asking about the mask!

283

"Well?" Mosely pushes, "what has dear Tracy had to say about it?"

"What do I have to say about what?" she pulls out her chair with an uncertain smile.

"The 'other' imports," says Mosely.

She freezes. "What do you mean?"

Neville turns to her, dumbfounded. "Wait, Tracy is in on this, too?"

Her balled-up hand smacks the chair. "For fuck's sake, George!"

"*Language*, my dear!"

Tracy throws her arms off the chair.

"That's the *least* of our problems!" Her fists clench before her eyes. "What about your insistent blabbing, to the heir apparent, about 'delicate' trade *secrets*?!"

"What do you mean 'heir apparent?'" Neville stands, "This museum was Pike-inspired, it's in my fucking name!"

"So, it's *yours*, all *yours*, is it, *Mr Pike*?!" She squares up to him, with knuckles tight at her sides.

A crash at the table shocks them. Tracy and Neville – now silent – turn to Mosely. His fist-turned-gavel rests on the table where the impact had rung out. The light behind his eyes, engulfed by the rings around them, darken as he stares.

"Sit the fuck down," commands Mosely. Even his voice is darker. A callous tone familiar to Neville…

Silence.

Neville and Tracy place themselves back into their chairs, not taking their eyes off Mosely, who sits unflinchingly folding his arms. All are still, as the cropped-hair server in jeans and a shirt arrives, miraculously carrying three plates at once. He places the all-day brunch in front of Neville, the panini with garnish for Tracy, and the curry before Mosely.

"Thank you," says Tracy.

"Thanks," says Neville.

Mosely's gaze remains fixed on both of them.

"Is there anything else I can get you?" the server asks, innocently.

"No," says Mosely. "Thank you. That will be all."

"Okay guys… Enjoy your meals." The server minces away.

"Eat," says Mosely.

Neville sneaks a look at Tracy, gingerly retrieving her cutlery. He follows suit. Mosely, unmoved by the presence of food, watches them put knife and fork to plate. He breaks the silence with the breaking of 'bread.' *Bones,* to be decided…

"Now that we are, *finally,* all caught up, perhaps we can continue discussing the business arrangements from now on, like *civilised* associates."

Neville clutches his cutlery in each hand, like a spoilt child waiting to say grace, "What the hell's going on here?"

"You, *Mr Pike*, bit off more than you could chew," Mosely states, "by trying to reinvent the wheel…"

Neville grips the cutlery, forgetting food. "Why was I not told any of this?"

"Following the untimely demise of your grandfather, business was supposed to carry on as usual, until my return from inspecting our Indian branch-"

"We have an *Indian* branch?"

Mosely glares at Neville's plate, then at Neville. Timidly, Neville tucks in.

I need to know everything. These resources must be

tapped!

"Bigger than you ever expected, isn't it? Whether it is indeed *yours* as well, remains to be seen, but imagine our surprise when we found the home branch was taken over by *you.* And, how the rest of the income resumed once you struck your petty bargain with Mr White – it was business as usual. Not that *I* knew about it…"

Knife-in-hand, he reaches towards Neville who pulls away his fork hand.

Come on, don't be sick…

Mosely spares a thumb and two fingers to retrieve two of Neville's chips.

"I thought you were a chip off the old block…" Mosely mocks, unblinking. "Meanwhile, Tracy *failed* to let me know that you were not, in fact, in the loop. That there was a break-in. Some *murders…* And that the *police* were sniffing around."

I'm not shaking. It's a wonder I'm not shaking!

Tracy opens her mouth to interrupt, but Mosely's voice denies her.

"I presume she thought she would keep you in check, or that she could steal the position right out from under you." As Mosely turns to her, a chill lessens before Neville. "Not that this company tolerates such underhanded behaviour…"

Tracy sits perfectly still. 'Showing no fear' somehow shows fear.

"In all fairness," Mosely shares his gaze with Neville again, "telling you everything before you imposed yourself would not have been feasible. Alas, you were not supposed to 'take over' the museum just like that, if at all…"

"Why not?" says Neville, mid-sausage.

"Do not talk with your mouth full," Mosely orders. "You were so well-ensconced in ordinary civilian life and your grandfather did not wish to tear you away from that."

But I wanted something more all along!

"*Ordinary civilian life*," Neville swallows… "Did 'Maxwell's' death have anything to do with this *line of work*?"

Tracy looks at Mosely, perhaps just as curious, then back at Neville.

"Well?"

"Strangely, he died not long after you separated from your wife."

"Really…" Neville's plate shrieks under the knife. "Are you saying he actually cared? And he died because of me?"

"Hardly. It's not necessarily about *you*. It is a *stressful* job, after all." Mosely finally picks up his knife and fork.

I can't believe any of this. What the fuck did I walk into?

"I see you've nearly finished, Tracy," says Mosely. "Just as well. Can't leave the front desk un-*womaned* now, can we?"

She stands, gulping down the last of her panini. "Of course, Mr Mosely, I-"

"*Please*," he says, stone-faced, "you get to call me *George*, from now on. Lunch is on Neville…"

Neville rolls his eyes…

"Th- thank you. George." Just short of petrified, she turns, pushes in her chair, and restrains herself from *running* for the door…

Mosely is unfazed, grazing on his curry as harmlessly as the other *cattle*. Neville fails to contain a slight sigh.

"You know," says Mosely, "that woman has been doing your job since she was in her teens."

"Impressive," says Neville.

"I made her to be."

"I… hope to live up to her standard."

"You will *surpass* it." Mosely rests his knife and fork at the edge of his plate.

What's he going to do, now?

"Your grandfather and I have not dedicated our lives to this business to be succeeded by workshy adults who cannot think for themselves. You showed promise following in Maxwell's footsteps, without instruction. You reek of ambition. Fulfilling it is wonderful. However, it is essential that you hide your scent."

"You sound like someone I know."

"Is this someone successful?"

"He will be," Neville then mutters, "…if I'm not careful."

"Our rivals," Mosely picks up his cutlery and elegantly manipulates the contents of his plate, "our *enemies*, often provide the best advice. It's one reason to 'keep your enemies closer…' Your bacon and egg are getting cold."

Closer than you would believe! It's a good job no-one else is here.

Neville cuts up a slice of bacon, and then the luminous egg…

I might not get another chance to ask about the mask.

…spearing one onto the other.

"Mr Mosely-"

His eyes snap up to Neville's.

"*George*," Neville corrects, "I wanted to ask you about this mask-"

"The one on the display? Yes, you seemed curiously interested in that piece. You may have noticed it is not all junk at the museum."

"I have… Up close and personally."

"Mmm?"

"Are the masks known to have any real significance? Any real effect?"

Neville rewards himself for finally asking with another couple of chips.

"Of course they are," says Mosely, "Masks have had cultural influence all over the world. There is a psychological experiment on how masks can grant us anonymity, distance from our own selves, allowing us to disengage from our inhibitions… To act without guilt or responsibility for what we do."

"Nothing about real magic, then?"

Mosely dabs his mouth with a serviette. "I never said *that*."

"So," Neville pushes, "if I were to put on one of *those* masks, it really would… change me?"

"The way this Devil mask has already changed *you*?"

Chips at the end of Neville's fork stop short of his gaping mouth.

"You may as well speak plain, Neville. We are sometimes required to authenticate exhibit pieces, and sometimes there is a lot of truth to them."

Neville lowers his fork, surrendering the pretence, submitting to relief.

But this cursed crap really does have influence?

"Tell me," Mosely enquires, "the mask must've influenced you to act as boldly as you have… particularly in running the museum… How did it manifest?"

Finally, I can talk to someone about this! I'm not alone!

"It's always been a *voice*," says Neville, "Like, your reading voice in your head, or hearing your common-sense, but this is sort of… independent. *Ruthless.*"

"'Was?' You don't have it anymore?"

"Well, we're not speaking at the moment. It's been trying to take over."

"This 'Devil mask', as you so tactfully put it, was lumped in with the Masked Performance collection as a Japanese Oni mask, but it is not even Japanese… It is in fact more closely related to Sri Lankan *medicine* masks, and is thought to help expel excessive negative energy, 'bringing the bad out of you,' as it were."

"I think I should've had a bigger mask…"

"Just like your grandfather, the self-pitying fool…"

Neville recoils with offence taken.

Being so much like Grandad is scary enough.

"*I* had…a different *face* for a time," says Mosely. "Things were changing around me. Going better, and then… going bad."

Neville's brow collapses as… *Mosely lived the same impulsive changes?*

"How long ago was this, exactly?"

"I've been a *wily* 'silver fox' for many years, I'll have you know."

The server emerges from their periphery and collects the plates.

Saved by dinner bell…

"Thank you," Neville faces Mosely as the clearer moves away, "Alright… But what did you do about these 'changes'?"

"Nothing."

"What?"

"I sated all of my appetites. Did all I wanted to do. And never looked back."

Who else do I have to kill before it stops and I'm free?

Mosely goes on, "Not that the wearer would have to *kill* anyone."

Neville stalls.

But you said some of these items are… 'real'!

Mosely is on a roll… "One who resorts immediately to murder would have to be incredibly bitter, and repressed, for the mask to manifest in such a way."

"But, once enough has been… *sated*… of the mask's urges, the wearer comes out the better for it?"

"More or less," Mosely shrugs. "I am no longer the babbling fool the world perceived me to be. My being an incessant talker was perhaps a symptom of frustration, or it is, still, because I have nothing to hide."

"You took back control when you were ready…"

"Oh, I was already in control. It is about exploring the self, realising one's potential. Whatever you do is whatever you wanted to do in the first place."

But I don't want to kill whoever is in my way. I just want my life back. I want my family.

"You're not in any other kind of trouble, are you, Neville?"

"No… Nothing I can't handle."

"Because if you are… you're on your own."

Thanks…

"We can't keep drawing attention towards the business now, can we?" Mosely stands up stiffly. "Now, this has been a most stimulating chat, but I must be off. The museum is in *capable* hands, after all."

Mosely circles behind his chair and pushes it in. He glares at Neville, "If anything changes, I am *sure* you or Tracy will let me know."

"Yes, for sure, Mr- *George...* Thank you."

"No, thank *you. You* are paying for this." He strolls right past Neville. "I will be in touch."

Mosely rips open the door and strides out, leaving it shy to close.

"Wow," Neville gulps.

I'm fucked.

CHAPTER 36

Glaring red eyes spur Neville to snatch his foot from the accelerator… before he can hit the rear of the van in front.

I love them… I've got to tell them I love them while I still can.

He stomps on the brakes and glances up at the rear-view mirror, as one car, *two*, approach behind. He faces ahead, hissing a sigh of relief into the windscreen. He has not hit the van.

And there is still only *him* inside the car…

Green light. Neville's VW rolls along in a string of vehicles, as long-legged adolescents in school uniforms gangle by on the pavement. Stocky stragglers stare at phones-in-hand or laugh with each other over nothing.

Spoilt little sods don't even know how good they have it…

He takes the turn towards his true home.

I've parked up before anyone else. See? These other idiots are bound by their respectable routines in their insipid little lives, but not me! I had to get away to see you both. I couldn't just finish a whole day at work. I love my family and I'm not afraid to show it. And I am done with that grotty bachelor's flat. It's finally time to come home…

Onto the drive, Neville turns off the engine. He snatches up the plastic-wrapped flowers lying in the passenger seat and gets out of the car. The door falls obediently shut.

I've been Kat's 'Knight of Sorrowful Countenance' for so long.

Neville crunches across the gravel to get, *finally*, to the front door.

She can't turn me down now. Not now that I'm certain.

Disregarding the bell, he hammers on the door.

If only she knew what I've been through!

Quiet. Again, he hammers at the door.

Knock, knock. Who's there?

No answer.

No-one. No-one's *there…*

"Come on, Kat," he mutters, "your car's here, dammit…"

Neville turns away, with rustling bouquet in hand.

Should've called first. I'll leave these on the doorstep, dammit…

He stoops to prop the flowers up against the door. Top-heavy, they flop onto the mat. Neville snatches at them and presses them against the door until they obey.

They wouldn't dare fall over now.

He stands, retreats, and glances back over his shoulder, but amazingly Neville does not turn to salt…

The flowers settle.

He turns back and steps into the car, still eyeing them to stay up.

The love of my life is not answering the door. Assuming she's there to answer it, and not off with some other man. Why would she do that – now – when I can finally come back to her?

As Neville's door shuts, he exhales at the house through the windscreen.

I left work early. I can't afford to piss off the real boss… of the drug business *he and Grandad had been running all these years! The police, bleddy sharks, keep circling around me for the murders and beatings… A mad woman knows about this and could have me by the balls… My best friend is still in intensive care and hates my guts… And I don't know what's going to happen to my daughter… Other than that, my life's not so bad! But then, there's something in me that wants to kill everyone and take over the whole fucking world – what's wrong with wanting to have your cake and… fuck it!*

All being still, Neville starts the car and backs out. Backs off… Recoiling with the car's brakes, he claws at the steering wheel.

Got to get the hell out of the Suburbian Republic before I'm abducted by Stepford W.A.G.S. Or worse…

Tyres screech as Neville's foot is down. The main road itself expands as if to swallow him…

The curtain falls behind in Kat's bedroom window, where her hand has been holding it up.

She turns away, facing the opposite wall, pressing her fist over her chest as Neville's car scrambles away.

***

His hands and feet move independently, as the car practically drives itself…

…anywhere but back to the museum.

Neville's *steed* knows *exactly* where to take him.

I can't go back there. Mosley's the least of my problems anyway. Fuck, Tracy can have the museum… for now.

The wheel steers Neville off the main road.

I'm getting ahead of myself. I can still have everything. But what do I do? What do I do right now?

Cobblestones line the pavements, where he turns again. He flinches, as the phantom grip squeezes his innards… he could pop…

Tabitha's flat is on this block. I meant 'what' to do, not 'who' to do.

The nervous grip slithers down, over his loins, tightening…

No. I can do something right today. Perhaps I can dip a toe in the water. See where she stands… and where we go from there…

A mind teetering between chaos and clarity manoeuvres the VW neatly and efficiently between two other cars.

I'm usually awful at doing these!

His hand slips off of the wheel and turns the engine off. Deep breath.

Time to pull the sword from the stone and be crowned 'King of Camelford.'

Clutching the key between his fingers, the Once and Future King draws his trusty blade and gets out of the car.

I may need to open the boot to air it out… At least I don't have to worry about 'dropping off' Nick somewhere in broad daylight.

"Urgh."

I wish I could tell her now, that I'm going back to my wife. I can't dare jinx it.

His guts sink as Neville wanders toward the flats, in the hope of retrieving his balls from the dragon.

Tabitha was right there when… Luke was killed. I've spent too much time with her since. What the hell can I do?

He turns a corner and ambles up the road... The world turns faster as its lifeblood whooshes past. Wheels carry multiple colours through asphalt veins. Traffic stops and starts with each steady pulse. A beat for every step towards yet another forbidding door...

I hope she'll keep quiet about what I did. But at what cost?

Through the front entrance at last. Nicotine and damp wrestle for dominance over the magnolia fortress. Familiar odours exchange blows. In the crossfire, Neville takes a hit to the nose.

Did I buzz? Did I even have to? I don't remember...

The world unfolds before him like a dream, beckoning Neville's feet to carry him across sinking carpet, while the buckling floor threatens to swallow him whole.

She might be in. She might not. I'll surprise her in person, that's for sure.

Thighs and knees burn as his stride takes bites out of the stairs. He rises from Hell into Purgatory... but the climb to Heaven could end in a fall...

Do I knock? I should've called first. And maybe saved the trip... but I've come this far...

He claps a hand around the knob and twists. Tighter than ever, the phantom hand squeezes Neville's loins...

I should be used to that by now...

An anxious smile permeates the dark cloud cover. A glimmer of Neville's old self as he pushes... Unlatched, the door opens.

"Hello? Tabitha?" Neville treads carefully into silence; a new silence, like debris settling after a bomb. He scans the room for Tabitha, *sensing* something.

An unpleasance I've not felt since...

In the still and colourful flat, Tabitha stands from the armchair in the corner, lighting up to see... "Nev?"

Opposite her, a man sitting on the sofa looks over his shoulder

What. The fuck. Is he *doing here?*

A most reptilian Detective Sergeant Tout curls his lips. "Fancy seeing you here, Mr Pike."

He stands to face with Neville, who inhales, puffer-fishing himself up.

"Same to you, Sergeant."

"So…" Tabitha interrupts, "do you two know each other?"

"Yes," states Neville, "Everything okay? Is someone in trouble?"

"No more than usual," Tout retorts. "While you're here, Mr Pike… Can you confirm your whereabouts on the first Friday night of last month?"

"I was… probably at the pub, stressed over my work."

"And with your friend 'Tabitha'?" Tout nods to her.

Neville's brow furrows, as if in attempt to grab hold of Tout's thoughts. "That particular Friday? Yes, I would've been there *every* Friday night last month."

"In that case, Mr Pike, you might remember a man who attacked your *friend* Tabitha. Apparently, another man, matching your description, stepped in and chased him into the nearest alley." Tout paces towards the door, between Neville and the way out… "The body of one of those men – the one not matching your description – was discovered the next day. His features were so badly disfigured from the beating that he couldn't be identified immediately."

"What an awful way to go…" Neville stands his ground, with eyes on Tabitha. Butter is slow to melt in her mouth. Her cat-like eyes follow the *Trout*.

What really brought you here, you ugly prick? Was it her*?*

"We finally had a witness come forward," says Tout, "putting both of you at the scene. And if *you* were there, as the last person to see Tabitha's *ex*, I shall have to take you in for questioning."

Tout's head jerks forward – a blow to the back of it brings him to his knees, and onto his front, like a marionette with its strings cut. The plant pot, surprisingly intact, droops at one with Tabitha's arms. The wonder blooms in her face…

…but shock shoots across Neville's… It diminishes, darkens, but for the baring of teeth. "What, the fuck, have you done?"

Tabitha meets his gaze, with her falling jaw, "I… I was trying to save us."

"He has a partner. She'll be close behind."

"He was going to arrest us!"

"Great, now there's *another* body to deal with!"

The groans of the undead reach their ears…

Shrieking, Tabitha drops the pot with a thud. It smashes into several pieces, soiling the carpet.

Neville whips round to see Tout, very much alive as he pushes against the floor to get, groggily, onto his feet. "Another body?"

As if this assault alone wouldn't draw enough attention …

Tabitha charges at Tout, but Neville rotates and catches her by the wrists. She struggles, clawing for the detective, but Tabitha's reach yet exceeds her grasp… Neville pushes her back, "Will you stop, you mad bitch?!"

Tabitha staggers to a halt, teary-eyed, "What did you just call me?"

Tout seems awfully quiet…

Neville glances over his shoulder at the detective, who winces with his hand at the back of his head. Tout's spare hand pats at his pocket.

He's looking for his phone… or his cuffs! Fuck!

A tatty smartphone buzzes, vibrating the floor before Neville…

Before Tout, who takes a drunken step towards the phone.

Neville lurches…

"Here, let me…" His helping foot kicks the phone across the floor and under the sofa. "Shit, I'm so sorry!"

"What are you doing, you bloody idiot?" Tout rages, "I'll have you for *obstruction* as well!"

'As well?' He's already got more than enough to charge me! What do I do?

Tabitha, suddenly behind the settee, creeps around for the phone…

Something stirs within Neville, "Don't *you* fucking move, either!"

A serpent uncoils from around his heart, unwrapping the powerful urge to inject long-dormant venom into his words.

Tabitha has stopped in her tracks, more hurt than scared.

What to do indeed…

"No, not *you!* Not *now…*"

Tout and Tabitha's eyes pan towards him.

I'm surprised you haven't killed these two. Make it look like an accident! Or that they killed each other…

"I'm not doing that. I'm better now. There's still a civilised way out of this."

"Nev? You okay?" Tabitha's concern divides between these two, indeed 'three', strange men.

Have you heard yourself, lately?! Think of the consequences. Do you dispose of these little people, cover yourself, and return to your little life? Or give the sergeant back his phone, knowing he will arrest you, and her... knowing she will sing like a chicken for the chop. And you'd be next. Decisions, decisions...

The Leaning Tower of Neville sways gently before them, with fists hanging at his sides.

"Pike?" Tout urges, "What the hell's the matter with you?"

They're waiting.

Neville stands, with sweat tickling every itch. He trembles, as tectonic plates shift at his very core.

Take too long and the decision will be made for you...

Tout glares at Tabitha, "Pike's gonna fuck you over. Look at him!"

"Spouting your poison are you, old man?!" She shouts.

"It's not like I can come back to normal life," Neville muses aloud, "with people moving on... moving forward without *me... forgetting* about *me...* I can't have them lock me up... taking my *freedom!* No, *I'll* have the last laugh. *I'll* take back control..."

Yes, you will...

"Nev?"

"Pike, what are you doing?"

"I'm not a bad seed," Neville continues, "but I am made of the same stuff..."

What's happening to me? What's gonna happen to Gemma? I don't have to worry about Kat, she can take care of herself. Always has. She landed on her feet alright, didn't she? In the end?

Deville stretches, creaking, clicking his body. His bellowing yawn is more the roar of a beast. **"This got boring a long time**

301

ago. Let's clear the board…"

"Pike," Tout growls, "whatever you're thinking of doing… *don't.*"

I'm gonna gut you. If you threaten me and my family, you'll be extinguished.

Yet these words do not leave Neville's mouth. Nor a primal scream…

"We've come *this* far…" Standing eerily right before Tout, Deville's actions speak louder… a punch, into the older man's gut, winds the tenacious sergeant.

Tabitha's hands clap together as she cries out, *overjoyed…*

He places hands on Tout's shoulders, and knees him in the chest. Soft tissue at Tout's core yields every successive blow to his buckling ribs. With a deep gasp, Tout flies onto his back. Lying still, his eyes brim with water, and his mouth is now a bowlful of blood.

Arms wrap around Deville. Tabitha constricts him with a hug from behind. Her bosoms press against his back, and her hair is smooth against the nape of his neck. Deville stands while Tabitha squeezes the love out of him. She releases the hold, with her arms melting to her sides. He turns away from the latest broken body to face her.

"You chose *me…*" she dreams. Her radiant glow, against Neville's bitter husk, casts the shadow of Deville, as he brings a palm to her soft cheek.

A smile warms his lips. **"No more ties."**

He slams her head into the wall, knocking a scream out of her. Tabitha's cranium meets the wall again, leaving a red impression. One more collision exposes the bone of the building. The noise stops. Fragments of Tabitha's skull protrude like thorns… no longer *in his side.*

Deville loosens his grip.

Tabitha collapses onto the floor.

What have I done? This has gone too far… How do I come back from this?!

"Oh, *enough* with your *inhibitions* and your *principles*… *and* your mundane, mediocre existence! You had your chance… Now it's *my* time to shine. I'm going to devour you… *and* your pathetic life."

He approaches the door. Sliding his sleeve over his wrist, he pulls the handle, and leaves no trace. On the other side, he pulls out a spare tissue and polishes the knob… Satisfied, he strolls to the stairs and descends.

The Deville strides out.

CHAPTER 37

Like a knife sliding under skin…

…the silver Ford parallel parks immaculately between two vehicles, one of which in front, is Detective Sergeant Mickey Tout's.

"You've been dragging your heels ever since that bloody museum, Mickey," Detective Inspector Lake muses, "Why the hell did you have to go on ahead *now*?"

She turns the engine off and gets out of the car. In one fell slam of the door, she approaches the driver's side of Tout's vehicle and knocks on the window before seeing… as if by a magic trick, the seat is empty. The man is nowhere to be seen.

Christina rolls her eyes. She fishes her phone out of her pocket, dials, and waits until… an answer.

"Hi, I need to know which flat DS Tout went to visit? He's not picking up, and his car's outside… Okay. Don't rush on *my* account… Great… Thank you." She hangs up and pockets the phone. "Twats."

Christina marches up to the flats, studying the disquietly quiet urban landscape. She mutters to herself. "It's been *so long* since the last victim… that we *know* of."

At the front entrance Christina pushes the buzzer and waits for the door.

"Well, *you're* still here, Mickey, so this woman *must* be in." She pokes at the buzzer again.

Stepping back, she looks up at the complex. "I'm not waiting any longer."

Supposedly ready for what is behind the door, Christina pushes each of the buttons. The panel growls rhythmically, as disagreeable as an unsuccessful turn at the children's game of *Operation*.

After a fateful, *weightful* click, Christina pushes the door open, stepping into a domestic tomb. The battle between dust, must, and nicotine rages on under her nose. Observing the doorframes before the stairs, she sees slight yellow scars where sugar soap lost the war long ago.

"How I *love* these aromas…" she grimaces.

The door slams behind her, she glares back at it.

Christina soldiers on. Her sturdy legs push her up, and ever forward…

Finally at the first floor, she finds the door for the address and drums her knuckles against it.

Nothing from the other side.

"Hello? Police, this is DI Lake." She knocks again and waits for an answer.

A raspy voice claws at her ear. "Curse…"

Christina's brow sinks under her curiosity.

The voice scratches at the door. *"Curse…"*

She knocks again and leans in to listen.

"Chris… *Chris…!"*

"Mickey!" Christina grabs the handle for a twist. It does not give.

She steps back, brings a knee to her chest, and launches a suit-trousered kick, but the door is solid. Christina kicks again. It resists. She charges with her shoulder, and braces against the impact.

Christina throws herself at the door once more. Her shoulder gives out from the pain. Frustration bares its teeth... and growls...

"Chris..." Tout moans.

Christina steps back. Savage breaths inflate her. She steadies herself, lifts her foot, and fires another kick at the door. Under the impact, the wood squirms.

Christina's partner's life is on the line. Like a coiled spring, she releases a kick, and her foot collides with the door... which flies open on a wing of splinters.

She stumbles in with a heavy shoulder. In the middle of the variably coloured décor, Mickey is down on the floor.

"Mickey!" she lunges into a kneel beside him, "I'm calling an ambulance, *right now*..." She feels at her inner jacket pocket, struggling to get her hand inside.

"Yes..." says a drippy voice from the landing, "the police, please..."

Christina looks up at a woman in ridiculously huge glasses, peering around the door frame with a phone to her ear. Christina pulls out her warrant card and snaps at the woman, "*No!* Call an *ambulance!*"

The woman jumps back and hides out of sight.

"Chris..."

"I'm right here, Mickey." She looks for his hand to hold, but it is on the move.

Tout lifts his arm, with a shaking finger, as he points towards a woman lying in front of the couch.

Christina snaps at the door, "Call for *two* ambulances!"

She can but hope the daft old *biddy* will not be contrary.

"I'm right here, Mickey, I'm not going anywhere." Still on her knees, Christina turns to the female on the floor and shuffles towards her, reaching for the woman's neck and placing two fingers under her jaw line. The pulse is faint.

"So... You must be *Tabitha*..." She turns the woman's head, easing her face from the floor for a better look.

The woman's flesh parts from the carpet with a soft kiss. Half her is face caved in.

"Nev... ille..." she murmurs.

Christina gasps with a sinking heart. "Okay, love... help is on its way."

She faces Tout again and crawls back over to him. Christina's shoulder throbs a reminder for her to go slowly. "Mickey. Who did this?"

"His face..." Tout sighs, "*changed*..."

"What? He was... wearing a mask? Who? Why'd you have to do this alone?"

"Shaddup..." he says.

Christina is still. Dumbfounded.

"Look," Tout struggles, "you... are *not*... a robot."

He stops.

"Mickey?" She places her fingers over his throat. "Mickey, stay with me. Mickey... *Mickey!*"

Christina reaches into her jacket pocket, lucky dips for her phone and retrieves it quickly.

"All this for my investigation... *Our* investigation..."

She makes a call...

"Send units to Neville Pike's house address, *now*. His wife and her daughter could be in danger. Find them and bring them back to the station!"

She struggles to her feet, with her burning shoulder.

"Please be okay, Mickey, please be okay ..." *Fuck* procedure, she limps out of the flat, blundering into the plump woman on the phone. Christina snarls, "Stay with *them*, and stay on the line!"

She hobbles downstairs to get out, to get there first, and get this *right*.

***

A roar charges up to his ear...

Si turns to face the beast.

Pale headlights flicker, as the grill of a car rushes towards him... with Neville in the driver's seat.

Si's blood chills...

He falls... awake.

Si snaps upright in the hospital bed. A car engine chases the air through the window, into the white curtain dancing around him.

His arms fail. Si falls flat onto the bed with a sensation of teeth sinking into his ribs. Even crying out would hurt. His bruised face bites back against the pain, creasing his cheeks. His eyes ache as he lets out a pathetic dry sob.

Si knows that car engine closing in.

"He's not coming for me. Don't let him come for me!"

He brings a heavy hand to his face to catch any tears that might escape, and to shield his eyes from the vision of this cruel, disgusting world...

Si at last finds some comfort under the darkness of his palm, obscuring his eyes from the cold hard light of the ward. As he settles slightly, he trembles. So does a tooth.

He lifts his hand, suspending it over his face. Si opens his mouth to reach in... *opening wide* for his fingers, which feel like stranger's, probing his mouth. Lightly, he pinches a molar on the left of his jaw... It wiggles to the touch.

Uttering a shrill wail, he lets go. His feeble hand rests on his chest with a tearful tremor... as his fingers fold towards his palm. The nails dream of digging further. Si clenches his teeth against a frustrated scream.

It is a nice change from crying...

*****

"Does he do this often?"

Moseley rests his hands on the reception desk at Pike's Museum, a deceitfully casual enquiry before Tracy, who stops typing.

She sits back, folding her arms. "He *often* comes in late or leaves an hour early... getting himself into trouble, risking our necks, no doubt."

"Obviously, the man is not *himself*. He did come into contact with one of our more *legitimate* artefacts."

"George... it's all junk. You know that as well as I do."

"The museum *needs* a non-believer like you, Tracy, my dear, to keep the place *innocent*... maintain 'plausible deniability,'" Mosely stands, beckoning with his hand, "It would be a shame if that poor fellow got into trouble."

Tracy opens a drawer beside her and reaches in with both hands. She pulls out three grubby surveillance tapes and places them on the desk.

"Especially after going to the trouble of cleaning up after him." Mosely picks up the top black box and turns it over in his grasp. "I'm glad to see the back of that *Nick White* thug, for good."

CHAPTER 38

Screams ripple repeatedly from the house phone. Each ring, each shriek, as brief and urgent as the last... A helpless little thing crying desperately for attention... No mother could ignore that, could she?

Kat approaches and picks up the phone. "Hello?"

"Mrs Pike?" the man asks.

What she would give even to simply be 'Ms Spike' and have no more ties to *that man*...

"Yes, speaking."

"This is Sergeant Pearce from the police. A man we believe to be your husband has just attacked a woman, and one of our officers, and then fled the scene. For your safety, we've dispatched units to your address."

"What? *Neville?* He couldn't have done that! This can't be right!"

"Mrs Pike, you should lock all your doors and windows and then stay on the line till the police arrive."

"Gem!" she calls upstairs. Kat takes a deep breath, trying to quell the rising panic. "Can you come here a minute, darling?"

Her hands tremble as she speaks into the phone. "How long will they be?"

No movement upstairs. She puts her hand over the phone to turn and shout, "Gemma, will you-?!"

Little Gem is suddenly standing before Kat, making her jump.

"When did you…? Gem, sweetheart, can you talk to the nice police officer while I just… do something?"

"Okay, Mummy," Gemma receives the phone with an outstretched claw. "Hello…? Is that the police?"

Kat dashes for the front door and locks it. She peers through the frosted glass to see the porch empty. As Kat huffs back towards the living room she hears no dialogue between Gemma and the man on the phone. She sees the phone firmly in the cradle. With her heart in her mouth and fear on her lips, "Gemma! Where've you gone?!"

Gemma runs out from the kitchen.

"What are you doing?" Kat shouts. "You're supposed to stay on the phone!"

"That man scared me, Mummy."

"Oh, Gemma! Whenever I ask you to do something you totally go against it!" Kat shoos her out. "Go upstairs, I've still got to lock the back door…"

"But *Daddy's* here!"

"What?" Kat looks up from Gemma.

In the kitchen, a figure bearing the same shape and face as her husband stands by the door, staring… serene…

Mother clutches child in the face of the Deville.

He casts his eyes over everything around him, sizing it all up, re-registering each exit… and then the phone rings.

"Such a lovely home… taken for granted," Deville ignores the shrill ring.

"Nev…? Is it true?" Kat asks, "That the police are after you?"

"Such a lovely family…"

"What are you doing here, Nev?"

The phone shrieks as Deville steps toward Kat and Gemma.

"Nev!"

"Yes?"

Kat recoils before this calm cold 'Neville.' "Why are you here?"

"I just wanted to see the *family*."

Gemma stares in awe. Her mother's arms tighten around her.

The phone rings again.

Deville's face lights up, **"Who wants stir fry?"**

"Yay!" Gemma cheers, trying to pull away from her mum, but Kat is frozen.

Frightened and fascinated, Kat watches her husband, this fearsome stranger, raid the cupboards.

Deville turns around to open the fridge, and roots around inside.

Kat turns with Gemma for the front door when-

Thump.

They jump. Kat faces Deville…

A wrapped-up, uncooked chicken lands on the worktop, blowing a chill towards her; the breath of the mortuary drawer.

He picks up the biggest, most unnecessary knife in the block, and cuts the cold dead poultry free. And smiles, all the while...

He is faster and stronger than Kat… and holding the sharpest object in the house. Kat *daren't* even try to run. Not while holding onto Gemma.

Clang, as Deville places the knife on the worktop. His hand curls around a frozen leg. He rests the other over the breast of the carcass. With a twist and snap he pulls the leg free. He holds it up with a smile, reflecting Gemma's joy.

Kat watches, certain that he's going to take a bite out of the raw chicken, but he places it on the worktop, next to the body.

Deville assumes the stance again, as if the poor bird was still alive to struggle. With a hand curled around the other leg, he rips it away from the body, while grinning like a shark.

Gemma laughs.

Kat can only wonder why, *why* does she have to laugh at this?

"Nev?"

He places this leg beside the other limb.

"Neville," she says.

"Hm?" His eyes dart up to meet Kat's. His hands are still at the breast of the bird, squeezing. Fingers digging in. Enjoying the mutilation…

"What are you doing here?" she pleads.

"I'm cooking dinner for my family." He throws his head back and erupts with laughter. **"I'm having my *family* for dinner!"**

A cheeky chuckle reverberates from Gemma.

Kat hopes desperately that this is just a nightmare. Yet there is no waking. No escape… "Why are the police after you?"

"After *me*? No, no, they're not after *me*…"

The flesh tears away from the chicken, pink and dark in Deville's hands.

"Yes, they are."

"Been on the blower, have they?"

"They'll be here any minute."

"Oh dear... Then I suppose there's no time to *cook*."

He snatches up the massive knife and throws it at Kat.

She turns Gemma away...

Kat shrieks as the blade plunges into her shoulder. The stabbing pain floods her side. As she stumbles forward, the knife slips out, too heavy to stay in her flesh. Tears run down her face. Blood runs down her blouse. She bites hard against the urge to scream.

Gemma gasps with eyes wide like ten pence pieces, "*Mummy!*"

She turns to her *not*-Daddy, stalking around the counter. His face is dimmer... the smile, brighter...

With her good arm, Kat shoves Gemma into the hallway. Nearly pushing her over, she shouts, "Get out! Run!"

As Gemma turns to acknowledge her, a hand slams Kat's face against the door frame with a hard thud.

A scream escapes Gemma.

Deville glares at her. **"Shut up, you little *bitch*!"**

She does. Gemma watches, seen and not heard.

Kat, fallen to her hands and knees, swings her bad arm at Deville, but he catches it with one hand and whips her over.

Not at all like when he used to her over in bed, but this is not the man she married. Kat yelps in agony, and then launches a foot squarely into his groin.

Deville stumbles back, wincing from the impact. He looks up. A chuckle quakes from the depths of his throat...

"Pity I've come this far. It might have been worth keeping you…"

"Why are you doing this?!" she shouts, "What the fuck's got into you?!"

"This fool's been half a man for too long. He could've been anything, but for *you*… *and* this mediocre little life… So much potential *wasted!*"

He lunges toward her, gathering so much momentum over the short stretch.

Kat pushes herself up with her good arm and ushers Gemma towards the front door. Top-heavy with pain, Kat falls towards the door. She launches her palm towards the handle to twist it, but it does not turn. Locked…

She turns to face Deville. The other end of the hall, at the foot of the stairs, his *predator* smile beams from his face.

Kat drags Gemma behind her, clutching her tight with her bad, bloody arm, while raising a shaky, good arm to at least try and keep him at bay.

Her voice trembles, "If you hate your life so much, then why don't you just kill *yourself*?!"

He steps closer, with his smile dropping more into a trance-like expression.

"Why kill *me*, when I could kill you and have no more ties?"

Deville's face appears to morph… angry… less human, and somehow… *redder.* Heat reverberates from his lips as he edges closer and closer…

"You know what I'm going to do? I'm going to start afresh. I'm going to take this body and get it into shape. I'm going to take what's mine – the whole *world*! But I can't just up and do that while I'm – while *he's* – tied… Tied to you… I'm going to cut those ties… and then I'll be free…"

"You're not Neville."

"No!"

Deville punches the wall. He walks towards Kat, dragging his fist along the textured paint, as his knuckles impress his will, and his skin, and his blood, into the foundations.

"*Neville* doesn't have time for you... And neither do I!"

He throws his fist at Kat.

Her legs buckle. She slips, somehow avoiding the blow, and falls right beside Gemma.

Glass bursts from the door as Deville's fist breaks through.

Gemma rushes for the stairs.

"No! Gemma!" Kat staggers in the same *wrong* direction, after her daughter, and away from the man – the *thing* – that is not Neville, as it pulls its bloody hand back inside the house.

"You see... he's even so much *slower* with you around!"

Kat finds her feet, but stumbles. She lunges up the stairs, favouring the side that does not continue to bite and dribble blood with every move. Gripping each and every step, she pulls herself up. Her legs push her as high as she dares, to reach the bend towards the landing. She sneaks a glance over her shoulder...

Her leering husband approaches, scraping his fingernails now, along the wall. He walks, swaying casually, as though he has all the time in the world...

Kat continues to climb. Her hands and feet snatch at grainy carpet, like grains of sand sinking under her, tumbling down an hourglass.

A slow, heavy creak behind – below – marks the predator gaining on its prey... tiring herself out as she tries to escape.

Kat's hand presses flat on the floor upstairs. She tries to gather momentum to stand, but collapses under the pain of her pierced shoulder.

"Gem?!" she cries out. But Gemma has gone ahead. Hopefully to hide… Better still, to flee the first chance she gets…

The heavy creaks follow Kat from below.

She lurches forward, hoping for a means of sneaking her daughter away from all this horror.

The creaking moves higher… louder… closer…

Kat seizes the cool magnolia-painted banister, closing the distance to Gemma's room. The blood she leaves behind could stain the house forever…

She grabs the doorframe of Gemma's bedroom and pulls herself forward to peer inside, to scan over the little bed and her stuffed T-Rexes and triceratops. Kat realises, if Gemma is already hiding, there is a chance that her daughter could get to safety… if Kat can lead *him* into the master bedroom.

Kat limps for the room she used to share with Neville. Her head is sore, ringing with disbelief and concussion. The creaking steps turn her aching head. The chilling shadow of her husband reaches the top of the stairs, joined by the Deville himself.

She shouts, "The police'll be here any second!"

"But they're *not* here yet. *Are* they?"

Kat turns, and practically falls through the bedroom door. Her fingers coil around the handle and she slams it shut.

She pinches the bolt and snaps it across.

This bolt would not be here, but for her beloved wanting her to feel safe, after that one dark day when he had a breakdown…

She steps back, watching the door. It is still. Kat's heart is not. The whole room is still, while her heart bludgeons her chest.

Thump.

Kat jumps with the door.

Sirens wail, distant on their approach. Their salvation!

"Even if they do turn up, dear... I'm still going to end you... After all, the real prison was the man you once knew as *Neville Pike*, so *I've* got nothing to lose! Today, I'm going to be *free*."

Thump.

A tattoo of pounds makes the door shiver, constantly, as if under gunfire.

Kat holds her shaky, bloody hands to her ears.

The noise stops. She looks up. The door is still. The house is silent. She dares not to even breathe.

"Gem?" Neville calls out from behind the door. Gentle, sweet, daft, loving Neville... "Come here to Daddy?"

Kat brings a hand to her mouth, failing to catch a sob.

"Won't you come out now... **so that your Daddy can gut Mummy while you watch?**"

Kat's eyes water. Tears escape as fast as the blood from her shoulder.

The sirens grow louder, closer... but the police are not close enough... not *fast* enough.

"**Better still... *you* can do it, Gem... Come to your Daddy. *He'll* put the knife in your hand. It's what *Mummy* really wants...**"

Kat roars at the door, "You leave her out of it, you sick fucking bastard! I'll *kill* you before you get anywhere near her!"

"**See, Neville? This is how your wifey *really* feels about you...**"

"It's not too late, Nev, you don't have to do this. Whatever's got hold of you, you can't hurt our little Gem; you love her so much!"

Kat breaks down again.

"**No. This family has held Neville back long enough. So**

hold still, while I *cut* you out, *Kat!*"

Thump. The bedroom door shakes. A volley of blows against it all but deafens Kat. She covers her ears. If only denying the sound would void this terror.

Thump – heavier…

One… Two…

Silence…

Kat's hands slip away. She looks to the door, listens beyond, hopes even to see through it. The danger knocking at her door is real. Her shoulder burns. Her head rings.

The door crashes open with Deville's kick. His strength eclipses Kat's disbelief in this nightmare.

Shriek is all she can do, and lurch for the en suite bathroom, as if this next door between them would be enough to keep her safe.

But her husband is already on her, the lion has pounced on the gazelle.

"Old habits die hard." Deville straddles Kat, pinning her to the floor. **"You didn't always *make* it to the bed, did you?"**

Kat wails against his weight on her, and her red remembered shoulder.

Deville snatches at her neck. His fingers curl under the back of Kat's head, as tenderly as Neville once held their *baby girl*…

Both thumbs press against Kat's throat.

She clutches at his hands, digs her claws into them, only for him to tighten his grip.

Deville roars triumphantly, screaming loud enough for the both of them.

She is strapped in for the ride of her life. The ride *for* her life. 'How is sex like air?' Nev would say. 'It's not a big deal unless you're not getting any!"

No airway, no neck… No neck, no airway…

Kat drifts from her body as her throat buckles under her husband's thumbs. Eyes drown in their own tears… Lungs pry their cage bars apart… The heart bursts into her ears… The strength drains away from her hands, and her arms. Even the pain is choked out.

The beast within growls behind her husband's gritted teeth.

"Daddy?" calls Gemma.

His eyes widen, unwavering…

"Daddy, please stop…" she pleads, in streams of tears.

Neville's hands loosen the grip. They clutch and tenderly cradle Kat's head.

A twinkle grows in the gloss of his eye. The tear falls softly onto Kat, blurring the face… of the man she once loved?

It is too dark for her to tell…

CHAPTER 39

Her hair sticks to Neville's hands.

Kat's blouse soaks with sweat... *His and hers* sweat... Her dark, red, wet shoulder glistens, clinging to Neville's white shirt.

He gasps, demonstrating fitfully to her how to *breathe again*. But Kat's eyes remain blank. The light behind them snuffed out, *squeezed* out by the hands that *now* hold her tenderly.

Neville wraps his arms around Kat and holds her tight. His knees grate hard against the floorboards. He loosens the hold. She is still... *sparkless*.

Helplessly, a moan trickles out of him.

The room, the house, is still.

Gemma stands in the doorway.

Oh god, how could I forget her?

"Gem," sobbing Neville pleads, "Gemma, I'm sorry, I'm so sorry. I... I couldn't stop him. I tried, but I couldn't. It's all my fault, I'm so sorry..."

One dull thud and another creaks up the stairs.

What now? Surely, it can't be him*!*

"Gem. Come here. Quickly!"

She stares, not hearing.

Delicately, Neville lays Kat down. His heart and stomach sink as he steps across his wife to get to Gemma. He kneels to put his hands over Gemma's shoulders and look her into her eyes.

He must resemble her daddy again, because she wraps her arms around his neck and clutches him.

Neville puts his arms round Gemma to shield her. His eyes focus on the staircase and whoever, *whatever*, comes to the top. Neville primes himself to scoop Gemma up.

A woman's voice reaches them... "Mrs Pike?"

"She's in here," Neville's voice breaks.

Thuds... up the stairs... DI Lake steps onto the landing, gripping a baton tightly in one hand.

"Mr Pike? Is that you?"

She edges towards the bedroom.

"Please," he says, "call an ambulance."

Lake creeps in with the baton primed against her shoulder. She sees Katherine Pike on the floor. Bloody. Still...

The grip on Lake's only weapon loosens as the hand that holds it falls to her side. The baton barely sticks to her fingers. Her jaw drops.

She turns to see Neville's melting eyes. And his little girl crying quietly into his shoulder. Lake's fingers tighten around the baton until it burns with her white-hot knuckles. "Did you do this? *Pike*?"

Staring at Kat lying before him, Neville coughs a dry sob, "I was too late. I couldn't stop him... Why the *hell* didn't you get here sooner?!"

A default ringtone sings out in Lake's pocket. She keeps her eye on Neville as she snatches the mobile out and answers.

"Hello? Yes, I'm with Pike now. There's been an attack… We'd best call that off now. Send several units… And call for an ambulance to their home address… Okay."

She hangs up and promptly stuffs the phone into her pocket, with her eyes fixed on him as if the call never happened.

"So… Neville… you're saying it wasn't *you* who did this? To your wife?"

"It was…" Gemma stands to interrupt, and turns, "…*another* man. It *wasn't* my Daddy. He was funny, but then he hurt Mummy. That man was *not* Daddy."

Lake stares in awe.

Neville – frozen – thaws… "Gem…"

I can't admit to any of the killings – it wasn't even me*! If I do, I'll lose Gemma too. She'll lose me…*

"Which way did he go?" Lake barks.

"Downstairs," says Neville, "I… heard the back door go."

Lake turns to leave, but then faces him again. She pulls out her phone again, with thumbs at the ready, "I'm having units sent to patrol the area. Can you describe the attacker, Mr Pike?"

Is Gemma really safe with me? I don't know if this is over. It's not fair, none of this is fair!

"No, I… I can't… I didn't see him."

Lake sighs onto her texting thumbs, "Why is this man targeting you and your family, Neville? We had our suspicious that Mr Pike Senior was involved with the local distribution of drugs, and if that's true, *that* could be the connection…"

"We're not discussing *that* in front of my daughter. Where's the fucking *ambulance*?!" He yells. "Oh god, I'm sorry, Gem."

"It's okay, Daddy." Gemma hugs him tight.

Lake keeps her game face on. "There must be some reason behind the recent attacks. Did you witness this man attacking any of the victims?"

"No. I suppose *he* and I have… kept *missing* each other, somehow."

"Mr Pike. If he's still out there, he's likely to attack again. Are you able to give me some description of this man?"

"Inspector," he crescendos, "I. Do. Not. *Know* this man!"

Lake grunts in recoil.

I've come this far, and I'm still lying. I don't know what's right anymore. What's going to happen about Gem?

As quiet as the blood on his hands, Neville clutches Gemma closer. The blood is on her now, too… with the law as his witness.

Torrential tears run down Gemma's cheeks and fall from her face, like lemmings off a cliff.

Wailing sirens close in, a tsunami Neville cannot escape.

When would I ever get to see Gemma again? Is it selfish of me to want that? She's taking it all so incredibly well, considering… Maybe I ought to tell…

Lake faces halfway away from Neville, still with one an eye on him. If only the tears were not pounding away behind the whites of *her* eyes…

The sirens wail ever louder, signalling the race to save her *failure*. But this man will *not*. Stop. Talking.

"What about Gem?" Neville panics. "Where will *she* go now? With her grandparents? Please no, she can't end up like me!"

Drier-eyed, Lake faces him again. Gemma's face is long buried into her broken father, with her eyes shut to all of this.

"She'll be safe with me," says Lake. "You should just say goodbye to each other for now."

Neville eases his little daughter away from him. "Gem... Gemma, look at me, madam."

She has her father's watery eyes.

He smooths away the tears. "*There* she is. That's my girl."

Whining over his voice, the emergency vehicles park outside. The sirens cease with a tone of a run-down battery-powered toy.

"But I want to stay with you, Daddy," Gemma clings.

"I know you do, love," Neville croaks, "but I have to stay with Mummy so she... So that she can be... *taken care* of."

Entranced by such a creep's unconditional care of his daughter, Lake discreetly sheaths her baton.

"Look, Gem, DI Lake here is going to take you outside and give you a little ride in the police car."

"No!" Gemma *stamp-trums*, "I don't *want* to *go*."

"Okay. Okay!" He steadies her arms. "Listen, Gem. In that case, I need you to take DI Lake outside, maybe to the garden, so there's enough room in here for the paramedics to... to look after Mummy, alright?"

Gemma nods, sombre. Calm.

"Good girl. Love you." Neville wraps his arms around her one last time. He fights to glance up at Lake, watching them. He eases Gemma free of their embrace, cradles his daughter's face and plants a kiss on her forehead.

Clattering downstairs as doors burst open. The footsteps of first responders move closer. Voices hum, crawling over each other like bees in a hive.

"Go on," he rotates Gemma gently, "Go. Take her outside."

"I've got her," Lake assures.

I wasn't talking to you.

Gemma stomps out of the bedroom, taking Lake's hand, and leads her away. She looks back over her shoulder at her father. "I love you, Daddy."

Rushing to the top of the stairs, two first responders arrive.

"I'll see you, Gem," Neville calls out louder as she and Lake pass them by, "as soon as I can, okay?"

As Gemma turns, her crimson complexion startles Neville. There are horns piercing the air above her head. **"No, you won't, Daddy,"** she *Devilles.*

With a black-lipped snarl, *Gem-mae-el* steps off the landing and descends the staircase.

Neville clambers to his feet and cries out, "Oh my god!"

Lake only glances back, as she and Gemma disappear behind the wall.

He screeches, "She's wearing the mask! Get it off her!"

Neville lunges…

…but catches his legs against a thick table, and falls back into a chair…

Neville looks up and scans the surrounding quiet darkness. "Hello? How the fuck did I get here…?"

Etching into the abyss, the corners of four walls surround him.

Gleaming to Neville's left is a tinted window. His own reflection, restrained, stares back. His wrists pinch under the pressure of handcuffs.

The door opens to the dim, dull interview room. Lake asserts her way in. "Do you know where you are, Mr Pike?"

Neville jumps at the chill of the table under his hands.

Foreboding steps bounce off the four dark grey walls boxing him in, as Lake approaches and pulls out a chair.

Panting, he looks up at her. "I think so... How did I get here...? *When* did I get here?"

She sits, hooking her hands together. "You really don't remember?"

He shakes his head.

"Your wife has been taken off to hospital."

"But it's too late for that..."

"No, she's still alive."

"Really?!" Neville lights up like an excited child.

"Barely."

Neville sinks. "And what about Gemma? Where is she?"

"She's safe." Lake sits back into her chair.

Oh, how very telling...

"When can I see her?"

Lake sits up, drawing breath as she stalls. "We'll need to get a few things in order before we can arrange anything. Including a formal statement from you."

Neville groans. "Are these necessary?" He holds up his handcuffs, jingling.

Lake glances down at his wrists and then up to meet his eyes. "You didn't exactly come quietly."

Neville remembers his story. The one he must keep to, at least. "Did you find the man who did this?"

"No." She folds her arms. "The search is still going on. And we're still looking for witnesses to come forward. So, we need a detailed statement from you... how you found your wife and your daughter... Everything you have already told me, and anything else that comes back to you."

She pushes a pen and clipboard across the table to him.

When did she put those there? I could be digging my own from here!

Clipped to the board is a sheet, an oasis of honest white in a box barren of colour. Neville's fingers pull the effects the rest of the way towards him and picks up the pen. He twiddles it between his fingers as he reads the above text.

Scraping the chair across the floor, Lake gets up and marches out. She opens the door and faces Neville. "We can call in a solicitor, if you like, Mr Pike."

No-one likes Mr Pike…

Neville shakes his head. "No, thank you. That… won't be necessary."

She steps out, shutting the door after her, when Deville, with his hands in his pockets, and far more kempt than Neville, approaches the table.

"Neville, Neville, Neville…"

"Fuck…! Is this you, speeding things along?" In the interview room of his own mind, Neville stabs his index finger into the table, "Is *this* even real?!"

"As real as you and *me*… All you had to do was let go. And trust your better self with your pathetic little life."

Deville pulls up a chair, reverses it, and then sits over the back of the seat, resting his arms over the top. **"It's 'make or break,' *mate*. Only one of us can walk out through that door…"**

"And as for the other?"

"As far as the *other* is concerned, this place will cease to exist. Along with him in it…"

"Will it now? Because it's going to be *me* that walks out."

"Oh, is it *really*…?"

"The world doesn't need a monster like *you* running rampant!"

"The same could be said of a monster like you, Neville… Another mal-adjusted citizen with his spoilt, fractured ego."

"I need to be back out there… so I can see it all through."

"*Why?*"

"I have my daughter to think about."

"Fool. You were supposed to *let go* of your family."

"No… I'm not."

"It's always been the only way you could move on."

"Move on, and you'll have me all to yourself. Don't move on, and you'll take over. Either way, you win!"

Deville smiles.

"I'm going to kick you out of my head. And out of my life!"

"While still in handcuffs?"

"Oh… You mean *these* handcuffs?" Neville flicks his wrists and blinks. His eyes open before Deville sitting at the table, in handcuffs instead.

Neville stands where Deville had stood before…

"Oh, very droll…" Deville glances down at his restraints over relaxed arms. He glares at Neville. **"Either way, Neville Pike emerges a better man."**

"*I will*. That trick I learnt from you." Neville rests his hands on the table. "Now, I'm going to get out, and be there for my family… Without *you*! So, this is the last time… Be. Gone!"

Deville pales in the face with darkening eyes… Greying skin… He stands, and the handcuffs break, crumbling off him like wet paper.

Neville shivers, shrinking with cold… and then steps back.

The *malifested* Deville steps forward, closer to him, and with one hand the phantom grabs Neville's throat… **"No. You are the**

329

weaker one…"

The chill will freeze Neville from the inside-out if the grip does not choke him first. Both hands seize Deville's slab-cold wrist to try and pry him off, but Deville is unfazed before the struggling worm that is Neville Pike, now *suspended* with one arm.

"Enjoy non-existence in the *shadow* of the subconscious!"

The worst of Neville's own greying likeness stares at him with void-black eyes. A smile prises free of his lips.

…And *Neville's* too, as he grips Deville's wrist, and then *releases*, with both arms falling at his sides. "Guess again."

Deville struggles to breathe, as he is now the one suspended by Neville's grip on the phantom's throat.

"It's an oldie now, but a goodie. It's not the *ol' switcheroo* if everything in *here*," Neville pokes a finger at his temple, "is already mine."

Teary black ooze runs down from Deville's eyes as he grabs desperately at Neville's wrist.

"The shadow of my subconscious is too good for *you*." He lifts Deville higher. "Enjoy *your* non-existence, *altogether!*"

His new-found strength crushes Deville's cold grey neck.

A bass, deafening hum burns the surrounding darkness from the walls of Neville's mind. The black room glows blue and bluer, luminous, inverting all colour like a photographic negative. Neville's hair and eyes whiten as his own skin *blues*.

Glaring lighter and lighter before Neville, as he suspends Deville, everything in the space bleaches warm white.

CHAPTER 40

Straps flex and creak with the shifting of shoulders.

Neville breathes a weep on waking. The air is clean. Cold. Sitting up is denied. Panic under straps holds him down onto a bed. Lying in an open casket for the death of sanity.

He only lost himself, he did not lose his *self*…

Bound Neville snatches a look to his right. He is one of many more strapped in beds… a row of *impatients* squirming, waiting, writhing for release, like larvae wriggling over leftovers gone to spoil. Some are already humming.

They all look alike… like me*!*

He lifts his head *ahead* to see reflected back, a row of man-shaped shells all tightly bound. In the mirror, lies *another* Neville, and another mirror, and another Neville… Infinite windows of infinite Nevilles…

One of me is more than enough.

The walls of white surround Neville but for a door… left… shut on the moans of the once-sane souls that will swallow his own.

But speaking *of*…

Screaming silence… no *Devilles* abound. Neville is half-empty. Free, dumb… but in captivity.

331

"Did *I* put me in here?" He mumbles. "Did *he* put me in here?"

Neville stirs, with wrists itching under straps.

"Either way, I'm a prisoner."

His keepers clip and clop through halls with voices afloat… "He's just had one breakdown too many. How is the wife? Lucky she's alive. Albeit barely… There's another woman in critical condition. And a detective, but it's unlikely they'll make it…"

"They survived?" begs Neville… as if he would be heard.

But a new voice, no, a *familiar* voice answers

Oh yes, but you heard them: 'barely'… You're not very good, are you?

"At *killing?*"

At anything… You're just not very good. You didn't even stop to think of your daughter, did you?

"What's going to happen to her?"

Exactly!

"Please! I need to know if she's okay!"

Silence. *Unquiet* silence.

Listen, this is your common sense talking. No more lying, false-promising evil here… You won. Congratulations. Now what did you think would come of all this?

"But it wasn't me…"

Do you know how many people you've hurt? Do you know many lives you've destroyed?

"It *wasn't me!*"

Liar…

"Where's my precious Gem?" He giggles, "my

332

preciousssssss..."

Neville's chilly feet wiggle and wave.

Hello. Good-bye...

"I had so much to do," he squirms. "So much to achieve, so much to cover up... And it all just blew up in my face."

You *blew it up.* You *threw the first punch. And the last...*

"Didn't think I'd accomplish this much before hitting *forty...*"

You'll find your way back to the family again... one day.

"I guess... but for now, I'm just a man again. And god, the drugs are *sooooooooooooooo* good..."

The door opens...

"Maybe now you can *finally* get the help you so *desperately* need..."

The door shuts on Neville... but somehow the wicked laugh is locked in the room with him.

Neville looks to the mirror in front. To his disbelief, Deville's expression is spread across his face, laughing back at Neville...

All of the squirming *impatients* strapped to their beds are just as high with sadistic joy, as the echoing voice chuckles...

"Remember! Life *begins* at forty!"

The squirmers snarl and laugh at panicking Neville as he writhes against the straps.

"Happy birthday, *Neville*..."

THE AUTHOR

Jack James Dixon studied a BA in Film, followed by an MA in Professional Writing at Falmouth University.

As a Cornish Writer – and now a published author – he will also continue to pursue a variety of creative work.

Printed in Great Britain
by Amazon